THE
TUNNEL
OF LOVE

by
PETER DE VRIES

PENGUIN BOOKS

Penguin Books Ltd, Harmondsworth,
Middlesex, England
Penguin Books, 625 Madison Avenue,
New York, New York 10022, U.S.A.
Penguin Books Australia Ltd, Ringwood,
Victoria, Australia
Penguin Books Canada Limited, 2801 John Street,
Markham, Ontario, Canada L3R 1B4
Penguin Books (N.Z.) Ltd, 182–190 Wairau Road,
Auckland 10, New Zealand

First published in the United States of America by
Little, Brown and Company, Inc., 1954
First published in Canada by
Little, Brown & Company (Canada) Limited 1954
First published in Great Britain by
Victor Gollancz 1955
Published in Penguin Books in Great Britain 1964
Published in Penguin Books in the United States of America
by arrangement with Little, Brown and Company, Inc., 1982

LIBRARY OF CONGRESS CATALOGING IN PUBLICATION DATA
De Vries, Peter.
The tunnel of love.
I. Title.
[PS3507.E8673T85   1982]   813'.52   81-13978
ISBN 0 14 00.2200 7   AACR2

Printed in the United States of America by
Offset Paperback Mfrs., Inc., Dallas, Pennsylvania
Set in Linotype Electra

Parts of chapters Six, Eleven, Thirteen, Fifteen, and Seventeen of this
novel have appeared, in somewhat different form, in *The New Yorker*.

PENGUIN BOOKS

THE TUNNEL OF LOVE

Peter De Vries was born in Chicago of Dutch immigrant parents and was educated in Dutch Reformed Calvinist schools. He graduated from Calvin College in 1931 and held the post of editor, for a short time, of a community newspaper in Chicago. He then supported himself with a number of different jobs, including those of vending-machine operator, toffee-apple salesman, radio actor, furniture mover, lecturer to women's clubs, and associate editor of *Poetry*. In 1943 he managed to lure James Thurber to Chicago to give a benefit lecture for *Poetry*, and Thurber suggested that De Vries should write for *The New Yorker*. He did. Before long he was given a part-time editorial position on that magazine, dropped his other activities, and moved to New York City. He has remained on the editorial staff of *The New Yorker* ever since. Peter De Vries is the author of some twenty novels, the most recent being *Consenting Adults, or The Duchess Will Be Furious* (published by Penguin Books) and *Sauce for the Goose*. He lives in Westport, Connecticut.

by Peter De Vries

Virtues are forced upon us by our impudent crimes.

T. S. ELIOT

The Tunnel of Love

One

I DON'T know whether you've ever been interviewed by an adoption agency on behalf of friends bent on acquiring a child, or if you have, whether any doubts were in order concerning the qualifications of either of the prospective parents, or of yourself to judge, for that matter, and whether in that case you were realistic with the agency or romantic. I don't know, either, what you would have done had you been in my shoes that Saturday afternoon the caseworker called to ask if I wished to offer any opinion on Augie Poole as paternal timber. "In my shoes" is a loose metaphor, for when she arrived I was not in them. I was stretched out flat in bed with symptoms for which no organic cause could be found.

This in itself was answer enough. I tried to guard its significance from my wife, who didn't know the half of what I knew and who only said to me, "Get up, lazybones," as she pulled the slipping bedclothes off the floor or otherwise tidied up the premises for the approaching visitor. Her hands were not hyssop, neither was there meat and drink in them. Lazybones indeed! How I should have liked to deserve that charge rather than the one implicit in my prostration. A lazy man would simply have got up and gone through the motions of giving a reference, whereas some vestige of moral fiber in me caused me to malinger. The burden I bore was a complex one, involving both

Augie and myself in a mess of matters quite intimately plaited. The Augie part of the hazard consisted in my knowing him, not only better than my wife did, but better than his own did. The ordeal under which I lay was one for which the name of the imminent caseworker struck me as abysmally apt: It was Mrs. Mash. That was enough to throw cold water on anything.

My wife, at length, began to look as if she would like to throw some on me. However, she called Dr. Vancouver when I finally convinced her how punk I felt. He arrived an hour later.

My symptoms were soon rehearsed: sore throat, heavy feeling in my chest, and feverishness. Dr. Vancouver took my temperature and found it normal. Then he examined my throat, peering down it gingerly and with great care not to get himself breathed on, for he is an awful hypochondriac. "There's nothing in your throat," he said. He chucked me under the chops with his fingertips. "Perfectly O.K. Let's have a look at your chest." I loosened my pajama coat, and he tappped my trunk in several places, holding his head averted. He tested it next with a stethoscope, telling me to look well away when I coughed. "I can't find a thing anywhere," he said at last.

I watched the jaws of his alligator bag close on the stethoscope. He walked over to a chair in the far corner and sat down. Dr. Vancouver is a bald man with a ruddy complexion (like most hypochondriacs he is in perfectly satisfactory health) and a jutting nose. He has a double chin, except that he has none to begin with, which makes him rather all wattles from the mouth down. He crossed his legs and regarded me the length of the room, with such a bedside manner as the distance between us afforded. By habit he was hygienic even with patients from whom he was unlikely to catch anything.

"Has anything been troubling you?" he asked. "Some situation you want to avoid?"

"Not that I know of," I said, reaching to my nightstand for a pack of cigarettes.

"The human system is the greatest counterfeiting machine in the world. I mean in its ability to simulate symptoms. You say this feverish feeling, it's as if the underside of your skin was tender. That's a perfect description of fever, but remember you have the benefit of previous fevers to go by. Are you sure there isn't a difficult situation you don't want to face? Something you want to get out of?"

"I just want to get out of bed," I said. Let him make what he wanted of it. I could take myself with a grain of salt any time there was a necessity, which was more than could be said for anybody else in this room. It was peaceful in here and I wanted him to go away. He irked me. He was dressed to the nines in the kind of country "togs" you saw all over Avalon, Connecticut (where this was), with a pullover sweater under a jacket of barleycorn tweed, pebble-grain brogans, and no doubt a tartan cap on the hall tree, as though he had come on horseback to see me and not in his air-conditioned Buick.

Sitting up, I leaned back against the headboard. "I feel kind of faint," I said.

"That's from the rapid breathing just now when I examined your chest. Please cover your mouth when you cough."

"Why make such bones about someone there's nothing organically wrong with?" I put to him.

"That's not the point," he answered irritably. "It's no more than you'd ask of a person sitting next to you in a bus."

Not wanting him to go away angry — and sick as a dog as I was — I started to crack jokes. "I've always suspected that feeling of well-being of mine was completely psychosomatic," I said with a rather charming smile. "That underneath I was riddled with complaints."

Vancouver opened his black bag again and rummaged in it. "I try to combine the old and the new, what's good in each," he said tersely.

"I know." I appeared to have wounded him. Feeling, therefore, that I should redouble my efforts to make amends, I went on: "That's the way to be — eclectic. So why don't you give me some sulfa and molasses?"

This had the peculiar effect of making him freeze up altogether. It's hard to understand the resistance of some people to humor, which is after all only laughing at our little troubles and differences. Dr. Vancouver addressed my wife. "I'll give you some pills for him to take. And see that he gargles every hour or so with either aspirin or salt water — I don't care which. You've got the week end to rest him up in, so if he has got a slight cold or grippiness that ought to take care of it. If he doesn't feel any better by the first of the week, give me a call then."

My wife saw him out. There was a huggermugger at the front door of which I caught only the repeated word "him." Once I thought I heard "humor" in front of it. My wife returned. She stood in the bedroom doorway. Her hands still were not hyssop, neither was there meat and drink in them, though I had demonstrably eaten nothing since the night before. "You might get up and have a bite," she said. "You ought to take one of the pills now, and I'll fix you either the aspirin or the salt water to gargle with. Which would you like?"

"Suit yourself," I said "It makes no difference to me." I closed my eyes and went on: "I'll gargle on the hour. That way it'll be easier to remember when to do it again. For you as well as me." My plan was to humor her before she did that to me.

"You don't have to gargle for me, or take the pills either. Doc says you're malingering."

"Is that serious?"

"It could be."

"How long will I have to stay in bed?"

"It's twelve o'clock. Mrs. Mash will be here in two hours."

I turned over from supine to prone. I lay for some time after my wife left, thinking, through the hum of a vacuum cleaner, about Augie. To begin with, how did he himself feel about pressing a deposition out of me, knowing what I knew? You assumed it was basically Isolde, his wife, who wished to adopt a child, though he protested he wanted one just as bad. But even if he didn't, Isolde's wanting one was enough, for he was devoted to her. I knew he liked me too, with perhaps a special amused affection for the wholesome advices with which (speaking of the fate of having met him at all) I had tried to brief him on our community after he and Isolde had moved into it. Such as, "If you get mixed up with *that* crowd you'll spend every night of your life at some damned party." Such homilies performed the function served by the inverted directions which used to appear on those wine bricks manufactured during prohibition: "Caution, do not immerse in water as it will turn to wine."

My wife and I were — to undertake as systematically as possible the task of putting the sinner in that perspective that is required by charity no less than by narrative — neighbors of the Pooles as well as friends. That made everything twice as ticklish: People are allegedly forever parting friends, but how can you part neighbors? From the time we and the Pooles first met to the morning I turned over from supine to prone was three years. Augie had in that period touched me for sums of which I had lost count; but the fact that I could estimate them as upwards of two hundred dollars can be taken both as a measure of my friendship for him and my anxiety at the thought of his acquiring additional pecuniary strain. After all I had mouths of my own to feed. I never expected to get any of my departed tens and twenties back: I saw them as gone in a flutter of jockey silks. Now, Augie was not a "sporting" type — not a bit; he understood perfectly that I was paraphrasing Shakespeare when, catching him out with a *Turf Guide* after a period of professed reform, I flung out something about a man who could "post with such dexterity to racing sheets." The effect on him could not have been more tonic than it was. No, Augie's interest in the sport was part of your intellectual's colloquial underside. A kind of fine self-consciousness made him lapse into some convenient dialect or other every time he put the bite on me. "Man, Ah ain't just flat — Ah is concave," he would say by way of preamble, or, "Divil a penny it is I've got on me this day. Is it a sawbuck you could be helping me out with?" He strove by these means to give my every fresh financial nick and scratch a quality of gay inconsequence, or nothing to worry about.

Of course it would be straining at a gnat to deny Augie Poole his "character" on the ground of thriftlessness alone. It was the trouble I had swallowing camels that undid me as a witness. My situation was not unlike that of the marriage guest who must, if he know any just cause etc., speak now or forever hold his peace. That I could do neither of these accounted for my being still in a horizontal position when Mrs. Mash arrived, and for my astonishing behavior when she walked unexpectedly into the bedroom.

My wife had worked herself into a state of suspicion by the time the doorbell rang. "You know something you're not telling me," she said. "I insist you do. Is it about Augie?" I shook my head. "Is it money? Is he head over heels in gambling debts?" I shook my head. "Is it that he doesn't really want a family?" I shook my head. "Has he fallen in love with another woman?" I closed my eyes like a wearied saint.

"Mrs. Mash is here. Go answer the door."

She did. "Surely you can get up for a minute," she said as she went. "The woman coming all the way from Haversham and all. . . ."

I heard the front door open and a voice say, "I'm Mrs. Mash from the Crib." There was an exchange of greetings and then, our children being dispersed among neighbors, the women spent an unmolested hour in the living room. The data fell softly and steadily from my wife's lips. "Isolde Poole is really a swell sort. Fine with kids from what I can judge . . . took care of mine several times . . . seem to like her . . . nice roomy house and all. . . . Oh, about three years . . . income? . . . Well, my husband knows more than I about the Mr. Poole side of it."

I crept out of bed and stood with my ear to the crack of the closed door. Suddenly I heard my wife say in answer to something of Mrs. Mash's, "I don't see why not . . . not that sick . . . your head in the door anyway."

I popped back between the sheets just in time. I lay with my eyes shut tight, like bars against which my caged conscience fluttered, when the door opened. My wife said, "He's not asleep. This is Mrs. Mash. She has only a question or two to ask you, and I think it would be a shame to have her make a special trip. *She'll have to see you sometime.*"

"I can — "

"Nonsense, Mrs. Mash. Come in."

My eyes blinked open. "Oh, hello," I said, in a very husky voice. "You'd be Mrs. Mash."

Mrs. Mash was a tall woman with a mouth like a mail slot and eyes the color of soy sauce. She stole apologetically in with the assurance that the merest word was all she wanted from me concerning Augie.

"They tell me you know him well. What say, do you think he has the makings of a solid citizen and a good father?" she put to me humorously.

A peal of cracked laughter broke from my lips, and then, sitting bolt upright, I pointed helplessly at my throat, from which no further sound issued. Not a peep. Mrs. Mash looked inquiringly at my wife. I sat gesticulating for some seconds, my legs plowing the covers in my effort to recover the power of speech, which had indeed quite fled. My wife burst into tears and left the room, followed by Mrs. Mash who marched out pad and pencil in hand.

At five o'clock that afternoon my vocal chords were still dead as a doornail. And I responded to my wife's hysterical displays by snatching up a sheet of paper and scribbling on it:

Now stop this, damn it! Can spill beans about Augie in ten words, but that not fair to him. Or to me — I deeply involved too. Only fair way is to tell all from the beginning. Will do so at earliest possible moment. This throat condition like when people victims of stick-up or frightened in some other way. Voice back in few hours. Now pull yourself together. This is no way to act in front of children.

Two

WHEN I try to analyze Augie Poole, I generally get about as far as recalling a movie I once saw about a man who could dive but not swim. Having tumbled adroitly through an aerial sequence, the man would be fished, threshing and coughing, out of the water by servants and friends before he drowned. Augie is something like that in his knack for the fancier turns of life, with little or no sense of its rudiments. I remember the first time he and Isolde had dinner at my house. We were eating at a table set with some imported place mats of which my wife was especially proud — Oriental mats, I think, with some kind of cryptic figure in the center. Twirling his fork between courses, Augie peered at his, lifting a plate to do so, and said, "I do believe these are prayer rugs." Augie knows about as much anthropology as whoever it was wove the mats, but that's not the point; the point is he could just as easily have said, "I love your prayer rugs." As it was, his pedantic flourish left enough doubt in the minds of his hosts so that their eating off the mats any more was out (even if they said grace). My wife answered with a mock mock wail, "Oh, and I was so fond of them — whatever can people like us do with prayer rugs?" Isolde said, "Shoot craps," and turned her beautiful China blue eyes on her husband like two gun barrels.

I began purely as a spectator of Augie's affairs. But I became so rapidly drawn into them, and was in the end so narrowly grazed by the absurd calamity which crowned them — of which the business that rendered me mute before Mrs. Mash was not even yet the last — that I felt a little like the Kansas farmer must have felt who saw his neighbor's house picked up and deposited elsewhere by a cyclone which then, crossing the farmer's own premises, swiveled his cap around on his head, leaving the peak behind. No more of that for me.

We met the Pooles not in Avalon where we all live but forty miles away at a New York cocktail party, as befits Eastern commuting culture — those numberless intact globules of metropolitan life that float on the surfaces of numberless New Jersey, New York State and even New England country-town populations. My first glimpse of Augie at this party is sharply chased on my memory. Reedy and handsome in chalk stripes, he stood talking about Kierkegaard with gestures perfected at El Morocco, waving his drink so it just didn't spill. Near him was an exquisite creature with a face like tinted Dresden, sipping a Martini. I have always prided myself on a gift for spotting people's vocations by circumstantial evidence. When I see a girl bent on standing at right angles to herself — a heel against an instep to form a T with the feet, or her chin lined up along her shoulder as though she's slightly out of touch with herself — I know we have a model striking the photographic poses of her trade. The Dresden beauty was so patently a magazine manikin to my practiced eye that I was interested to hear the hostess say at my elbow, "That's Isolde Brown, the actress." As we watched, the object of our regard broke into animated conversation. Isolde Brown's smile was a plagiarism. It gave me no trouble. Joan Fontaine. Of course. The sort of half-smile, a one-cheek smile, the lips just parted. . . .

"And that's her husband over there — Augie Poole," the hostess said.

"Is he in advertising?"

"He's a cartoonist. Why, he must send his cartoons in to you, come to think of it." This was not my day, but what my hostess was referring to was *The Townsman*, a weekly whose picture jokes happens to be my editorial responsibility (to take care of the occupations for the moment). "I don't seem to place the name," I answered, not making the slight mental effort that would have spared me so much embarrassment later. I was mesmerized by the virtuosity that went into Isolde Brown's small talk.

"They've just moved out to Avalon, so you must come meet them," the hostess said, taking my hand.

I permitted myself to be towed across the room, reflecting on the basic connection between modeling and acting, the latter being but a series of successful postures, etc. I was soon at Isolde Brown's side, hearing her introduced as Mrs. Poole. "Tell him your story about Helmholz," the hostess said, after the presentation, and was off in a gasp of taffeta. Helmholz was a half-baked theatrical character who was then in the news in connection with a fashionable gambling raid. "I'll tell you about Helmholz," Isolde said, settling herself in an unoccupied chair and patting the ottoman for me. The woman she had been talking to had twisted off through the crowd, leaving us together.

In the press of a cocktail party everyone is in bas-relief. Friends lose a dimension; their talk, nervously disbursed for quick consumption, becomes all surface in a way that curiously drains them of characterization. Familiarity is undone — even one's wife appears at times a chattering alien. With strangers the trick is reversed. Having nothing previous to go by, you take at face value what account they give of themselves, and out of small details erect a character, for whatever it may be worth in accuracy. Quite quickly I had a full-blown version of Isolde Brown, which took a lot of checking up on later. For the moment, I could but let her represent herself as she would.

"Helmholz," she began, running the ball of a forefinger around the rim of her glass, "is a fool, sure. But then perhaps ambition makes fools of us all, at one time or another."

I have by no means yet lost the capacity for wonder, and I hung on her words, which her pretty mouth fashioned with a somewhat overprecise diction, like shapes turned out by a cookie cutter. And for the benefit, no doubt, of any producer who might be within earshot.

"I went to see him about, oh, seven years ago, when he was a producer, or trying to be. He said he wanted to know how well I could project an emotion without saying anything. So he gave me an assignment from real life. He wanted me to go to the Empire State Building and be rejected."

"He wanted you to go to the Empire State Building and be rejected?" I said softly.

She nodded, drinking. "The Observatory. That was before they had the high fence around the roof, and they were more careful about jumpers. At the window where you had to get your ticket, they watched for people who seemed moody or preoccupied. Anyone who answered that description, no ticket. That was my exercise — to be refused a ticket. If I couldn't convince the people at the ticket window that I was brooding about something, Helmholz said, how could I convince an audience in the theater?"

"This isn't what they call the Boleslavski Method, is it?" I inquired.

"The Stanislavski? No. Oh, I forgot to tell you — he wore felt slippers in his office."

"And did you do it?" I asked, flabbergasted by an image of a girl shuffling up to a ticket window to register anxiety with a mouth that reminded me of nothing but that fine old-fashioned simile about snow in a rose.

She tipped the dregs of her Martini into it. She was a moment chewing the olive — business, as they call it in the theater. I relieved her of the glass and set it on a table with a little craftsmanship of my own.

"I left Helmholz's office at one o'clock that afternoon. Two hours later, Helmholz got a phone call from a distracted girl who said she had not only been stopped at the ticket window but had been taken to the police station. I was there now, I told him hysterically, and would he hurry over in God's name and straighten this thing out. Well, I was calling from a phone booth in the drugstore downstairs of his office. His office was on the second floor. I hurried out of the drugstore and met him as he came running down the stairs, felt slippers and all, and sort of clawing his way into his overcoat. 'How was that for an imitation of a woman in distress?' I asked him. 'Did I convince you?' His eyes went so." She lowered her lids in a graphic rendition of reptilian menace. "I never got an interview with him again, let alone an audition."

I was curious about one thing. "Did you do this with your tongue in your cheek or were you serious about it the way he was?" I asked.

"Hm? Well, Helmholz never did put on a play. His only plays were the plays he made for the gals. I don't even know whether he had a script then. Oh well, so it was no loss. Poor old ham," she said sympathetically, and again I saw the derivative smile.

Well, any number can play at that game, and while waiting to fall asleep that night I gave her her head as Joan Fontaine, playing myself the man Helmholz could never be. The action of many of my daydreams took place at an imaginary lodge I have on a remote promontory of the Maine coast, which I call Moot Point. "Because of some legal kink in the deed," I told her, sucking in my cheeks in the manner of Clark Gable. We were strangers who had collided on the beach in a sudden downpour, and now she sat in the cottage propped among my hypothetical cushions, after a hot shower and dressed in my pajamas, which were way too big for her. I emerged from the bath myself wearing the terry-cloth "blotter" robe also essential to this scene, my neck scarved in additional toweling, and as I shuffled off in matching mules to the kitchen to brew some tea I drew taut the cord and said, "I probably don't own the place at all."

Sipping the steaming oolong we got better acquainted.

"I like to take absurdly long walks in the rain," she told me about herself. "And I like Pogo and Edna Millay and those crazy puzzle shops along Sixth Avenue. I love those foolish little flower carts in the Village. And I like men who don't worry about deeds to things, and smoke a pipe held together with adhesive tape." The eyelashes swept downward and there was the half-smile, with perhaps a touch of some winsome and muted early wildness. "Oh, and deep woods and the smell of pine. I love pine."

"I love yew."

"We mustn't."

She was soon unmasked as an aspiring actress who had contrived the encounter on the beach, knowing I was a noted producer holing in at my Maine retreat to read scripts. I had her recite to me in pear-shaped tones. Later we went to town and bought tone-shaped pears. Oh, we were silly like that for a month or more, silly and insanely lazy, knowing the hard work ahead, for I had decided to undertake her debut. More than merely talented, she had drawn me out of a husk of misanthropy into the sun and the fun again. . . .

This was among the reveries with which I detained myself in the days following the party, during which I wondered when I would see her again, of which I naturally had every expectation. Three weeks passed without my running into either her or Augie, whom I had met at the party long enough to shake hands with, and I forgot about them. I saw their house, once, for though it turned out to be on our road it wasn't on the way to the station I commuted from. Then one afternoon as my train was rolling into the Avalon station I caught sight of Isolde swaying in the aisle. She flashed a smile of recognition down the length of the coach, over a shoulder draped with a scarf of crimson wool. That evening, my wife being dug in at the telephone, I settled down with an after-dinner bottle of beer and was soon far away at Moot Point, deep in divagations of a worldlier order than previously. Then, I had arisen to breakfast from a couch on which I had all night humorously revolved in search of a comfortable position, for I had given the girl my bed. This time it was another story, and she expected to be made an honest woman.

"Yes, I've given a lot of thought to marriage — that's why I'm single," I said, striding out to the porch and pitching my cigar into the disreputable sea.

Friends have noticed — or at least I have noticed — a resemblance between my diction and that of George Sanders. There is the same closed-mouth delivery, the same urbane sense of everything being murmured. These and a knowledgeable fatigue, a sort of offhand *Weltschmerz*, together with features at once fleshy and sensitive, complete the similarity, which is marked enough for purposes of meditation.

"You're trying to make me hate you because you think I'm just grateful to you for making me a star," she said in a later scene, as the surf of applause beat undiminishing against the dressing-room door. "But I don't want this — now — I want us. Oh, Bruce, we'll go where we can hear the larks again."

"Larks, my dear, should be had, not heard. Take another bow now, and I'll see you at the party."

But the chit had proved unquenchable. Now she had followed me here to Connecticut where all along I'd had a wife I'd never admitted. Presently the two must meet — all three of us. What a nasty mess, to be tidied out of whatever faith and courage and plain sense we had between us —

I had been aware of my factual wife hanging up a real-life phone, then of the phone having rung again. "Swell, we'd love to," I heard her say, and hang up again.

She came into the living room where I was nursing my lager.

"That was Mrs. Poole. You remember — we met them at the Crandons' cocktail party," she said. "It seems they live up the road in the old Shively place."

"Oh, yes." I slid up in my chair and got a grip on my glass of beer. I was a bit startled, I must say. "What did she want?" I asked, picking up my drink.

"She wants us to take in a movie with them. Come on. Get up and put a tie on. It's that mystery we both want to see. Snap out of it. I'll call Mrs. Goodbread and see if she can sit."

Three

I HAD chance enough to be of service, though I didn't know
it yet. Not, to be sure, to make a star of Isolde, but to edit into
printability the cartoons her husband kept turning out and
sending to *The Townsman* — the more Herculean of the two
challenges you may be sure. They knew about my magazine
connection, but I still hadn't tumbled about Augie's name:
some stopcock in charge of my peace of mind held the recognition back. They had the grace not to bring the matter up
deliberately and nothing was mentioned after the movie, when
we dropped into a bar for a drink.

Isolde had on the bright wool scarf above which, and beneath
hair the color of ripe wheat, her smile played, ionizing my
stream of consciousness. Augie had on a brown tweed coat
and a turtle-neck sweater, which gave him a vaguely profligate
air. They were a handsome couple all right in their casual
splendor. Spattered brogans completed their accommodation
to the country. I felt like a hick in my banker's gray flannel
and tie that went well with it.

Trying to keep an ice cube submerged in a Tom Collins with
two straws, Isolde asked: "How many children do you
have?"

"Four," I answered sheepishly.

"Jesus," Augie said ambiguously. Isolde looked at him as, Fontaine all forgot, a smile split her face like a coconut. "We'd like to have some. Ever so much."

She had, as the philharmonic commentators say of horns and woodwinds, stated the theme of our relationship; but it passed undetected, as a musical motif will slip by the unapprised listener. The talk went from this to that, and we parted with the Pooles asking us to dinner the following Friday. We could make it.

When we arrived, Isolde let us in. She was wearing raspberry-colored slacks and a white peasant blouse, and blowing at an errant strand of hair, for she had been busy in the kitchen. Augie hove into view, wearing a denim coat and a silk scarf knotted with the proper casualness, even a touch of contempt. He was suavely stirring a shaker of Martinis, which he had just poured out of a bottle of Heublein's ready-made. We were ushered into a large living room through which cats slightly less in size than lynxes freely charged. There was a slight lawn of hairs on things in general, and I reflected how under another code of honor I might be permitted to invert the cushion on which I was invited to sit. I furtively did this, as a matter of fact, when the host and hostess were momentarily out of the room, to find more of the same on the underside. It's not a grudge I don't hold against my own house, reading dog for cat. The room soared to "original" beams, and on its lower levels illustrated its owners' allegiance to forthright fabrics and affirmative hues: there were large bright comfortable chairs almost haphazardly disposed, patternless drapes of the coarse, pleasant family known as homespun, scatter rugs offering splashes of further candid color. A heretical hooked rug or two were the effect of people not conscious of antiques but oblivious to them. Isolde flew between the kitchen and the living room, shading the oven flame in the one, the volume of a phonograph going in the other.

During cocktails, Augie told a story that I remember. "When Stephen Douglas was a young man debating in the political campaigns in Illinois," he said, "there was always a sort of lanky boy sitting in the front row, in one of the best seats. Grownups resented it, because seats were at a premium when Douglas spoke. But when they wanted to put him out, Douglas protested. He asked the boy why he came to the debates so regularly. And the boy said, 'Because some day I hope to be up there on the platform myself.' 'That's fine,' Douglas said. 'What's your name, my boy?' And the boy said, 'Abe.' 'Abe what?' Douglas asked him. And the boy answered, 'Abe Feldspar.'"

"Dinner!" Isolde called. It was a casserole of chicken cooked in red wine, and superb. But while we were eating it, fate chose to move in with his ruffian tactics.

The winds of conversation swung around, from God remembers where, to the subject of cartooning, and a question was put to me that, for some reason I can't fathom, I am constantly being asked. "Is it true that cartoonists draw themselves?" I answered that a lot of them did and that a few of them drew their wives, (but had drawn them before they'd met them). "Not friend Poole," Isolde said, laughing in her husband's direction. "Thank God. I'd hate to think there were any popeyes like that in this family. Maybe a popeyed girl jilted him once."

That was when the stopcock opened. "Good God," I said. "A. Poole. I'm sorry I never tumbled. I'll be damned."

"That's all right," Augie said, picking a shred of cork from his wine with a corner of his napkin, as though he were taking something out of somebody's eye.

Of course it wasn't. The identification was anything but a happy one. The "popeyes" I had now suddenly connected with my visual memory of the signature, A. Poole, were rejected regularly with letters bearing my own. That was half the story. The other half was that the ideas in them were swell. Poole was a third-rate artist in whom a first-rate gagman was trying to claw his way out, or rather that I was trying to claw my way to. For years The Townsman's editors had been trying to buy his ideas to send on to our good cartoonists, many of whom were indifferent jokesmiths and often becalmed at their drawing boards on that account. But he wouldn't sell. He went on doggedly resolved to prove the reverse of our view — that the gagman we saw was a cocoon out of which an artist would one day burst. "Thank you, I don't think I'll release this idea. I'll take another crack at a finish and maybe this time . . ." How choked my files were with letters beginning like that. How choked his own must be with my end of the correspondence. And how choked I was on this chicken.

Sensing that her wonderful food had turned to gall, Isolde laid a hand on my wrist and said, "We won't talk shop tonight, will we?"

"Hell, yawl so grim about?" Augie said. "Mean why get so grim? Miro, Klee, Saroyan, they all tell us to relax." However, he was wiping his palms on the sides of his pants.

"I wish I knew what this was all about," my wife said.

"I send my work to your husband's office. They don't want the pictures, only the ideas."

"Oh, that goes on all the time, don't let that upset you. There's one artist he gets off the train wailing about. It's been going on for years and this man never will . . ." The pressure of my foot on hers brought her up short. "What's that cartoonist's name again, dear?"

"Spittlefield," I said, fetching up for some reason with the name of my stationer. I very nearly said Feldspar. My wife said, "Oh, yes. Well, that's the way it goes."

"Yes," I sighed, "that's the way it goes." I reflected what a damn sight better this conversation would have gone at Moot Point, and made no secret to myself of wishing I was up there now.

"I keep thinking of myself as an artist," Augie went on. "They prefer to think of me as a gagman. Right?" The query came at me across the table like a fast Ping-pong shot.

"The best," I answered with a grin, "of our time."

Isolde put her napkin down. "Leave us repair to the living room," she said.

Coffee had the quality of religious proceedings, despite its being accompanied by a crème brûlée so delicious it was almost obscene. There were silences in which cups lowered on saucers sounded like pistol shots. When Augie was standing over a coffee table some time later pouring brandies and I was hovering in his neighborhood, I bent down and said in his ear, "I'm sorry I called you the greatest gagman of our time."

"Oh, that's all right," he said. "That's quite all right. Christola."

"It's just not constitutional," Isolde protested from elsewhere in the room, where she and my wife were perusing an architectural organ together. "All this shop talkety-talk. We'll have no more."

"Where do you work, Augie?" I asked, calling him that for the first time.

He pointed a thumb over his shoulder. "Old barn back there."

"I'd like to see your studio." I knew what the impulse that had made me say that was. That's the impulse to swallow something hot to get rid of it.

"Better put on your overcoats if you're going to stay in there and chin-chin," Isolde said. I knew what that impulse was too. She thought that now was the time to have Augie lay it on the line with me once and for all, and ask, "All right. Why don't you buy any of my stuff? What's the matter?" So we could get on with the business of becoming friends.

Augie and I bundled into our overcoats, rather in the mood of men being egged out of them to have a fight.

"Shall we take our drinks?" I suggested.

"Take the bottle," Augie said.

Playing the beam of a flashlight behind him like a movie usher, Augie led the way across a long yard, past a disused chicken coop to a red barn. "You haven't had any roughs in the last few weeks," I said, to show I wasn't afraid of him, and springing round a decayed poultry crate. "Done got me involved fixing this place up," he answered in the same tone. He opened a door in the barn, snapped a switch, and led the way up a steep stair to a freshly paneled loft with large windows the length of one side, and a wood stove about which hovered the odor of defunct fires. The room had the comprehensive disorder of a junkyard. Files and tables inclined toward one another, papers lay about like a compost, pictures in varying stages covered everything including the walls. At one end was a drawing board on which was a captionless sketch of a goat in a vacant lot eating a copy of Duncan Hines's restaurant guide.

Augie dropped into an armchair, after a sidelong glance at me taking this in, and waved me hospitably toward a ruptured day-bed. It was like an icebox in there. He sat with his overcoat spread open, but I buttoned mine to the chin. We lit cigarettes, and between the plumes our breath made and the tobacco smoke we blew in one another's direction we all but obscured each other from view, which was just as well for we were both twitching with anxiety.

"What shall we talk about?" Augie said, setting the flashlight on a table, still turned on. "The king of Spain's daughter?"

I finished off my brandy and he did the same with his. We refilled our glasses from the bottle which I had carried over in my overcoat pocket. Augie took a sheaf of drawings from the table and began to shuffle through them. "How about a stroll down Memory Lane. Remember this?" He thrust a picture at me.

I remembered it very well. It showed a woman patient peering furtively down into the street from the window of a psychia-trist's office, with a pistol in her hand. The psychiatrist was ask-ing, "What makes you think your first analyst is following you, Mrs. Meyerbeer?" I smiled and said, "Yes." It was one of the first ideas I had tried to wangle away from him. He'd worked over it at least twenty times, always ending up with something too unfunny for tears. Since then he had become if anything more wooden still, out of his drive to "perfect" himself. He handed me a picture showing an artist's studio, inexpressibly squalid, in which a gloved visitor was saying to a painter in rags, "Boris, I wish to God I could get you out of your ivory tower." The editorial mouths had watered in vain for that idea too. Done by the right cartoonist, it might have made a memo-rable piece of social satire. Now it was another souvenir of a joint frustration, moldering in the attic of a man in an ivory tower of his own.

"Why do you keep sending my stuff back?" Augie asked abruptly.

"Well, I mean hell." My knees came together in a spasm of cold. Dared I say, "Because it's as stiff as a new shoe and will never be anything else" — to be cruelly kind? I said, after a pull on my brandy, "We don't set ourselves up as critics. We just feel whether a thing is right for us or not."

"My stuff isn't right for anywhere else," was his rebuttal to this. I have found only one thing richer in non sequiturs than a woman's logic, and that is the logic of an artist about his own work.

"The thing you ought to try to do is loosen up a little," I said. This was, after all, the terminology of his own trade. "Tightness," "stiffness," these were a curse all cartoonists were rightly in horror of. I knew an artist so bedeviled by them that he went to every expedient including, so help me, that of working for a few weeks on transcontinental trains in hopes that the motion of the cars would rock his line free.

"Oh, the joke business!" I groaned. Augie chose that moment to drop all the papers he was holding to the floor with a smack, and didn't hear what I said, so I had to regroan it. I felt a spring in the daybed twang under one haunch. I threw a look toward the stairway.

"Do you think I should give up?" Augie asked, pouring another drink. "Is that your opinion?"

"No editor has the right to say that. I'll just say I've given up myself," I answered with a laugh, handing him back his fine jokes. He saw me roll an eye around the remodeled interior and guessed my thought. "Isolde has a grandmother with money," he said. "She bought this house for her. For us. I didn't marry Isolde for her money, but it's because she had money that I could marry her. Mean the money problem is the artist's perennial one."

"Of course," I said.

Augie brought his hand down on a nearby cabinet with what was neither quite a caress nor altogether a blow. "Well, if I ever get pinched enough to have to sell my ideas, it's nice to know there's gold in them thar hills."

"There sure are. Is." I sneezed and added: "Thousands of dollars."

"Shall we join the ladies?"

"If you like."

I was a time getting to sleep *that* night. In bed, I saw our new friends as having a last cigarette before putting out the lights, talking their guests over with special emphasis on my critical level as illustrated in the frozen loft. Isolde's moving to the suburbs would imply a surrender of her own career, never, I gathered, a very hopeful one, and a consequent deepening of her interest in her husband's. So I couldn't help thinking of them as talking things over, maybe in the kitchen as they did the dishes — another couple huddled together over the blundering wheel of fortune. A wave of pathos washed my fretfulness away, but I did wonder whether business and friendship must be mixed in yet another case, and whether to the detriment of either or both. Had my chances of wooing A. Poole's jokes away from him brightened or declined? But it was too trying a reality to rehearse long at this tired hour. And since I can't count sheep, because I keep trying to guess their sex as they jump over the fence, I was soon again in the land of revery. More wish-fulfillment. I imagined Augie to possess a talent of the first order, which I discovered and nursed into stardom as that of "one of the finest comic artists of our time" (*New York Herald Tribune*), to the undying gratitude of Isolde, and, what was more, the satisfaction of Hugh Blair, my volcanic editor in chief.

Four

THE next time I heard from Augie it was to find the goat eating Duncan Hines on my desk. Which picture was soon again restored to his possession. With the novelty of our not this time beseeching him for the gag.

It was later that same week that my wife got a phone call from Isolde that was to prove important in the lives of all four of us.

It was early evening. Our family were all in bed without the house having in the least retired. My wife lay in hers reading a book in which she was using a bus transfer for a marker, a fact which obscurely vexed me, and whistling tunelessly through her teeth, a grievance on which my hold was firmer. What a greater cumulative toll the small irritations of life take than its major woes; if instead of the thousand perennial gnats a man could pay in one good snakebite! My wife's name, I'm afraid, is Aurora. Since her majority she has gone as Audrey, which she regards as short for it though I take it to be an outright substitution. A woman's name ought ideally to steal over one, and not come up like thunder out of China 'cross the Bay. Our four children are Phoebe, Marco, Ralph and Maude, and some of them were discussing the names they were going to change to when such alterations were within their legal reach. A dog, a hound rich in separate strains, was down in the basement, asleep in a bisected cello. His name was Nebuchadnezzar, and though he was in no position to oppose it there were times when his dark eyes seemed to me liquid with reproach. I felt foolish myself every time I called him.

"We need more air in here," my wife said, turning a page. "And while you're up, get me a small brandy."

She is the soul of service by day, but at night is partial to being waited on. I'd be more willing to consider her whim my law if she didn't tend to regard it as such herself. And tonight it was my own whim to see how long it would take her to prop her request with a complaint about her physical condition; I knew all her gambits and was ready with a stock of medical repartee. Also, I wanted to show her that taking an executive tone with me was not in itself enough.

"My back is stiff as a board," she said presently.

"In through here?" I laid a hand on the small of mine.

"Yes."

"It's supposed to be stiff as a board there. That's called the lumbar region."

The caprices devised for my marital hours had of course both the rewards and the risks of actual testing that could never affect those at Moot Point. At the same time, I was trying to garnish the passing years with some of the prepared glitter of Moot Point, and so my surprise can be imagined when she scowled at me from her bed and lowered her book to her stomach. "I wish you'd have just one of these cricks of mine. Like this afternoon when I sat down a minute to play the piano, all of a sudden I got a twinge down my whole back."

"Possibly you struck a spinal chord."

I bounced over on my side, away from her, and laughed till the bed shook. She would purchase my services dearly! Of course we had some of the stresses you will find in any normal household, and she elected to have no share in the scene, nicely as it was going. I sensed from her silence that she was looking over at me with a slow burn. Those were more or less our positions when the telephone rang.

She was out of bed like a hound over a stile, no sore back now. I heard from her greeting that it was Isolde, and the two of them were soon dug in — something about babies but I couldn't make head or tail out of it. I fetched her robe and mules to the telephone, also the brandy as requested, and then made a patrol check of the children's two rooms.

First that of the girls — Maude, aged twelve, who believed in a monarchical form of government, and Phoebe, four. Maude asked me about everlasting life, but Phoebe goaded me about her name, which was definitely in her craw. I feel rather touchy about the name, having argued for it against my wife when she was pregnant and too drained by the object of the dispute to wage it with much spirit; now here was the child itself carrying on the fight against me. Phoebe had early divined that her name had comic value, also that it had been my idea; so it was that I came home, evenings, to find libelous profiles of myself on the walls, salt to have been discerned in the sugar bowl, and my studs and cuff links wedged into pots of cold cream by a child with a knack for improvisation. "I'll change it to Eleanor," she said as I left the bedroom after turning out the light there the third time. "Go ahead — and be like everyone else," I said.

I crossed the corridor to the boys' room. Something in the arrangement of details struck my eye as screwy. Ralph was standing in a corner trying, of all things, to fall asleep like a horse. I whisked him smartly out of his "stall" and back into bed. "I never heard of anything so asinine in my life," I said. "Horses can sleep standing up because they have four legs." I turned on Marco as a nine-year-old who should be more responsible in keeping his eye on a brother of five.

"Maybe I've got other things to think about," Marco said from his bed, his blue eyes bland in an oppressively circular face. "Whoever heard of a name like — ?"

"That's enough of that," I said with lethal moderation.

"Well, whoever heard of anybody with a name like Marco?"

"Your name is Marco and I've heard of you," I said, borrowing a retort from a Two Black Crows routine of the twenties. I was sick and tired of the fuss about names around here. "Did you have anything else on your mind, that you couldn't see your brother was standing in the corner like a horse without a blanket on?"

"Yes. I was thinking about the arithmetic problem Maude told us. I bet you can't do it. The poor mother has eight children and five and a half apples for supper. How does she divide them?"

"That's better. Don't fuss about your name just because Phoebe does. That's being a copy cat. Learn to have a mind of your own."

"I have. I'm going to change my name to Art as soon as I can."

"Learn independence now. Remember, the child is father of the man."

"What did you say?"

"I don't chew my cabbage twice," I said, wasting no urbanity on the likes of him.

I settled myself in bed with a highball this time, and a book selected from the headboard behind me.

As I was reading or drinking, I have forgotten which, something told me to move my eye and glance under a desk in the corner. I did. A rat, looking like Andy Gump, was watching me. He had an aspect of alert but forlorn protest, as though disclaiming the tradition against him. I drew back my book and let fly at him. He flowed along the wainscoting like a blob of rather dirty quicksilver and disappeared into the closet. I grabbed three or four more books from the headboard and hurled them into the closet, frightening myself half to death; then having given the rat ample time to clear out if he had an exit in there, I went after him. I scrabbled among shoes on the closet floor and found no rat but an arch-shaped hole in the far corner. I wedged the toe of a slipper well into it, retrieved and straightened the books, and hopped back into bed. I was glad when the bedroom door opened and Audrey reappeared, about ten minutes later.

Her face wore the expression that goes with News — the smiling, briefly hoarded relish of the female courier.

"Well?"

"The Pooles want to adopt a baby." She shook off her robe and got into bed. "What are you smiling about? I don't think that's very nice."

"Well, I mean they just moved out here and all," I said, grinning uncontrollably.

"That's why they moved out to the country." Then: "Isolde called to ask us a favor — or rather to tip us off. They gave our name as a reference to the agency."

I slid up to a sitting position. "But we hardly know them," I said.

"We're practically the only people they do know out here. And getting a character reference won't be the only thing the caseworker will come to see us for."

"What else will she want?"

Audrey sipped from her brandy, which she had carried from

the phone, and set it down on her nightstand. "Since we're friends as well as neighbors of the Pooles, with children of our own which theirs will probably play with and all, why, we're part of the applicants' environmental picture. The welfare agency will want a look at us."

"I see," I said, glancing into the closet. I didn't like the turn the conversation was taking, and gave it one of my own. "The main thing the agency will want to find out from us is, do we think the Pooles would make good parents? Just offhand, what would your opinion be?"

She pored over her nails, as she habitually does in a state of thought. I asked presently:

"Are you of two minds about them?"

"Yes and no."

I asked her to explain what that meant, and she said she meant yes for one of the aspirant parents, no as regarded the other.

"Exactly my opinion!" I said. I was eager to compare notes. "I wonder if we've passed and flunked the same people."

"I'll tell you what I think," Audrey said.

It's not a point on which anyone has been successfully sententious, to my knowledge, but I think women's reputation for intuition is based on the speed of their judgments rather than their accuracy. They're no more acute than men in their evaluations but neither are they any less so, which leaves them with some balance in their favor. Penetrating façades gives them more pleasure than seeing frailty in perspective, hence their "I told you I was right about him" is more familiar after someone has discredited himself than after he has brought himself distinction. Women, to their credit, never spare themselves in reversing their own appraisals, under fresh evidence, and their verdicts, if my wife is any gauge, can be astonishing. I remember an epithet with which she officially changed her mind about an acquaintance who fancied herself a sensitive aesthetic type far above distaff chores. Audrey had gone along with this slant, but after disillusionment had crept in, her revised estimate ran: "She's a bitch and a sadist and a good housekeeper."

Well, it turned out we differed about the Pooles right off. I spotted Isolde for "nice, but probably not very practical," and Augie as having "a lot more to him," despite his kinks and quirks, his slightly jazzed-up literacy. "It's just the other way around," Audrey said. "She's basically a sound girl, with all that actress fluff on top. She's serious about canning things this summer. In the short time they've been here she's gotten a line on the best adopting agencies — made work of it. No, that girl's O.K. Augie now. He's got something wrong with him that I can't put my finger on. Something in his, well, beams and timbers. It's as if I can *hear* termites in there that I can't see. It's very frustrating."

"You've got to admit Augie knows more. Has a lot more depth."

"Only on the surface. Deep down, he's shallow."

"Deep down he's *shallow!*" I exclaimed, scarcely able to conceal my delight. These are the word sequences for which I live. I liked a man being shallow at bottom even better than I had her recent "Winter sports leave me cold," and "Penicillin is a drug on the market." Such effects are a kind of specialty of hers, effortlessly come by you might say, which I had detected early in our union. The first, "When I woke up and found I had the flu, I was sick," I had pricked up my ears at on our honeymoon. Topsoil in Connecticut is far from dirt cheap. There is literally no end to them. She was surely the first to feel that anybody who goes to a psychiatrist ought to have his head examined. I don't think she suspects how dear these convolutions are to me, nor that I keep a mental file or "collection" of them. Well, anyhow, to get back to the argument. Her last words were: "Watch."

That was the long-range program; the immediate order of business was to get to sleep. An hour later, I was lying in the dark with my hands laced under my head, thinking about what the caseworker might be told. Audrey's bed gave a sharp creak as she raised her head alertly. "Do I hear a mouse?" she asked.

"No," I said, my lips curled in a faintly ironic smile, which of course she could not see for it was pitch dark. And which was not of long duration, for I thought: How will I handle that problem? Could Nebuchadnezzar be banked on to any extent? He had a terrier ingredient in him, to judge from the zeal with which he worried slippers through the house, but the question remained whether the instinct could be brought to bear on a more cunning adversary.

I was about to drop off when something popped Marco's arithmetic problem into my head. What was it the poor mother had had? Eight children and five and a half apples. Well, let's see, eight times five would be forty, so if she cut the apples into eighths she would have forty slices to divide, or five slices for each child. But what about the half left over? She could divide that into eight pieces, of course, but that sounded too simple; the problem must be to find a way of cutting the apples into slices of equal size — otherwise what would be the sense of putting it in an arithmetic book? Let's see now, how did the poor mother work it out? Oh, the hell with it, I told myself — go to sleep.

I settled resolutely on one side, kneading the pillow under my head. I tried to get my mind on the rat again, but the way back wasn't easy. Problems and puzzles have a way of getting their hooks into me. Give me farmers with acreage to parcel among their sons and canoes with distances to travel upstream and I am soon out of my wits. I lay stark awake. What composer was it — was it Mozart — who as a small child would torment his father by stealing downstairs at night, striking an unresolved chord on the clavichord, and sneaking back up to bed again, leaving the old man to toss and turn till he had left his own bed and gone down and resolved it? No connection. Yes, there is. The raveled sleeve of sleep. He who has children gives hostages to fortune. The Pooles want children and this is very laudable of them, for could they not just as easily go on spending all their money selfishly on themselves? Isolde's grandmother's money, rather. Would the agency ask me about Augie's finances? Would he ever be self-supporting? It was tough for the head of a family to make both ends meet. The poor mother has eight children —

I threw the covers back and got out of bed. I turned the light on over the desk. I sat down, drew pencil and paper to me, and started in. Now, the thing I must do is find a common denominator for eight and five and a half. Of course. Then I'd as good as have it. I was scratching away when Audrey stirred sleepily. "What are you doing?" she asked.

"Going over some figures."

She dropped off again. But presently the same inquiry was mumbled. "Just something I want to do before I forget," I answered. "You go to sleep."

Then for the third time: "What are you doing?"

"Nothing."

It was true enough. Even finding a common denominator and letting the poor mother divide accordingly would not, I guessed, be the answer; for the suspicion now began to gnaw me that the whole thing was a riddle, with a pun or something for an answer. A hell of a thing to get into in the dead of night. I might lie here fussing till daybreak, unless I "gave up." I gave up.

I snapped the light off and picked my way down the hall, flicking on a succession of others, to the boys' room. I shook Marco awake.

"In that problem, you remember, what did the poor mother do?" I asked him.

He uttered a startled cry.

"Shh!" I said. "You'll wake the others. It's just Daddy. You forgot to tell me the answer — you know, about the five apples and eight and a half children. I mean the eight children and five and a half farmers," I whispered in his ear. "Daddy gives up."

"Leave me alone," he said.

I saw that he would be no good to me. I recalled it was Maude he'd gotten the problem from, so I went into the girls' room and shook *her* awake. "That problem about the mother and the apples," I said. "You remember. What did the poor mother do?" *She* muttered something in protest and turned away on her side. I shook her by both shoulders. "What did the poor mother do?" I demanded.

"Made applesauce."

Climbing back into my bed — for what I trusted would be the last time that night — I wondered how Augie would have done as paterfamilias, given tonight as a sample, say. Then the reverse suggested itself: what would the agency have thought of me? A heavy drowsiness began to overtake me. That, I mused, was one of the fortunate advantages of having children the normal way — nobody was around to say whether you should. With such comfort as I could extract from that thought, I fell asleep.

Five

WHEN the caseworker arrived I was making faces at my children to show that I ought to have them. Funny faces, eyes crossed, cheeks squished in, that were great sport. I had been watching for the caseworker from the picture window, and managed to time a tableau of sorts for her benefit on the above lines, when her car turned off the road and came up the gravel drive to the house.

It was now some five weeks since Isolde's call forewarning us of her and three since the caseworker herself had called to make this appointment. This wasn't the Mrs. Mash before whom I was stricken dumb but a predecessor back in the relatively azure days when I didn't know anything much about Augie. It was two o'clock of a Saturday afternoon in mid-April. The children had been bathed, brushed and scrubbed till they looked sullen but simonized, for was it not avowedly among our objects to pass muster with the welfare people ourselves? There was not a member of the family who wasn't dressed in his best from the hide out.

It had not been easy. The day had begun portentously, with a contagious crossness among the children building by noon to that kind of uproar that sometimes seizes pet shops. Phoebe had awoken in a vile humor; she was going to kill Ralph, cut the fringes off the rugs, go to Egypt. She and her mother were at the breakfast table together when I sat down there. I flapped out my napkin and said brightly to Phoebe, "Eating your breakfast?" No answer, and I picked up my orange juice. My wife checked me with a shake of her head. "Phoebe, your father asked you something," she said. Continued silence. The girl's no good till she's had her milk, and then is nothing to brag about. "Maybe you didn't hear him. He will say it again." She gave me a sign to repeat.

"Eating your breakfast?" I said, with somewhat synthetic spirit. Still no reply. I lifted my orange juice and again my hand was stayed with a look. "Phoebe, your father asked you a question," my wife said sternly now. "Must everything stop till you're civil?"

"Forget it," I said, anxious to get on to my breakfast. "It's a rhetorical question, just a remark really. I don't mind."

"But I do," my wife said, with a look which said she was surprised that I could not see when an issue should be made of a thing. "Now, Phoebe," she continued to the girl, "we'll give you one more chance to be polite. If you aren't, I'm afraid we'll have to do something about it." She cued me with another nod. I took it from where I'd sat down. Flapping my napkin out once more, I said with a threadbare smile, "Eating your breakfast are you, Phoebe?"

We both watched her. There was a short silence. Then, somewhat darkly into her cereal, she said, "Yes."

I fell to, and my wife returned to the paper she'd been reading. The next order of business made more sense.

"You're not eating your breakfast!" we both observed to the tot, who was shoving her cereal about in its bowl. At that moment Ralph came in clutching a stuffed horse and revealed plans to spend the day in the MacPhersons' barn, which were promptly countered with the reminder that we had an important visitor coming today, and that cleanliness was of the essence. I dilated on the prevalence of this theme in nature. "Look at the cat," I said, pointing to one of the Pooles' eunuchs, which we had on loan to see if it could help eradicate the rats. "Cats are the healthiest animals in the world. And why? Have you ever noticed how they're always licking themselves?"

"Yes," Phoebe said, "it's a filthy habit." Showing that she can make breakfast conversation when she wants to.

When Maude and Marco arrived we were discussing why cats don't come when you call them, the way dogs do. Now, at one stage in the getting-acquainted scene of my Moot Point fantasies — where the girl is wearing my pajamas and sipping hot tea after the thundershower which had driven us to refuge there, you will remember — at one juncture she tells me that she is fond of cats. I reply with a sort of quip which struck me as apropos of what we were talking about here at the breakfast table. So I threw it into the family discussion.

"Cats are merely live bric-a-brac," I said. My wife gave me a shake of the head to tell me not to confuse the children. I returned to my coffee. Maude tried to call the cat: "Here, Figaro! Here, Figaro!" — with no results. Marco piped up, "Maybe he's another one who doesn't like his — "

"That's enough of that!" I said. I stamped my foot, starting the oil furnace. "Children today are let speak their piece about everything," I complained to my wife. "They're pampered and indulged and kowtowed to. Back in the great pioneer times of our country, people had names like Cotton and Increase. Those were the days of stamina."

In the midst of minding all the children while my wife cleaned the house that morning (with no help, the cleaning woman being sick), I took time out to deal with the rats. I had seen no more since that evening, but my wife had sighted "something" running behind the Bendix in the basement. I went down there toward noon with a broom and a BB gun, and with bicycle clips fastened around the ankles of my pants. After clattering about behind boxes and barrels, flushing nothing, to my considerable relief, I got Nebuchadnezzar aside as I had before. I took him to our bedroom closet. I got down on all fours and showed him the hole there. Then, pointing alternately to that and to the picture of a rat on a box of poison, I went through a series of sounds and motions, which would elude reproduction here, by means of which I tried to drive home the fact that, rather than the footwear which it was his wont to chew, here was his rightful foe, whose challenge was his birthright and whose prompt and faithful dispatch was essential to the preservation of my esteem. Then I wedged back into the hole the beer coaster with which I had been keeping it stopped up.

By this time the children were boiling to some sort of climax. They had been listening to records under the supervision of Maude, the oldest, who had set their backs up by insisting the music played be "good." She had going the Magic Fire music from Die Walküre, the story of which I had related to her. "There's the fire," she explained to the circle gathered round on the floor. "Hear the crackle of the flames." She said this so prissily that I could not resist telling her, "No, that is needle scratch." This put her out of sorts with the enterprise as such, and she began to practice a piano piece of her own with the phonograph still going. Above the whine of the vacuum, this was an interesting phonic experience. It seemed as good a time as any to give the girls the shampoos which had been decreed.

I obtained some rather unique effects. In calling out instructions for rinsing, my wife told me to use the juice of half a lemon for each, diluted in a little water. Pouring this over the head was the penultimate step — I got that. But I understood her to have said a cup of lemon juice for each. In addition, nobody said anything about straining the juice (though I did flick the pips out with a spoon), and the resulting pulp in the tresses was more than a simple rinsing could handle, and my wife had to wash the girls' hair all over again. It wasn't till I was drying their locks with an electric blower that I noticed the resemblance to clotted straw, and turned them over to their mother. I stood in the bathroom doorway as she lathered the heads anew, doing my best to keep up everyone's spirits.

"I should think you could spare me at least this," my wife said, "with my back. Yesterday I got another of those twinges driving to Bridgeport. But driving the car," she puzzled. "Must be some nerve."

"Possibly involving the motor area. What," I went on, leaning against the doorjamb with my hands in my pockets, "did you go to Bridgeport for?"

"See about musical instruments — where you're not much help either. What did you suggest to Ralph he take up a shoehorn for? Now the child thinks you can play on one."

"You can — footnotes."

You can understand my surprise at the irritation with which these attempts to lighten the burdens of the morning were met, likewise those I made in the living room from which I called over words of encouragement, advising her to avoid all agitation and to keep calm in the teeth of adversity, which would soon enough be got through. "Oh, go find Ralph and give him his bath," she said.

He was found, easily enough, in the proscribed barn, and was such a mass of filth and bruises that the one could not be told from the other. Nor did I eliminate the one without adding to the other, so brisk was the drubbing I administered in the tub. Tearful howls attested the thoroughness of my efforts, and a faint smile my satisfaction with the results.

I had not been in the children's bathroom for some time, and now found scraps of paper glued to the enamel of the tub, which I paused from time to time to scratch at with my nails.

"What is all this you've got stuck to everything? Are these stamps?" I said.

"You told us to keep our Christmas seals in the bathtub — "

"Oh, for God's sake!"

Fatherhood is an art, and it took as much tact and beguilement as it did muscle to get both the premises and the children spic and span by two o'clock, but we did. I trust the caseworker was well struck by the tableau we presented at the picture window where, in addition to the faces I was making at my family, I believe I also had my thumbs inserted in my ears and was comically waggling my fingers. My wife answered the door, wearing a blue housecoat and leisurely dropping a magazine to the coffee table as she rose to go to it, smiling at the scene we made. "I'm Miss Terkle from Rock-a-Bye," said a resonant voice.

Miss Terkle was a woman of fifty in tweeds the color of summer sausage and with straight brown hair drawn into a yam at the back. She glanced round the living room with what appeared to be approval, and then beamed at the children. They were radiant, and there were glints in the girls' golden hair, undoubtedly the remains of citrus mash.

"Now then," she said, settling into a pull-up chair. Now then indeed.

There are times when parenthood seems nothing but feeding the mouth that bites you. It never seemed to me more so than that afternoon. Phoebe, who knew she had us, led off with a request for eating matter. Which I met by reminding her that, on that head, she had done nothing with her lunch but rearrange it on her plate.

"Sounds familiar," Miss Terkle laughingly remarked. "I guess all parents have different ideas how to cope with the food rebel, but none of them appear efficacious. What do you do when a child won't eat its food?"

"Send him to bed without any supper," I said.

I felt a pressure on an already aggrieved bunion, applied under the coffee table by my wife's foot, as she smiled at Miss Terkle and said, "Would you like a cup of tea?"

"A cup of tea would be fine."

"I hope you take cream," my wife said, rising. "We haven't a lemon in the house."

"Are you going to give her cookies?" Ralph said.

"If you're good," I answered, meeting his ellipsis head on. I glanced quickly at Miss Terkle to see if I'd made another gaffe by thus laying down a pragmatic, or "reward," basis for morality; but her expression told me nothing, that being rather a matter of watching with interest as Ralph's hand advanced toward a bowl of nuts on the coffee table in front of her. The hand closed on a fistful of them, and mine on it. I tried to make him yield his booty, but the hand was as hard to pry open as a clam. I prised a finger at a time away, the nuts dribbling back into the bowl and onto the table. Miss Terkle sat forward, as if witnessing some prolonged and misbegotten act of legerdemain. "Lick the problem not the child," I panted with a smile. She nodded, watching intently. Rather than the principle I had enunciated, I longed to illustrate that more venerable one of "knocking some sense into them" — though if I'd got started on that boy just then I doubt if I'd have been able to stop short of knocking it out of him. I got his hand open at last, but in a final lunge of resistance he stumbled against the coffee table, overturning it at Miss Terkle's feet and emptying the bowl of nuts in her lap.

"Can we go now?" Marco asked, when Miss Terkle had been tidied up.

"You not only can but you may," I said. "Out in the relative sunshine with you! Play nice together, all of you, and when we have tea maybe we'll give you cookies and ginger ale."

I was convinced now that the caller felt herself to be slumming. In the need to recover status, I studded my conversation with as many terms like "substitute situation" and "plastic suggestion" as I could, to show that I was familiar with the latest terrain on child guidance; but I felt her expression to be deteriorating steadily, as though, that is, it were now no longer a question whether I should have had children but whether my father should have. A sudden vibration of withdrawal, a lowering of my eyelids, signalized a dangerous glut on my part with this subject, which I now left to the women. Vaguely I heard them talk about the Period of Protest (when the child throws dishes on the floor), then about the Period of Co-operation (when he insists on carrying them in from the dining-room table). I was in my Period of Resignation (the realization that the adults sweep the fragments into a dustpan in either case). Then Miss Terkle was recommending what she considered the definitive volume on dealing with children from five to seven. "I think five to seven is the most crucial period in many ways," she said.

"Right," I said, sliding up in my chair. "That's the cocktail hour."

Miss Terkle glanced at her wrist watch. "I won't keep you any longer than I have to," she said. "This has been very interesting. Now, what about the Pooles?"

"The who?" I said.

"The Pooles. Your friends."

"Oh, yes." We gave our view of the matter, the gist of which was that, yes, we thought it would be fine for the Pooles to have children, whom they could give a good home. What else was there to say? What else was there to think? The Pooles were an intelligent young couple with means, with enough money for a nurse. . . . So we gave our recommendation, and Miss Terkle took her leave, shortly before four o'clock.

"I'm sorry about the nuts," I said.

"Oh, that's all right."

"No, it isn't," I said, and meant it: The nuts that had been swept up and thrown out were roasted almonds costing a dollar and a half a pound, which I had looked forward to nibbling on with my imminent Martini.

I was setting about the concoction of that when the children came tumbling back in, offering to tired spirits a burst of animal health. They talked about Miss Terkle, and I felt there must surely be some substitute situation for this. At last I hit on one. I put on my hat and went out to a bar instead.

The upshot of everything was that the Pooles appeared to have been turned down. Oh, not in so many words of course; they just didn't get any child. By the end of the summer the implications were clear. I took the disappointment resentfully to heart, feeling it one in which I personally shared by having failed to come up to snuff as part of somebody's environmental picture.

"It's hard to tell why agencies turn down couples," my wife said. "It could be some one thing in the Pooles' setup, or a little bit of everything in it. The Hurlbutts haven't been able to find out to this day why they flunked."

"How did it all happen? Where did we go wrong?" I went on, flapping my hands at my sides.

"Don't let it get you down," Isolde said, taking my arm one afternoon as we were leaving their house to go for a drive. "We'll try another agency."

"You're damn right we will," I said. "The hell with Rock-a-Bye."

But Isolde was by no means in perennially level spirits. When October came and they were given neither a child nor a reason for the refusal, she stamped her foot furiously at her home one evening and said, "Why not? What's this all about? Is there some skeleton in our closet or something? That we don't even know about ourselves? How do caseworkers find things out?"

"They snoop," I said. I remember that my wife was watching Augie, who was mixing drinks at the bar.

Snooping is probably the term for what I now undertook myself. For as the Pooles plunged doughtily into a fresh try with another agency, one in New Haven, I thought about them, listened to things about them, asked about them — bent on finding out what I could. My curiosity was thorough and it was systematic. I became a caseworker.

Six

FOR months there was no data — the mystery seemed unsolvable. Then suddenly it poured in from all directions and without my prying for it.

Rather than merely at dinners exchanged in one another's home, we now began to see the Pooles at parties everywhere — the parties I have come to think of as "those Saturday-night strip teases."

How well I remember those Saturday-night strip teases that were such a cardinal part of Avalon social life, yet how they all seem to blur into one: I mean those gatherings at which familiars favored one another with something of the nature and origin of their personality structures, revealing stage by stage the libido or ego or inferiority drives that made them what they were. The next morning they might shudder a little at the intimacy of their disclosures, but not while they were at it; I was often detained by total strangers with accounts of their complexity. "Did I ever tell you about my aberration?" would seem to be the latter-day variant of an old gambit. Women, I think, made freer with themselves than men, stopping short only of some ultimate secret suited to the analyst's ear alone — indeed like dancers one garment short of final revelation, deterred, perhaps, by a warning frown from a husband across the room. At such times it was often all I could do to keep from clapping my hands and yelling, "Take it off!"

There were at these strip teases specialties to suit all tastes. One woman I recall analyzed the whole of her foliation in terms of erogenous zones. This was more interesting to an advertising executive who was present than it was to the rest of us because he listened to the entire story under the impression that erogenous zones were red-light districts. But under whatever skies their peculiarities had burgeoned, in whatever family bosoms they had been separately irked, these people together formed an aristocracy of ills; nor was membership in it to be had merely by being in possession of the glossary, as the ranking neurotics soon gave me to know. There was an implication quite deeply rooted, namely that discomposure is the price of civilized subtlety, and freedom from it the boon of less evolved types. The neurotics were those oysters, so to speak, in whom the abrasive grain of sand had produced the pearl, Sensibility. I myself took this on faith; so that when the neurotics slung an arm around my shoulder, as they often did, and said they envied me my untortured simplicity, I had a feeling of resentment and chagrin. And when they referred to me as "levelheaded," "steady," "a good sort," it was like a goad in my side, for it amounted to being called names. None of this would have carried the sting that it did were it not for a certain professional aspect to this whole matter, which involved a man's pride.

Avalon is full of artists and intellectuals. They set the social tone in the circles in which I found myself afloat. Since artists were so numerous, the connection between neurosis and talent was widely aired, and the view of a genius as someone not accountable to normal standards highly thought of. I found Augie very vocal on this subject.

"Name me one genius who wasn't a son of a bitch," he said one Saturday night at the Blooms'. He was standing at the mantel, waving a highball in one of those gestures that seemed always so patently to typify the Eastern seaboard. "Name one. A son of a bitch in his domestic life, or his sexual conduct, or money matters, or his relations with people at large."

We sat a moment in thought, as if playing a game.

"Plato?" I said at last.

"Very little is known of Plato. Socrates? He wants to know about Socrates," Augie said humorously. Since this mere mention seemed enough for most of the others I didn't ask for particulars, not wanting to appear an ignoramus.

"Shakespeare," I gave him next off the top of my head.

"Shakespeare he says. He wants to know what kind of a bird Shakespeare was. Well we don't really know — luckily for him!" Augie said, smiling at those in primary-colored shirts and wool ties, who smiled back. "Coleridge caused his wife constant embarrassment. Who next? Dickens did I hear somebody say?" He hadn't, certainly not me, but he singled me out as the target of these apparent ripostes because I had sent the goat eating Duncan Hines back to him. "Dickens turned his wife out of the house," he affected to fire back at me. "Gauguin told his family to go to hell. Flaubert had intercourse with a courtesan with his hat on and a cigarette hanging out of his mouth."

"What for?" I asked.

"To show his contempt for bourgeois standards. Wagner had three children by another man's wife, while he was working on his best operas. Byron was a son of a bitch. Smollett wrote all over the walls, or was it Trollope? No, you can't ask a man to be a good artist and a good human being both. The artist is a washout as a husband."

Isolde smiled admiringly up at him during the bulk of this speech.

"And the better he is the worse he is," he finished, and drank. A man in a primary-colored shirt nodded.

"He's right about that," said the man, a painter whose canvases were dubious, but whose inability to get along with other people was monumental.

Now all this began to get to me. Little by little, as the mosaic of implications completed itself, I acquired the sense of lacking caste among subtle and gifted spirits, many of whom were validly that, though with the most articulate it was of course often a case of "howling loudest who had drunk the least." All the artists and intellectuals I knew personally and dealt with editorially had periods when they didn't do a tap of work, which they called, as you know, blocks. Then they would have to go see their psychiatrists, or blockbusters. They frequently interpreted these blocks as sexual, just as they had their drive to produce. It was enough that the real painters talked about their blocks, but when one afternoon at a cocktail party I heard a commercial artist going on about having one, I thought that was a bit thick. This commercial artist had done a series of posters for a chewing gum which were outstanding of their kind. On top of him bragging about his block, his wife chimed in with something about his being "all tied up in knots lately." That did it. I figured if he could have blocks and be tied up in knots, anybody could.

I cast a glance over my life and temper. I could point to days when I just damn well didn't see how I could go in to the office. Why weren't those blocks? I was on salary, true, but there were weeks on end when I was in a "funk" about my work, had no "stomach" for it whatsoever. Those stretches, why couldn't I call them periods of being immobilized about the magazine game if I wanted? As to the shortcomings-as-persons that are the bruited hallmark of talent, why, I could adduce instances in my own case, of which such things as treating tradesmen shabbily and spasms of irritability with my wife and children were only the beginning. There were times when I think I could honestly say there was no living with me. There were other things along these lines. I couldn't reasonably expect much in the way of public testimonials from my wife on that score, but I felt I had a right to at least as much loyalty as the commercial artist got from his. So I brought the subject up as we were driving from the party in question to another party, and we had a spat about it.

"Why don't you ever build me up?" I asked her, out of what she no doubt took to be a clear sky.

"What do you mean, build you up?" she asked.

"You know very well what I mean. The way other wives build their husbands up."

"I don't see how you can say I don't build you up. Why, only tonight, at the card table, I was saying how pleasant you are at breakfast."

"Sure, make me out a cheerful moron," I said. "How about the dumps I get into about my work, and then the states. I'm a dethroned elder child, remember. My temper isn't so damned long as you sometimes like to think!"

"What are you talking about?"

"Sometimes I wonder if you ever know."

She had been slumped abstractedly down in her seat, but now straightened up.

"*Really!*" she said.

"Yes, really," I said, feeling the wrangle was going well; feeling that if some of our fine-feathered friends could hear me now they wouldn't think I was such a bland mediocrity.

"Have you been drinking?" my wife asked me.

"No, but it's an idea. I need one — all that guff tonight. That commercial artist's wife going on about the stews he gets into. Chewing-gum posters, for Christ's sake! Who the hell does she think he is? I should think you'd resent it. Why, there are days when I come home limp as a rag from tension. You know that. I'm just as tied up in knots as he is any day. I'm just as much as any of these bastards around here. And don't you forget it!"

She gave a weak shake of her head and looked out the window. "I never know what you want," she said.

Well, I knew what I wanted. I wanted to be treated with some respect in my home community. I wanted to be regarded as somebody. After all it wasn't as though I was a magazine hack; I was creative to a large extent in my work, suggesting changes and even complete switches to artists that they might never have thought of themselves, working with them from the idea stage, and so on. My editorial contributions were thus an integral part of the generative process, in whose extreme ferments I often as not wore my secretary thin. I was in any case fed up with being branded as levelheaded, which I felt certainly to be unwarranted.

I was still brooding on these matters when we reached our destination, a lawn party at some friends named Winchester. The party is important because it was there that Augie gave me my first inkling of the scale on which he practiced what he preached.

There was on hand a nobly hewn blonde who had arrived

with a local painter, the spoils of a recent excursion into the theater, which had consisted of his doing the sets for a musical comedy. She wore a shimmering coral gown which advantageously set off her arms and shoulders and the snowy cleft between. Looking accidentally in Augie's direction I caught his long, carnivorous glance as she crossed the grass to take her seat, but gave it no second thought, there being not a man there on whom her vibrations did not rain. She even made me salivate; I say even me because I am normally plunged into despair rather than excitement by such presences, which are but part of the world's weary wasted stimuli. As intimated, it has become somewhat my pleasure to see women qualify on the more abiding ground of colloquy, and so when I heard the newcomer remark, on her entrance, "Tom has been handing me the usual baloney about how long women take to dress," I knew she was not likely to be among those guests who were regularly seen at Moot Point. Augie was not so given to caviling. Early in the evening he was à deux with her on the lower slopes, helping her to seconds from the buffet spread as well as from his store of learning concerning the living habits of the great. Once I saw her throw back her head and laugh at something he'd said, and it was not much after that that I didn't see either of them at all. I learned afterward that his progress was based in part on her impression that he was a playwright with a work nearly ready for production, a misunderstanding he did nothing to correct and may have done something to create. This all came to a head quickly, to the consternation of more than a few people.

The grounds here were of estate size, almost a small park, an expanse of lawn and manicured privet in the center of which lay an oval pond. Augie in piloting his friend from view had skirted the outer hedgeworks and come up well out of the dusky glow of the Japanese lanterns; but the damn fool had not reckoned with the notorious acoustics of open water. We could hear every word he said, the ten or dozen of us who were sitting just then at the side of the pond near the house. We were presently treated to an aphorism.

"Most women only strike the quarter hour, some the half," came Augie's voice in a murmur transmitted with high fidelity across the calm water. "A few strike the hour. You're one of those."

We writhed as if sitting on nests of ants. Someone called, "Who's for dancing?" To which an eager chorus demanded that the radio be gotten out and going on the terrace without delay. Then there was silence. Into which came Augie's voice again:

"Who was it that said, 'Let us all be terribly Spanish, for there is not enough time to be Greek'?"

It was no doubt the speaker's acting on the injunction to be Spanish that brought the next sound we heard — that of the smart clap of a hand on a cheek. It's one of the most rending adult sounds witnessable, and is almost never heard in real life. Whatever its effect on its object, that on our group was to disperse it like a dropped shell. We scattered in all directions, angrily demanding to know what was keeping the music.

My wife couldn't wait to get into our car, when the party broke up. She had been among the witnesses to the incident, which thank God hadn't included Isolde.

"Well, what did I tell you?" she said, before I had the car quite in second.

"Hm?" I said, being concerned with a stuck window on my side, and also mentally engaged in weighing the merits of garroting, strangulation and poison for Augie. "How's that?"

"You know what I mean. About your fine friend. I told you so." She sighed and shook her head. "I'm surprised at him."

"You told me so, but you're surprised at him."

"That's just an expression. I'm really not surprised at all. Really! Making a pass at another woman. Well, what do you think of your boy now?"

I steered the car around a large hole in the road. "It goes on all the time," I said.

"You certainly don't sound as if you disapproved of it."

"I'm no censor of other people," I said. "The trouble with you is you don't take people as they are."

"Thank you."

"You're welcome," I said, with as much an air of repartee as the nature of the exchange permitted.

We rode on in silence for a while. I could sense that she was a pod bursting with contention. At last, sighing sharply now rather than meditatively, she said: "That's the male viewpoint all right. Sticking together like — union members!"

"I don't think it was the male sex that started what went on tonight. That dress — designed solely for the purpose of showing off her excellent recreational facilities." My wife made a repressed, grinding noise. I shrugged and said. "It's one-thirty."

"Don't you condemn that sort of thing?" she inquired abruptly.

"Yes, it was a foolish thing to do. At a party and all."

"That's not what I mean and you know it. Don't you condemn it as such?"

All might yet have been well if she only hadn't said "and you know it." That was what stoked me up again. I could not find it in my heart to say, "Yes," and make an end of it. I asked:

"Who was it that said life would be perfectly enjoyable if it were not for its pleasures?"

"What does that mean?"

"Why, that the by-products and botherations that go with pleasures make it hardly worth it. Sex is supposedly life's greatest pleasure and look what it gives you. That," I said, jerking a thumb over my shoulder at what we had left, "and — this."

"Thank you."

"You're welcome. We're the victims of our morality as much as of our sins," I continued acutely, guiding the car around another pock in the road. "Perhaps more. If marriage wasn't made so much a corral in which to confine us we'd all be more content to stay inside it. All you have to do to make Augie forget that bag of sachet is make her available. As it is, he'll probably spend the night tossing and turning."

"I see. Free spirits."

"Oh, for God's sake."

"Maybe you wish you were just dropping me off instead of going home with me."

"Make no mistake about that!" I said, piloting the car into the garage, for we had reached the house.

"Well, go right ahead!" she said, slamming the car door behind her after getting out.

"All right I will!" I said, following her up the walk to the front door.

Mrs. Goodbread took her money, summarized the evening, and left without having to be taken, for she lived only a few houses up the road. I locked the door behind her and turned to find my wife, who had checked on the children, walking into our bedroom. "You're right about one thing," she said from in there. "There are times when you're impossible."

"Thank you."

"You're welcome."

Retirement was a travesty. We occupied our respective beds in one of those marital silences that are so much more corrosive than any words can be. Each lay building up his charge of static electricity, not only out of the friction of the moment but out of the materials of ancient grievances as well: in her case the long maternal grind, thanklessness, fatigue; I as the tethered male who could identify himself with a friend's digression.

"I suppose this isn't just general talk. Maybe you're trying to pave the way for the future. When you might have an affair of your own some day?"

I punched my pillow somewhat and said: "Intellectually speaking, there's no good ground for condemning it categorically. Why is at least one affair almost universal among couples we know? Most anthropologists agree man is not naturally monogamous, remember."

"I'll remember." She settled on her side. "Any time you want to hole up in town with some flea bag, go right ahead. It's O.K. with me."

"Hole up *in* a flea bag," I corrected her. "*With* a floozy, *in* a flea bag. I wish you'd get terms like that straight. It reflects on me."

I spent the night tossing and turning. When I arose the next morning, Sunday, about ten o'clock, I found her alone at the breakfast table. The children were playing outside in the bright sunshine. She was behind the *New York Times*. I poured myself some coffee and "joined" her. I slipped a slice of bread into the toaster and sat nervously watching for it to pop. She cleared her throat.

"I see Reverend Bonniwell — that minister Mother went to school with, you know — died," she said.

"Death is no respecter of parsons."

It was no good. Her silence on receipt of my reply sharpened the constraint and worsened the mood between us, though she seemed not to notice this. She folded the paper, laid it aside and said, "I've decided to forgive you."

Now this had the misfortune of being precisely what I had planned to do to her.

"Oh, you'll forgive me, will you?" I said. "And suppose I refuse to be forgiven. For an argument that's been made a logical female hash of, like every other — "

"Don't give me any more to overlook," she advised, buttering a remnant of toast.

"Overlook, forgive. If there's any forgiving to do around here, I'll do it! What have you got to say to that?"

"Nothing," she replied with spirit, and rose and threw her napkin on the table. "I don't want to talk to you today or even see you."

"That's easily enough arranged," I barked in return, rising and chucking down my own napkin. Since she had taken the dramatic offensive by sailing out of the room, there was no way for me to top it except by sailing out of the house, which I accordingly did — out the open front door and slamming the screen door behind me.

It can be imagined how little placated I was by the sight that greeted my eye — that of Augie and Isolde approaching down the sunlit road, hand in hand. They waved, but awkwardly, for the report of the screen door had echoed like a rifle shot through half of Avalon. I waved tersely back and made for the garage. I climbed into the car and, when the Pooles had passed my driveway, backed out and made off up the road in the opposite direction. I could see them, in the rearview mirror, looking perturbedly after me.

I had breakfast at a village lunch counter. I roosted on an end stool, perusing some fat metropolitan tabloid and sipping infamous coffee. After about forty-five minutes, I went back home. Augie and Isolde were in the living room, talking with Audrey.

"Hi," the visitors greeted me, with some reserve.

"Good morning," I said.

"Warming up."

A few words were exchanged about the threatened resumption of a hot spell we'd just been through. "It's hard on a person. It gets everyone," Isolde said, smoothing out a crease in her skirt.

Augie said, "Audrey here has been telling us you two haven't had a vacation in four years, apart from some visit of hers to her mother's. That's bad. You look a trifle chewed up. Everybody has to have a holiday now and then. Off the old reservation, you know."

"I know," I said, glancing out the window.

"We'd be delighted to take the kids," Isolde said. "No, now, I mean that. You could bring us back something terribly expensive from Bermuda or Lake Banff or whatever."

When they had gone (looking fresh as daisies), I turned to my wife and said, "Well! Isn't that fine and dandy? What did you go and tell them?"

"Tell them? Was there anything left to tell them after that fancy exit of yours? I was in the doorway when they came by, and they waved and stopped, and I told them we had a little spat, to play it down. That at least was better than letting them speculate. By God, I won't have the neighbors thinking we're a couple of brawlers!"

I realized that I had suddenly lost a great deal of ground in the quarrel. And since I had no one to blame but myself, I became twice as hostile toward my wife. Nor did I lose any more time than was necessary in attempting to extract a penalty. I spotted a chance to get even the very next day — by walking the three miles from the station in the broiling heat, under circumstances that I saw a way of pinning on her.

That Monday, the temperature reached ninety-six, and it was well on its way to it when my wife drove me to the station in the morning. My regular train home was the five-thirty. I told her that I was going to try to clean up my work at the office in time to catch the three-thirty, or at least the four-thirty, but that I couldn't be sure. I would phone her from the station when I arrived.

I caught the three-thirty, got to Avalon a little after four-thirty, and entered the telephone booth in the station, sooty and clammy, and hoping that when I rang my number the line would be busy. I needed a grievance of at least that size (the implication that my wife was thoughtlessly chatting on the phone when I might be trying to get through to her) to recover the ground I had lost and get back in the running. Presenting a footsore and bedraggled spectacle at the front door would put her at a distinct disadvantage, one from which she might never really emerge. I dropped my dime in the slot and dialed the number tremulously. I got the busy signal. I clapped the phone on the hook, and, murmuring "Yackety-yack!" gratifiedly, folded my crumpled seersucker coat over my arm and began the three-mile trek that was to punish her.

The sun was still high in the sky and beating down mercilessly. I hadn't gone a tenth of a mile before my shirt felt like a poultice. I crossed from side to side of the road, in quest of shade where it appeared (not to be too vindictive with her), but this was a technique that I presently realized offset any respite from the sun by adding a marked percentage to my mileage. So after that I stuck to one side of the road.

I lifted a wet cuff to consult my wrist watch. Five-twenty. I was not a fifth of the way. At that rate I wouldn't be home before eight o'clock, for much of the journey from there on lay uphill, and it had become increasingly necessary to pause for rest even on the levels. It would be mad to proceed faster than a stroll; a mile an hour was plenty. At that pace, when would my wife begin to wonder? When worry? When grow alarmed? Well before home was in sight, I'd be bound. Two or three motorists slowed to offer me rides, but I shook my head and plodded on.

My clothes were now not only soaked but steaming; at least it seemed so to me. I threw my coat away — or didn't throw it away exactly, but chucked it under a culvert from which I could retrieve it when next I drove by. A wallet I had taken from it made a disagreeable bulge in a hind trouser pocket. I hit a long open stretch where lengthened exposure to the sun had rendered the tar in the road so soft that I had the feeling of slogging through rarebit.

I sat down on a large stone to take a small one out of my shoe. Nursing my foot a moment, I forlornly compared the trite hassle of which this was the fruit with those bright, deftly negotiated spats by which marriage is idealized in drawing-room comedies. I mentally revised parts of our wrangle with some better dialogue (such as might be heard most any night at Moot Point, as a matter of fact). In my breather, there by the wayside, I imagined it as an adroit exchange conducted before dinner guests, which, uncorking a wine or disheveling a salad, I would crown with, "Marriage, my dear, has driven more than one man to sex."

I put my shoe on and rose, and, after pausing to draw fabric away from my person at various points, resumed my march. I sensed the birth of a blister on one foot. Presently, too, I began to have moments of vertigo in which I wondered whether I hadn't perhaps punished my wife enough. I tried to divert myself by repeating over and over the pun, "You haven't vertigo, you haven't vertigo." I had neglected to water myself at the waiting-room drinking fountain before setting out, and now a great thirst, which a little thought amplified into panic, parched my throat. My general condition, plus heat shimmers in the road and blinding flashes from the chrome of passing cars, resulted at last in a fogging of my vision. Fogging may not be precisely the word, for the change took the form of rendering commonplace objects adventurous, and objects visible that may very well not have been there. Thus distant elms and willows appeared for fleeting moments to have the look of date palms, and once I thought I saw a camel on the horizon.

I stepped off the road, crossed a ditch, and sat down on another rock. I ran my finger over my forehead in the manner of a squeegee. I noticed several burs on the cuffs of my trousers. I was breathing heavily and feeling a dense throbbing inside my head when a car approaching down the hill ahead of me slowed and came to a stop on the other side of the road. My wife was behind the wheel. I waited for her to speak, prepared to consolidate my gains.

"What's the matter with you?" she asked, through the open window.

"I'll be all right," I said, plucking at my shirt buttons. "It's just my heart."

She put her head out of the window and looked back up the road to make sure nothing was coming. Then she turned the car around and drew up near me. She reached over and opened the door on my side. I got to my feet, made my way across the ditch, and climbed in. I pulled the door shut and she put the car in gear. I made sure my window was all the way down and adjusted the wing glass so the draft would strike me the instant we got under way. "I tried to call you a couple of times but you were busy talking," I said as we did. "So I had to walk. What brings you over this way now?"

"I tried to call the butcher several times — the cold cuts I ordered didn't come — and our party line was busy. That meant you couldn't reach me, and I got to worrying. I figured you might well have been on that three-thirty. I couldn't be sure, but rather than risk keeping you waiting in the hot station, I thought I'd take a chance on a trip for nothing."

We drove in silence for a stretch, and then she said, "Isolde Poole called just as I was leaving. She suggested we all have dinner together."

"Well?"

"An air-conditioned restaurant sounds good."

"I thought you didn't like Augie," I said.

She heaved a long sigh of resignation. "Well, it comes down to what you said," she answered. And, glancing off across the frazzled fields, she added, "You've got to take people as they are."

Seven

FAILING other certifications of his genius, Augie was deep in the long, symbolic process of building himself up as a son of a bitch. I was a willing witness: Curiosity could not resist what conscience must groan over. Our intimacy progressed from uncertain beginnings for Augie's first revelations were not voluntary but the product of incitement. I threw the incident of the lawn party up to him in a sort of peeve for his picking my brains about the spat, as he presently did, not to mention its having been over his sins that I had spent the week-end in the doghouse.

"You're not in any danger of splitting up, are you?" he asked the following Wednesday when he dropped into my office to leave some new cartoons (which I declined to look at in his presence following an editorial rule set up in deference to my nervous system).

"No, we're not in any danger of splitting up," I said with my head bent over my desk.

He set the drawings on a table, where I had motioned for him to put them, and sauntered to the window. "I wouldn't want anything to happen to you and Audrey."

"Just keep your nose clean and nothing will," I answered.

"What the hell are you talking about?"

"How does your garden grow?"

"My garden?"

"The blonde. You were quite smitten with her."

"Oh, that." He shot me a speculative look. "Anything she ever gets, she's asked for. All that come-on."

"Next time remember that water is a great conductor of sound. I speak as a friend," I said. "And, also speaking as a friend, if you mean business put this down as rule number one: Never waste your time with a flirt."

The sagacity of this so got his goat, especially as coming from a tenderfoot as I know he took me to be, that he asked me to lunch and was soon deep in accounts designed to assure me that he not only meant business but was and always had been fairly well established in it. I have listened to my share of males making a clean breast of their conquests, but Augie singled me out as a special confidant in a way that I always felt had something to do with the fact that I kept rejecting his drawings. Some special need must have driven him to play his own Devil's Advocate to a man he knew was down for a character reference for him, even granting that that fact was all a by-product of his wife's having submitted mine. "I suppose I'm a bit of a cad," he said, performing some surgery on a lamb chop. (Why does a man always look so smug when he calls himself a cad?) "But I pay for it."

I fed him the expected straight line, after a leisurely pause. "How?"

"I — no, I've told you enough already."

Tune in next week to this same station and see what happens, I thought. Next week was drinks on me at a Manhattan bar we began to frequent. I wheedled and needled more out of him by taking my wife's line of disapproving; then out came the private psychology. For his explanations were, again, à la mode (it seemed to slip his mind for the moment that the artist didn't need any explaining).

"You see, I have these devilish feelings of guilt," he said. He talked in a quite standard vein for a few minutes and then my ear, practiced from all the Saturday-night strip teases, picked out a complexity it was not accustomed to, a slight offbeat in the popular rhythm. "You see, part of the idea is that I deserve this guilt and when I don't have it I feel uncomfortable. As though I'm being delinquent? There's this masochistic urge to go *after* the guilt by sleeping with as many women as possible — what other way is there for making myself feel rotten? I feel the guilt, it wears off, and then I get to feeling guilty because I'm not feeling guilty."

"Why sleep around then, if it's that much trouble?" I asked, masking my fascination by breaking a pretzel on the top of the bar.

"It's the only way of getting back to the guilt."

"Why should you want to get back to it?"

"Because I feel I have it coming to me."

"What for?"

"For sleeping around."

I took in a house cat that was arching itself against the leg of a patron in a booth. Augie bent a plastic muddler back and forth. "I've really got myself on my hands," he said. What he wanted me to say was, "Augie, you've got to stop crucifying yourself." Instead I said, "What time is it?"

He looked at me reproachfully. "What do you mean, what time is it?"

I shook my head when the bartender glared at my empty glass. "Isn't it a little rear-end-to? Your complex."

"It's a vicious circle," he agreed, nodding. He plied the

swizzle stick a moment longer. Then he set it aside and revealed, "I'm going to an analyst."

"Does he tell you all this? What you just told me?"

"No — I tell him.'"

There was a pause. I glanced at a wrapped parcel of rejections on the bar, which he had just picked up from the office. Guessing my thought, he said, "This man is very reasonable. And he doesn't dun me for what I owe him either. He's interested in my case."

"I can believe that," I said.

"Not that the sledding isn't tough enough without doctor bills." He shifted his feet and hunched over the bar. He took a drink and for the moment looked the picture of a man with nothing much on his mind. "Divil a penny — "

"I've got to get back to the office," I said. "I'll see you at the P.T.A. thing tomorrow night. Be sure and come now, do you hear, because you're being watched."

Our local Parent-Teacher Association was putting on a fund-raising jamboree for which I had been asked to write a skit preferably satirizing the town Board of Finance which, by cutting the school's appropriation, had put them in the position of needing this benefit. I never went to P.T.A. meetings, they weren't really my speed, but I agreed to turn out a little something for their do. I also let it out that I was not averse to playing the lead. Plans for the project had been some weeks afoot, and now the various committees involved were to get together to discuss the show, the food, the publicity, and the decorations for the school gym in which the shindig was to be held. There was to be an opening rehearsal too — all at the gym, which has a stage at one end.

My piece was a two-character diversion. By the time the evening of the rehearsal rolled around, I had spent many mental hours with my leading lady (Isolde), casting about for the right vein in which to approach my role, assuming she would do hers as Joan Fontaine. I had smoldered in the style of Olivier, had ground my jaws and talked with protracted blinks like Spencer Tracy. With something of Cary Grant's animal charm I had taken advantage of that April heart. I had worked out a system of uttering all my labials with my upper teeth against my lower lip, similar to Humphrey Bogart's, and had even whispered everything like Jimmy Stewart. None of these seemed right for the part. It was while driving to the school gymnasium that I lapsed into an improvisation that struck what seemed to me the indicated mood.

I dissolved to an ocean liner on which we met at table. It was as George Sanders that, taking leave of her in the dining room, I rose and, pushing back my chair said, "If you care to take a turn on deck, you'll find me forward. Possibly even a bit unscrupulous."

That was sailing to the States. When we docked in New York, we made a date for cocktails the next day. "Let's make it fivish," she said.

"Fine," I said. "In front of the Biltmorish."

Five-fifteen found her waiting alone before the hotel door. Five-twenty came and still no me. At five-thirty she found me a block away, browsing at Brooks Brothers' windows. That was how I cured her of that suffix, and, oh, what fun we were going to have if this was any gauge.

I locked the door of my car and walked up the steps to the lighted gymnasium. There must have been forty committee members there, all jabbering away in groups from one end of the floor to the other. Isolde, sitting in the bleachers, raised her head from a script and waved. The P.T.A. secretary, a large woman named Mrs. Blenheim, had said she had connections in the theater and would get us a director. She saw me, and taking a tall, slim man by the hand, towed him across the floor and introduced him as Ernest Mills. He was a TV director who registered omniscience by shrugging one shoulder, and wore a white beret which, on top of a sunburn he had, looked like a poached egg on an order of hash. He was known as Putsi, though not by me.

Suddenly he turned around and, moving his arms above his head as though he were waving off flies, called out, "Kids, we're going to run through the first sketch. So please go out in the hall for your confabs, or if you have to stay inside here, keep it down to a dull roar, so we can hear."

About half of them stayed. Isolde and I mounted the stage. While we were waiting for comparative silence, I spotted Augie in the back of the gym, sizing up the walls for murals and posters with someone in a print smock. Evidently another P.T.A. officer had connections in the art world. But it was all right, I was later assured: two heads were better than one, and the newcomer and Augie were getting theirs together fine. Her name was Cornelia Bly.

The racket subsided and Isolde and I began our reading. Mills and Connections in the Theater sat together on a couple of folding chairs. The sketch was a what-if satire: what if a husband applied the same despotic methods to his family budget as our Board of Finance did to the town's. The M.C. was to set it up with an introduction ending, "Now we meet him as he enters the terrace to join his wife for their annual budget hearing." I explained all this to Mills who hadn't yet read the script.

I strolled out in flannel slacks and a houndstooth jacket and extended an imaginary dry Martini to the lounging Isolde, murmuring as I did so, "One for the Gibson Girl." I then kissed her and sat down with a cocktail of my own, whereupon "my wife" worked the conversation around to how much she had saved on redecorating the house and by skimping on clothes, with me deflating her at every turn in a way that was as foxy as it was deft. In the course of all the persiflage, I fetched her two more Martinis, kissing her each time I handed her one to show that I was flesh and blood beneath this fabulous exterior (and ad libbing repetitions of the Gibson Girl mot, which I assumed my hearers had not caught as they had not laughed). My wife tried to explain to me the difference between cord and seersucker. I reached for my glass and drawled, "I had supposed, my dear, that a seersucker was someone who spent all her money on fortune tellers."

Mills clapped his hands for us to stop and came forward.

"This has been going on for twenty-two minutes," he said. "Where's the action?"

"Why, in the grain, the subtlety of the give and take," I said.

"But this is a skit. It shouldn't take more than five minutes at the most. It isn't a three-act play."

"It isn't?" some card out front whispered.

I said, "There's some conflict coming up in a minute. Where she says she's going to Lord and Taylor's tomorrow. I say, 'What do you have to go to Lord and Taylor's for?' And she says, 'Because I want to go to Saks Fifth Avenue next week and I haven't a thing to wear.'"

"And your diction — " Mills continued with his strictures.

"I'm playing him with my tongue in my cheek," I said.

"Maybe that's why I can't hear you."

It got the first real laugh of the evening, and we resumed with some sense of the ice having been broken.

"One more important thing before we go on," Mills said. "Just how do you see this character you're playing?"

"As a sort of George Sanders type," I said.

"George Sanders." He turned with a frown to Connections in the Theater. "Does that strike you as right? For a P.T.A. sketch?"

Connections in the Theater rose and came down, shaking her head. "No," she said, "it doesn't. Not for what we want — local audience identification and all. And I agree with you about too long with too little action, now that I see it on the stage. It bothered me when I read it."

Mills went on to say that he saw the man as a stuffy middle-class suburban husband. Another P.T.A. official joined the discussion and the three of them went into a huddle. I turned back from the footlights and had a cigarette with Isolde, while those with humbler chores looked on.

"Making headway with the Crib?" I chatted.

"Mmm," she responded with an affirmative bob of her head, as she took a light from my match. "I've put your name in, so I expect they'll have someone up your way soon." She laughed. "If this isn't where you came in."

"It isn't that," I said quickly, "but I think you ought to get completely new references. For luck. We sort of jinxed you once. So you feel free to count us out, you hear?"

"You're sweet." She leaned over to kiss the tip of my ear. "And I think you're an absolute genius getting us mixed up in this sort of thing. I hope the Crib has a representative snooping around here. The P.T.A.!"

He glances to the rear and sees that Augie and his collaborator have their heads together indeed, and as duenna it is his task to calibrate the distance between them as they bend consultingly over a sketch.

"I wouldn't think of asking anyone else," Isolde said.

He mops the stage with his withdrawing gaze and wonders, Does no shadow of suspicion ever cross that April heart? Maybe Augie's very openness disarms it. Maybe she doesn't personally condemn the tangents repugnant to Rock-a-Bye? Did these agencies put a tail on a man, like a private eye? He glances toward the bleachers again, and again calibrates the bent heads. The distance between them has dwindled since his last reading. He knows Isolde is looking at him, the tinted-Dresden face in its winsome half-smile, and something shoots along the surface of his heart like ice cracking, and he knows his role at last. It is as Herbert Marshall he must go down the infested years, the faithful friend, somehow loyal to both, suave, meticulous and dear.

"You'll love this. The new caseworker's name is Mrs. Mash!"

He crosses to left center stage and, his back to her, squashes out his cigarette in a soup ramekin.

"I'll do all I can. You know that."

The huddle on the floor breaks up, putting to an end the intolerable scene.

"For this skit to get across," Mills said as spokesman for the trio, "we see him as definitely a conventional middle-class husband. Practical but stodgy."

"In that case, of course, I'm not suited to the part," I said pleasantly, laying my script on a chair, and started to walk off.

"Well, now, not so fast," Mills said. "Your build is O.K. Just boom the lines out — no muttering in your beard — and bang your fists and harrumph around. You can change the lines to suit the character later, but let's just try him for size. You can do it; stuffy — as — the — devil."

Coming on the heels of an afternoon in which Blair had praised me as good at routine details, a relief after all the creative-type editors, brilliant but erratic, who had preceded me in the job, this struck anything but a responsive chord, and I advised Mills quietly not to be optimistic; dryly adding that, as to the diction thing, he may have heard of something in the theater known as throwing your lines away. I didn't catch his answer, but a local electrician who had been asked to handle the lighting, and was already clambering about back there like an eager beaver, audibly remarked that I should have thrown mine away as soon as I wrote them. He was not the worst of the Philistines I was up against. There was additional conferring on how the skit might better depict a recognizable family situation, and Connections had a suggestion. "Putsi, how about putting in a daughter?" she asked him.

"Make him a sort of Edward Arnold type," he said.

"Edward Arnold!" I cried in a spasm of pain and bewilderment.

"The daughter's extravagant, spends money right and left on clothes, phonograph records, runs up telephone bills," Connections went on. "The father huffs and puffs and says, 'Do you think I'm made of money?' "

This excited my tormentors further and they went into how they "saw" this girl as to age, etc. By an odd coincidence it turned out that Connections had a daughter just back from college, where she had studied dramatics. "I could have her here in five minutes," Connections said. "She's home, just up the road."

That was all I needed. To be judged capable of delineating a stuffed shirt was unsettling enough; but the assumption that I could with no trouble suggest deciduous middle age was more than I could take in one night, and, wishing them luck in their plans for a new Ma and Pa Kettle, I turned and strode off the stage. As I did so, I caught my foot in a mess of the electric wire that lay everywhere like spaghetti and pitched into a crate of costumes. Mills sprang forward with the assurance that this sort of thing was the rule in the theater, where tempers were thin and plays not written but rewritten. The battering mine was taking was a measure of its resilience and potential. "This guy a pulp and paper magnate?" I said derisively, disengaging his fingers from my coat lapels. "Or do you see him as a big shot in the trucking game?" Mills and the chapter president, a bull-dozer of a woman who stood solidly athwart my path, detained me long enough for Connections' daughter to be fetched by car, an interval which they improved by assuring me that, as to the age matter, a ponytail haircut to peg the girl as a teen-ager, no more, and some cornstarch in my own thatch to grizzle me up a bit, and the same for Mrs. Poole, should do the trick. Isolde was asked if she'd mind, and she smiled through the wings with a shake of her head. I gave in for the sake of the show when I saw Connections' daughter, who turned out to have been hewn by Rodin, and whose flesh tints were evocative of ripe fruit. I sat down right then and there and dashed off some lines to audition her with, in the frenetic tradition of the theater.

The first speech we gave the girl to try went, "If you don't give me enough money to dress attractively, Pops, you may not find any boys around here to take me off your hands." Mills told her to stand over me as I fumed at a table on which were strewn the monthly bills (wearing on my face that grimace that goes with the legend "Grr!" in comic strips) and also gave her some pointers on how to say the line. "O.K.," he said, returning to his seat. "Go."

The girl read the line approximately as directed. But she prefaced it with a full half minute of aphrodisiac breathing so intense and vehement that I could feel it in my hair and down the back of my neck. It was pointed out to her that the rendition would have been ideal if this were a drama dealing with incest, and she were called upon to sexually inflame her father. It was, however, a cozy domestic comedy aiming at lots of audience identification, so omit the palpitations — and forget about keeping her chest in profile. She caught on and we had little trouble with the remaining lines so far written for her. But she drowned the stage in a perfume so heady that I left the gymnasium with my senses reeling, and dropped into bed exhausted and wretched, and wondering how old the girl really was. Twenty-one or -two probably, if she was just out of college. I was breaking my rule never to get my feathers fussed. And Augie — he was probably in his bed planning a campaign to get into Cornelia Bly's. Some P.T.A.

The show was put on three weeks from that Saturday evening. My wife and kids saw it. My sketch went on between an original ballet and a humorous slide lecture. As finally played it was a satire about a tightwad with a brain like a steel trap, who couldn't solve a simple riddle about a poor mother dividing her apples up. We made him a member of the Board of Finance. The next morning, Sunday, the following scene was enacted at my breakfast table:

MAUDE: (Studiously spooning her cereal about) Daddy, you were wonderful last night.

MOTHER: (Who has obviously been coaching the children and now shepherds them through their exclamations) Yes, wasn't he! The whole program was wonderful, but his skit was the best of all. (Chorus of "Yes, yes!")

MARCO: You could hear a pin drop.

FATHER: That'll be all of that!

MOTHER: (In a tearful collapse of her brave front) The child did not know it was supposed to be a comedy.

FATHER: Who said it was?

For as the hour had approached, and it could be seen how matters might go, I had changed my tune. It was now my story that the skit was a bitter parable of misguided thrift rather than a comedy aiming at easy laughs. The switch was made just in time, for the result had been precisely as the boy had said — you could hear a pin drop. Our hopes had been briefly nourished when one of the flats wobbled and threatened to collapse on the stage, to resolve in that way the conflict with which the drama grappled; but someone back there (no doubt the electrician who'd had it in for me all along) righted it in time, and we'd had to play through to the end. In front of an audience, Connections' daughter couldn't resist the chance to show what she could really do with her teeth in a part, and returned to Cheyne-Stokes breathing, fluttering my hair and offering me advantageous views of her hocks, which I had already repeatedly and exhaustively ratified. She wore the subversive perfume again, and wherever I walked on the stage or sat, she had just been and left her spoor. In the demoralizing boredom, I had an impulse to seize her in an incestuous embrace and then maybe extemporize to some sort of O'Neill finish. But we finished as rehearsed, and the audience gave us a pretty good hand at that, no doubt in a flood of gratitude for their deliverance.

MOTHER: Why do you object to the child's saying you could hear a pin drop? You've been claiming it's a savage indictment.

FATHER: (Rising and leaving the dining room) Oh, what's the use trying to talk to this family? (He slams the door behind him, starting the refrigerator.)

I was sitting in the living room when the dining-room door opened and Marco was gingerly piloted over to apologize. Which he did.

"That's all right, Marco," I said. "Forget it."

He drew his mouth taut and said: "My name's not Marco any longer. I've found the name I want to change to."

"Oh?" I said, glancing at my wife. "What do you want us to call you from now on?"

"Alphonse."

As the choice of one who had soured on his own name because people laughed at it this was a substitute for which we were hardly prepared.

"Alphonse!" I said. "Where did you ever get such an idea?"

"Your play."

It was true; I had used it for the husband. The thing was, as the hour drew near and it was plain how things were going, every expedient for injecting comedy relief into the skit had been advised, including that of funny names for the characters.

"But Alphonse is a *humorous* name — " I began to explain to the boy, but that avenue was forever closed to me; the tribe of Digger Indians to whom we had apparently been playing had greeted the principals' open-armed exchange of "Ermingarde!" "Alphonse!" with such gloom that the watchful Marco had decided that here, certainly, was a name void of comic implications, and it had winged its way straight to his heart. I held my breath all morning, fearing a similar announcement from the dissatisfied Phoebe — we had called the daughter in the skit Melba. But that at least was spared me.

"So from now on, you might as well call me Alphonse," Marco said levelly. "Because I won't answer to any other."

That alone would have been a disastrous enough result of the Avalon First Annual P.T.A. Supper and Jamboree. But there were grimmer dividends to be reaped.

Eight

ON a day otherwise unmarked except for Phoebe's circulating a report among the neighbors that I was dead, I saw Augie lunching in a New York chophouse with someone who looked familiar: it was the conjunction of the heads. He had spotted me too, and the next time we met he spoke of her.

"She's got something I can't put my finger on — at least not yet," he said.

"Everything takes time," I said dryly.

It wasn't long before he had progress to narrate. Two weeks later I ran across them in a midtown restaurant called the Somerset, and this time I got caught in a traffic jam beside where they were sitting and had to stop.

The Somerset was a packed grotto among whose tables, which were the size of throat lozenges, the waiters flowed by some kind of osmosis, and the celebrities, wearing dark glasses in an already crepuscular gloom, picked their way by a power presumably like that of the bats they must be blind as. Some illumination was afforded by the incendiary dishes that were eaten there, but that was fitful. The customers were about equally divided between celebrities and people wearing dark glasses in the hope of being mistaken for one; but they must all have by now developed that eerie dexterity by which bats are said to "feel" things just short of touching them, because they never bumped into anything, except occasionally one another. It was a new, contemporary habitat in which I was less adept with the naked eye. Add to the perils of darkness those of wires getting underfoot from telephones being plugged in at tables, as well as the flaming skewers borne aloft in the general press, and it was worth your life to go in there. Only the wonderful food drew me. I never saw menus squinted at from so many angles — because while the celebrities removed their glasses to consult them, the third-string columnists and unemployed bit players kept them on so as not to be unmasked in the interval as nobodies. There was an incessant waving from table to table, though I don't know what anybody thought he saw, or whether it made any difference. Unless it was owls they resembled after all.

I didn't immediately recognize Augie, because he was behind a pair of smoked goggles himself — he had just sold us a two-inch spot page decoration of a cornucopia full of frozen foods, which we might find a place for next Thanksgiving. He affected instability, throwing his charcoal down and grinding it underfoot when the cornucopia wouldn't come right, in repairs to it at the office.

"Hello, hello," a familiar voice said. "Setzen sie sich." And there he was, looking like a hunted gambler. "Sore eyes," he said, a little self-consciously, and lifted the cheaters to rub them. "You remember Cornelia Bly." I congratulated her on the party murals, as I already had Augie.

"Thank you," she said. "How did your skit go? I couldn't make it that night."

"You could hear a pin drop," I said. It got a laugh. She invited me to sit down, though God knew where I would have, unless in one of their laps. I said I had to get back to the office.

"Your artists have it easier than you do," she smilingly suggested.

Augie said: "We must all have lunch together sometime. And I want you to see Cornelia's paintings. She might do a cover for us."

"Love to," I said, taking my leave, and inside of ten minutes had gained the street.

Cornelia Bly was on the short side, shorter than I had remembered her, with her hair done — or I should say left undone — in one of those tossed salad sort of close crops. Her smile was a pink and white semicircle of short teeth and bright gums, which rather put me in mind of a slice of watermelon. She had a habit of ducking her head when she laughed. She wore no make-up and her finger-ends were square. She was dressed in snuff-colored tweeds, and a brick-red porkpie, which I took to be hers, hung on a peg over Augie's head.

"She doesn't have your obvious kind of attractiveness," Augie said to me later. "A woman like that totally escapes your callow romanticist. They wouldn't look at her twice."

"I don't know about that," I said, picking up my beer, for we were at a bar.

"You realize what a fraud the whole sexual paraphernalia is, your Hollywood sexless cakes and pies. How much more mature the French are — throwing a disheveled heroine at you on the screen. A man is like a moth driven insane by indirect lighting, by the interfering fixtures of glamour. Then he finds that bright light that's shed best by the naked bulb."

There was a little more to it than that. Cornelia had a glamour that wasn't alone anti-glamour. She had at the moment a kind of prominence. She had leapt into vogue on the crest of publicity springing from legal action she was bringing against a firm for one of whose advertisements she had done a semiabstract portrait which, she claimed, they had changed without her consent. She charged that the face had been mutilated by the addition of a second eye. The case had gained wide newspaper attention, and one news magazine had run a picture she had drawn over, showing the face as she had orginally done it with its single eye, side by side with the mutilated version containing the two. "The Eye for an Eye Girl" she was called, and was pointed out in restaurants and theater lobbies. So Augie liked to be seen lunching with her and strolling through art galleries.

When it reached the point of my trying to phone the boulevardier at home and being told by his wife that he was staying in town that night, where he had business, and would I like the number of the hotel where he was staying, I laid the cards on the table.

"Look here," I said, after a few pre-lunch drinks had loosened me up, "I've got something on my mind. Let me begin by saying that my personal opinion has nothing to do with this. I don't care who you play house with, but circumstances have made it my business and I can't beg off or back out. To beg off would in itself be an answer to the people I'm accountable to, and one not in your favor. You must know by now what I'm talking about. Have you forgotten that you gave me for a reference?"

He frowned into his cocktail. "I've been meaning to talk to you about that," he said. "Putting you on the spot is the last thing in the world I want to do. It was of course Isolde who gave you two for a reference."

"I assumed as much. Also that it's mostly Isolde who wants a child?"

"Not at all," he said with an injured air. "I want one just as much as she does."

I'd like to have seen the expression on my face as I answered, "You act like it. Do you know why you flunked out at Rock-a-Bye?"

"They knew I was an artist with no regular income. They think it's too risky to put a child into a home with a financial picture like mine."

"Does Isolde know how much trouble you go to to keep contrite?"

"Did you ask me to lunch or was I subpoenaed? Isolde is broad-minded."

"Isolde is not a caseworker," I answered. "I'm broad-minded too. But the Crib isn't. The Crib is just folks, the same as Rock-a-Bye. If they hear about the husband sleeping with other women, they don't understand that he's doing that to keep his guilt feelings tuned up. And I don't want to be the one to explain it to them, though I'd like to be around when somebody else does. Neither do I want to have to explain to them the tradition that the artist is part son of a bitch. Agencies size a couple up by asking, for one thing, if the husband is a good provider — yes, granted. But they also ask themselves if a child they give them might one day be the victim of a broken home. Lots of children are, you know."

"Yes, I know. And when I can no longer bear to think of the victims of broken homes, I begin to think of the victims of intact ones." He had me there, and I was grateful he didn't pause for an answer but went right on, with some heat, "I don't see what the hell my sex life has to do with whether I'll make a good father. If Isolde and I have an understanding about these things why isn't that enough for the rest of the world? Why must people go around looking for fleas in one another's hide, like monkeys? Our marriage works as good as anybody's we know with natural children. Look at the Arkwrights with their three, and the Johnsons with their six. I wouldn't give ten cents for either of those homes. Let welfare workers go to homes like that and make them deserve their own children or give them up. Why don't they give all couples tests before they let them have children, or stop trying to find flaws in marriages that don't exist? Western culture! The way it mauls and mangles the individual to save him for society. It's time we turned it around and organized society to let the individual live — yes, let him indulge impulses that don't hurt anybody. Soon enough we'll all be dead, or what's worse, old. When are we going to get civilized and let the whole man live? The French — "

"I know. But this isn't France. And if it was I'm not sure Cornelia wouldn't be chaperoned till she was safely married. Is she married?"

"Certain African tribes — "

"There's no time for certain African tribes. A woman named Mrs. Mash, who lives in Haversham, is coming to see me any day and ask for a clean bill of health about you. So answer yes or no — are you keeping your nose clean?"

"Of course I am. I'm walking the chalk line these days. It shows how much I'm willing to give up to have a child."

"What about Cornelia Spry?"

"Cornelia Bly. I'm not sleeping with her, if that's what you mean."

I looked at him and then looked away. What good was the question? How could I tell whether he was lying or not? He even owed it to me to lie, to clear my conscience and get me off the hook. But it didn't get me off the hook. Our talk only lashed me into a state of curiosity bordering on prurience itself. I was now that censor whom if you scratch you will find a satyr. In the half-wretched relish with which I now threw myself into the role of snoop, it was all I could do to keep from picking Augie's brains every time I saw him. Then a totally unforeseen incident occurred which uncorked my friend without any prompting, as well as shed some light on him from a fresh quarter.

It happened at a party, a typical Avalon evening studded with intellectuals who listened only to jazz and read principally the avant-garde funnies. In addition, there was the beautiful and jumpy Monica Stern, the dress designer; old Thaddeus Hall, the connoisseur of doorknobs; and Sid Walters, the clear poet. Mills, my director, was on hand. Whether or not he came with the beret I don't know because I came late and left early. He was there with his wife, a large, pleasant chandelier of a woman, covered with costume jewelry. It kept falling off her like decorations from a Christmas tree, and once I saw her angling for something in her Tom Collins, though that may have been a cherry. At one point Monica Stern sat next to me, rapidly draining me of interest in the servant problem. I had slipped away to Moot Point and was deep in didoes with her there, altering her to suit the tenant, when I became aware of a peculiar thunderhead building up out of the conversation around us. It went like this.

There was a bachelor named Morley who ate ice. He had brought up something he called mannerism tests, in a discussion about the sexes. When pressed for details by interested guests, he rang Mills into the discussion.

"Oh, you have a subject do three or four things." Mills explained. "There's a typically masculine and typically feminine way of doing each. You give the person a score accordingly."

"Let's try it," a woman proposed. "Who'll be It? Morley?"

"I know the tests, or at least one of them — how you drink

from a glass," Morley answered, grinding up the cubes out of his fourth or fifth highball. "The rest'll come back to me the minute I hear them. What we want is a fresh subject."

"How can there be two ways of drinking?"

"There's two ways of doing everything. And you can't cheat. Come on, who'll volunteer?"

Everybody was cagey. But at that moment who should turn from a *tête-à-tête* he'd been deep in with a woman a little apart from the group but Augie. He extended an empty glass to the hostess. "Could I have another?" he said. Everybody laughed.

Morley rose and spread his arms like a traffic cop. "Make way for the gent," he said, and taking Augie's glass went to the cellaret himself. "What are you drinking?"

"Scotch and soda. What's the matter with all you people?" Augie asked, grinning. Here a small knot gave off twitting Sid Walters about the clarity of his verse, and we became one. Morley shouldered his way back with a hastily conjured highball. The company watched in silence as Augie took it, glanced into it, and drank.

"Female," Morley said with a consulting look at Mills. "Women look into a glass before they drink, men not. Right, Putsi?"

"Not female — feminine," Mills corrected him. "It's not sexual as such — just strains in the make-up, characteristics. Like — well, masculine and feminine endings in poetry."

"Augie does move the needle to the thread, not the thread to the needle," Isolde said with a laugh. "Remember that business in *Huckleberry Finn* where the woman sees through Huck's disguise?"

But Morley was not to be put off. "I just remembered another one — the way you look at your nails. That right, Puts?"

"Well, yes," Mills said, sauntering toward the cellaret with his own glass.

"What the hell is this?" Augie asked, his smile a little frayed.

"Just look at your nails," Morley said. "Don't be bashful. Go on — they're yours."

"Let somebody else. I don't want to hog the show."

"What good is the test if you let everybody do a part of it? Go on, look at your nails. Don't be a spoilsport."

"All right if it'll make you happy." Augie obligingly spread the fingers of one hand in a fan and examined the tips.

"I think I'd like a drink too," my wife said, rising and making her way over to the bar. "And, Julia, do you still have the shuffle-board downstairs?" she asked the hostess. "I'd like to play."

Morley screwed round in his seat to find Mills, who was trying to bail out of the lark. "Puts, he looked at his nails like this. Isn't the idea that that's the way a woman would examine a polishing job? As distinguished from closing your hand up in a sort of fist?"

The latter was what Augie was now doing with both hands, having set his drink down. "For God's sake," he said, giving his belt a hitch. As we sat wondering how we were going to dismount this tiger we'd gotten aboard, Augie shook a cigarette from a pack and twisted a match from a book, remarking that Morley had probably had too much to drink — a fact which had also penetrated the rest of us.

"What's the next test?" my wife called over. "Let me be the guinea pig for the next one."

"He just took it," Mills put in, nodding at Augie. "It's the way you strike a match. Most women strike the match away from them, men toward them — the way Augie just did."

"So what score does that give me?" Augie inquired.

"Sixty-six and two thirds," Morley said. "It's all in fun of course," he added with a nervous laugh.

"Don't laugh in that tone of voice," Augie said. "It ain't lady-like."

"Now look here, pal."

"If you're so interested in masculine behavior, I've got a suggestion. Step outside and repeat that score."

"We are outside," someone said in a hopeless whisper. It was the case; we were out on the terrace, where we hung suspended largely on canvas in attitudes of stylish prostration, behind screens which moths had begun to batter in the late-summer-evening half-light. "There's boxing gloves in the basement," the hostess said facetiously.

"You people run this stuff into the ground," Augie said. That's what the rest of us thought too, suffering there in the gloom, and he should have let it drop. "All this bushwa."

"It's not bushwa, exactly," Mills said, strolling around behind a stout chaise longue from where he now proceeded to try to make peace by pouring oil on the flames. "The point is this: everyone is, and should be, a mixture of the two. Now wait a minute! A perfectly masculine man would be a monstrosity, just as a perfectly feminine woman would. Van Appledorn has worked all this out in exhaustive studies. The ideal is a balance of ingredients, is what Van Appledorn says."

"I don't give a damn what Van Appledorn says. Just watch your own lip. I fished a miller out of my last drink, so why shouldn't I look in the glass first?"

"You were quite right. Oh. Women usually hold a cigarette between their fingertips is another. I notice you've got yours well down against your hand, like a truck driver," Mills added graciously. "Of course these tests aren't Van Appledorn's. Schmidlapp's working on that."

"You can have Schmidlapp too."

Someone whispered in the ruined twilight: "Abraham Lincoln wore a shawl."

"I still think — " Augie went on, ignoring the emollient and kindling his expired fag from a table lighter someone had the presence of mind to extend — "I still think a man is a person who likes women and a woman is a person who likes men." He thanked the guest who had given him the light and glanced down at the unattached Morley, who now sat in a dejected slump, as though a jag had worn off. "That's perfectly true to a point," Mills said. "It doesn't hold for your Don Juan. He's trying to prove something. . . ."

The discussion, to still call it that, was going on when several of us went downstairs by way of falling in with Audrey's shuffleboard suggestion. We had been playing for some time when there was a muffled hubbub overhead, and a woman's face appeared at the top of the stairway. "They're at it!" she called, and was gone again.

We clomped upstairs and out to the yard where we found a circle of spectators standing on the grass, watching something in the center that wasn't instantly discernible. By an accident of confusion I thought first that Augie was fighting Mrs. Mills. Then I saw that in the cleared space were Augie and Morley, supporting one another in a comradely embrace.

"They're pooped," our stairway narrator explained. "Should we break them up? Most people think not."

"It started all over again when Morley accused Augie of symbolic virilization," someone else said.

"And then Augie called Morley a battle-ax."

"My daphne," the hostess moaned, glancing worriedly at a flower bed.

"Look, could you come over more this way, fellows?" her husband said, drawing the pair toward the house. The two staggered over together, interlocked.

"Isolde, put a stop to it."

"Why? It's what they want," she had sense enough to answer.

"*I'll* put a stop to it — the second he's sober," Augie said with great honor.

"I'm sober," Morley retorted. "What are you going to do about it?"

"Let go of that and I'll show you," Augie said, trying to wrench free his necktie to which Morley clung like a swaying subway rider. "More toward the house, away from those flowers," the host insisted testily. The combatants swerved obligingly down a slope in the lawn, with elaborate menace but around opposite sides of an intervening sour gum, as though they were stalking a common foe rather than spoiling for one another. Suddenly Morley took a cut at Augie that caught him straight on the nose. Augie cocked back a lean arm and planted one in Morley's middle, dumping him over backward into a clump of bushes. Augie stood over him and inquired after his health. Morley rose and grasped him around the waist with such determination that what they were doing changed to wrestling. Dancing erratically, they carried on an insulting banter full of epithets like "bigot bastard," and during which they stumbled about more or less buttressing one another. The host and I tried to pull them apart, but they were inseparable. By now a subtle bond had developed between them which seemed to consist of *their* being linked against their discouragers. At length, however, they stumbled against the sour gum with such impact that they were not only shaken free of one another but knocked, breathless, to the ground.

"It's a draw!" Isolde declared. We rushed forward and hustled the antagonists inside into separate bathrooms, from which they emerged cleaned up, and ready to shake hands, which they did with foolish grins. Everybody felt better all around. Everybody, that is, except Mills. He sat with a preoccupied look, which I later learned arose from his not being sure there hadn't been an error made in the drinking-glass test. It turned out that it's men who do tend to glance into a glass first — women by and large not.

But the incident did not lose its importance as a cause. At our weekly luncheon, the following Wednesday, Augie was not long in getting around to the triviality of the entire occurrence. "Mean, of course, there are these differences between the sexes. It's just that I don't like the idea of guys that lay their palm on their chest when they laugh being umpires," he said. "Or look at the toe of their shoe and waggle it, like women."

"Have you ever noticed that women pick a flake of tobacco off their tongue while a man sort of spits it out?" I said, sprinkling salt into my soup.

"Women have a different walk from a man," Augie said, looking away. "A woman throws her leg forward from the hip. A man from the knee."

"Yes, I remember that from physiology class."

I bit off a crust of roll and chewed it thoughtfully.

"Women and men get into bed differently," I said. "You've probably noticed the way a woman does that."

"Mmm," he said with a nod. He twisted round in his chair. "Where's that damned waiter with my beer?"

"A woman sits down on the bed first, then sort of swivels her legs around under the covers. Unlike a man who thrusts himself in foot first."

I have said that Augie was not prompted to the revelation he now made, but I guess I did irk him again with my insight into women and knowledge of their ways and all. However, I knew he had come stoked up and ready to tell me how many women he had slept with even without my cueing him by remarking: "I was thinking about your point regarding just plain taste for women being the real male gauge. What would be your guess is the number of women the average man sleeps with? The average American let's make it. In his lifetime?"

"That's hard to say," Augie answered. He took a pull on his beer, which had been served him, and looked away. "I've slept with forty-three."

"Forty-three!" I exclaimed, lowering a laden soup spoon.

"Isn't that many?" he asked with a negligence that I thought was really too much.

"Do you keep count, for God's sake?"

"I won't swear to the figure. Mean I happened to be thinking about it the other night, wondering where the women I'd known were that very minute, the way you do, and I started to count them."

"How many of these are since you've been married?" I asked. "If I'm not being too personal."

"Not at all. Ten."

Ten. So he had gobbled more sex on the side than I had partaken of in my entire thirty-five years, wild oats included. "What's the largest number of affairs you've had going at once?" I asked, biting down on an aching tooth.

"Three."

"Three. And do you think," I demanded indignantly, setting my soup spoon down altogether, "do you think I should be asked to give you a reference in the light of this information? Do you sit there with your bare face hanging out and ask me to recommend you to Rock-a-Bye and the Crib and Itsy Bitsy and God knows what else yet, as they flunk you out one after the other, do you ask me to say of a man who has laid over forty women, 'This is my idea of family timber.'? Do you think this is the sort of thing we want in our community? Do you now? What will people think when they find out I turned a goddam ram loose in the P.T.A.! Forty-two women!"

"Forty-three. Shh! People are looking. Now then. *Don't you think these very facts speak in my favor?* Because they show what I'm willing to give up to be a family man."

"You're not giving up Cornelia Bly. Because I phoned your hotel that night you stayed in, and they said you had left a message not to be disturbed," I put up to him. I hadn't phoned that night — it was just a trick. In my wretchedness and my wrath I wanted all the facts, however they might discommode my conscience. "I never asked to be a reference," I said. "But the only way out of this is straight through it."

"That's the way I look at it too," Augie answered. "So O.K. I'll tell you about Cornelia Bly." He studied his shrimp cocktail with that kind of frown that precedes the birth of an intricacy. "I can only put it this way. It's Cornelia Bly who's put me back on the straight and narrow."

Sensing a fresher nuance than those with which I was normally visited by articulate friends, even Augie, I spread my elbows on the table and listened keenly.

"You see, even if my wife might stand for a certain amount of nonsense I have a mistress who won't. Cornelia Bly is — how shall I put it? — a Puritan of the intellect. She doesn't care that much for conventions, but imposes her own rules on human relations outside of them, like your true radical. No promiscuity for her! So while my wife wouldn't mind my sleeping with Cornelia, Cornelia wouldn't stand for a minute for my sleeping with someone else."

"You mean you feel morally accountable to the woman who's led you astray?" I asked.

"Exactly," he said, gratified by my grasp. He shifted forward in his chair and went on eagerly, "You see, I wouldn't dare two-time her."

"Is she a battle-ax?"

Augie laughed, but gently, as if the walls had ears. "There's this, that most men do want a certain amount of domination. It's what I've always missed in my home life. I never got it from Isolde. Can you understand all this?"

"I may in time. I could understand it better now if it was the other way around — that you were married to your mistress and sleeping with your wife."

"That's exactly the way it feels! That Cornelia *is* my wife and Isolde's the Other Woman." Augie smiled. "We have a little domestic joke, Cornelia and I. I call her C.B. Like a vice-president?"

"What about your guilt feeling?" I asked. "What ever became of that?"

"That's been transferred to my marriage."

"You mean it's when you're with your wife you feel pangs of conscience?"

"That I'm cheating on Cornelia," he said, nodding.

"But won't this undermine your marriage?"

"Undermine it?" he said, with a tolerant smile for my opacity. "Just the contrary. Don't you see, it gives my home life the quality of an affair, and what takes longer to wither than that? Isolde's even suited to the role physically — sitting around the house in those velvet slacks and subversive necklines, greeting me with cocktails and roses in her hair. It's for her I buy the jewels and the expensive perfumes, believe you me!"

"I believe you," I said.

"So now I think I've answered all your questions. I've settled down into a reasonable groove, and my marriage is in no danger as every hour I spend with my wife has this tincture of cheating on another woman. Must you leave?"

"I have an office appointment. I'm not really very hungry, but you take your time. Here's my share of the check," I said, tumbling some money on the table and rising. "I'd like to hear more about this later."

What did I think of what I'd heard, after settling down in my office (and combing the snarls out of my hair)? This. That if Augie were put out for adoption, preferably to C.B., who would brook no nonsense, and Isolde married someone else, we might hope for a reasonable solution to all this. But failing that, I figured I might as well go along with Augie's elucidation and see what we'd see. For if Cornelia Bly had succeeded in pruning his trespasses to within that degree of rectitude, that degree of the stern standards by which the agencies were bent on measuring man, who was I to quarrel with the alchemy by which these ends were gained? Furthermore, once he and Isolde got a child there was every reason to believe the progress would be completed by the responsibility that alone perfects growth. For who of us is mature enough for offspring before the offspring themselves arrive? The principle of society is forced growth. The value of marriage is not that adults produce children but that childen produce adults.

It was on the basis of this thinking, and a few of the points Augie himself had validly made in his anger, plus a dash of mercy and a pinch of hope, that I at last made a settlement with my conscience. I would give him the testimonial.

"When," I therefore impatiently asked my wife, "is that woman Mrs. Mash going to get here?"

Nine

SEPTEMBER slipped into October, summer into fall, and still no Mrs. Mash — except at the Pooles' where she called for repeated interviews. She preferred to go slowly, letting her impressions steep and simmer. "It takes nine months this way too," said Augie, who chafed under what he called the woman's X-ray eyes. The exhilaration of the turning year was felt in the city's quickened tempo. Autumn is the spring of the spirit, when the sap flows once again in wilted urban man. Also in wilted urban man who lives in the country. Audrey and I went for Sunday drives with the Pooles, improvising rides along the blazing back roads and through little towns whose names we didn't catch and to which we fled without the aid of maps. There was an epidemic of some respiratory nuisance which all the children caught. Phoebe got it first, and she was pumped so full of penicillin that the fumes from her cured a cold I had. The others followed, and in addition to the miracle drugs, electrically driven croup kettles were set going in various corners of the house. There were so many hissing plumes of steam on all sides that the place looked like a roundhouse. We had no fears about leaving the children with Mrs. Goodbread, a skillful mechanic, who watched the croup kettles with all the care with which in the old country, she said, she had tended smudge pots to guard the orchard fruit from frost. You have an instinctive faith in anyone who has sat up all night with trees. Dr. Vancouver was all right in there too. He carried a supply of surgical masks which he put on the patients, when examining them with stethoscopes, explaining that this was indeed an epidemic and his first duty was to the community, for whom he must keep himself in fettle. Setting out on one of our foursome jaunts, we saw him parked beside the road in his car, taking his temperature. He waved as we went by, the thermometer sticking up out of his smile.

It was on that trip that I first began to notice Augie wasn't himself. He sat slumped in the back seat beside Audrey, managing to look glum even in the yellow tartan cap and houndstooth jacket which comprised his plangent motoring gear. Cornelia Bly was in Florida for a month. Did he then miss her that much? Isolde said the picking, poking painstakingness of the agency was wearing his nerves down, as it was hers. It was an awful mental hazard. Augie, who had claimed such attunement to the autumn season that he could smell the leaves turning in their faint combustion, "exactly like something burning," and held reveling in her melancholy to be the highest joy open to man, didn't feel like reveling in the melancholy now. He was too miserable. "Wenn du fehlen willst, fehle gut," he said.

"Don't talk like that," Isolde said. "What does that mean — something about not feeling good?"

"No, it's from one of the great Germans. 'If you're going to be a failure, be a good one,'" Augie said. In the rearview mirror in which I could see him as I drove, he seemed to be disappearing into his getup, like a turtle into its shell.

We were to lunch that Wednesday and discuss his latest try — a drunk lying in the gutter of a bowling alley — but there wasn't much to say about it. "Make him look dreamy and happy there, and you might put in a spectator — someone looking over and doing a 'take' on it," I suggested. He nodded vaguely. Our food came — a sandwich and a bottle of ale apiece. Pouring myself a glass, I asked: "Heard from Cornelia Bly lately?"

"I got a letter Friday," he said.

"You get letters from her at home?" I asked.

"No, I pick them up at general delivery, Norwalk."

"How's she doing? Still down in Florida?" I was sure from his expression that she'd given him the air, but I sensed that he wanted to talk about it and was doing my best to prime him past his reluctance.

He brought the letter abruptly out of his pocket.

"You might as well know the whole story," he said. "It's all in this. First she tells some gossip about where she's staying, local history and one thing and another. How we're still technically at war with the Seminole Indians." He poured himself some ale. "The tribe was originally formed by splitting with the Creek Indians. The name means 'seceders.' They fought the United States bitterly in 1817–1818, and later under Osceola. Toward the middle of the century that was. There aren't but three hundred Seminoles left in Florida. It seems a treaty was never signed with them."

"But that's not what's eating you."

"No." He bent his head again over the letter. "I told you Cornelia went down there to paint, but that's not the whole story. She went down there to think things through. Come to some conclusion about 'us.' That's all right, ours is a special relation, outside the pale. She felt she had to go over the whole thing objectively and without any emotional kibitzing from me. And now she's come to a conclusion about 'us.' Only down here she explains what she never told me before she left. It seems 'us' will soon be three."

It was a moment after his words reached me that his meaning did. There was an interval of dreamy disbelief during which the meaning floated dreamily toward me, like a shuttlecock over a badminton net well after the drive that sent it there is finished.

"I see," I said. "And?"

"And she wants to have the child and keep it."

"I see," I could only unresourcefully repeat. Then I asked: "How do you feel about that? Don't you stand on the right to live your own life, outside the pale as you say?"

"What is the matter with you?" he reproved. "A child . . ." He raked his hair and wet his lips. He shook his head distractedly. "I blame myself. . . . What's so funny?"

"Blaming yourself. I'm sorry."

"Who else is there to blame? I don't know what's the matter with you sometimes. Put yourself in my shoes."

I kept a straight face by pretending to probe a molar with my tongue. I said:

"It seems to me this is her own affair. She's sort of tricked you, hasn't she?"

He seemed not to have heard me. "My old will to fail," he said.

"How many months is she pregnant?" I asked, smiling helplessly now.

He held up three fingers, as though he could not utter the word. "Too late to do anything now but see it through."

"She knows you're married of course?"

"Of course. But that has nothing to do with it in her view. She feels she has a perfect right to be a miss mother if she wants."

I asked: "Can she afford a child?"

"She's banking on the ten thousand dollars she's suing that

flour company for. Her lawyer says it's a sure thing. He's got a critic who'll testify that there's been damage to her reputation. Thousands of people who never heard of her before have read about the case. So she figures the ten thousand she's asking will see her through the first few years, and by that time she expects she'll be making enough on her paintings to support the child. And of course she's hoping to get more advertising commissions as a result of the publicity."

The case was by this time already on the New York court docket. It came up very soon — in fact Cornelia's lawyer called her back from Florida by wire.

We all followed it with great interest. It was a libel suit, that being the category under which damage to professional reputation comes. The trial consumed two full days of expert testimony, disputed opinion, and legal and aesthetic wrangling. The pictures were of course placed in exhibit, and a long argument raged as to which looked more mutilated, with distinctions drawn between literal and artistic mutilation. The audience was all ears. The critic who testified in Cornelia's behalf was the editor of a surrealist quarterly called *Bloodshot*. I was in court with Augie the afternoon of the second day, and also two afternoons later when the judge rendered his verdict. He awarded damages to the plaintiff in the amount of twenty-five cents — in other words, Cornelia had lost the case. Augie gripped my arm and hauled me to my feet. "Let's go have a drink," he said.

"How the hell is she going to support that child now?" he said, in the bar to which we hurriedly repaired. "In France she'd have gotten a judgment. The artist has some rights there — what they call *moral droit*. Not here. I tell you, this country is a nest of Philistines."

"Won't she get more work, as you said?" I asked.

Augie shook his head. "Not a chance. The advertising agencies are laughing up their sleeves." He took a long pull on his beer and lowered the stein to the table. "She's got to give the child up now."

"Would she lay it at your door?"

Augie gave me a slow burn; and when my face began to get out of control I hid it with my hands and said, "Oh, God," holding them there till I had steadied myself enough to remove them and ask: "She has no other moneys?"

"Not enough. She lives with her brothers in a sort of homestead they inherited from their parents, who are dead. In Norwalk. She comes from a fine family," he added a trifle smugly. "I've never been there — we only met in New York. And where would I get any extra dough?" We glanced simultaneously at an envelope full of rejections in the pocket of his topcoat, which hung on the wall, the week's rejections which he had picked up from the office that morning. I remembered what I'd told him that night in his studio, about all the potential cash there was in his files, if he ever needed any. The same thought must have crossed his own mind because he brought his fist down and said, "She's got to give it up."

"Don't tell me," I said, "tell her."

He did, the next night. His report was that she tended to agree, but he didn't trust her. Women were too emotional. "Look at the cold, calculating way she sat down and figured this thing out from beginning to end — about having a child," he said. She needed further persuasion, he was sure, pressure perhaps from another source. "I mustn't run the risk of being seen with her from now on," he told me across the table at which we were again lunching. "I'm being watched closely — very closely — by the agency at this stage. So I've got to keep my nose clean, as you say. I don't suppose you'd talk to her?"

He had another guess coming if he thought I was averse. "I'll be glad to," I said, emptying a bottle of ale into my glass. He turned on me a look of canine gratitude, which I must say ill became a stormy petrel. "You're a brick," he said.

That was only part of it. What appealed to me was the opportunity of acting as proxy for a rogue. It was not only a role to which I was temperamentally drawn and by nature inclined, but one in which I was thoroughly grounded and even finely trained by the practice in which this picaresque side of me had been developed: I mean the hours spent at Moot Point honing my wits on just such romantic imbroglios as this. They had been literally without number, as I have perhaps adequately suggested. I had been embroiled there with women of all ages and from clinging vines to flinty intellectuals like Cornelia Bly, with no demonstrable damage. With this one a summer's dalliance, through a squall of passion with that, and out of it all had come a fund of dexterities and attitudes, aphorisms and ripostes all ready and waiting in a reservoir of dialogue at which I was letter perfect. Put myself in his shoes indeed! When was the week in which I had not? Lucky for the collapsed rebel that there was someone available to step into his role who had been thoroughly rehearsed.

Sympathetic as I was and ready with my good offices, however, I could not forego one final, somewhat reproachful remark as I rose from the table at which my deflated radical yet tarried.

"I guess you realize now," I said, laying a hand on his shoulder, "that you've been living in a dream world."

Ten

TAKING over for Augie was a grave responsibility. I felt that. I spent the next days getting myself in the mood for the part. What did that call for as I saw it? Strict conformity to the character in which it had begun — that of a moral independent. Of that I was convinced. It was all right for Augie to reform in his private life, but any show of faintness on the other front, any faltering, gelatinousness of heart would be instantly taken advantage of to the possible detriment of the innocent. Perhaps beneath the girl's bravado I would find another soft center? Then I must the more show no soft center myself, in taking it from here at the point where the rapids remained to be shot. There is only one way to shoot the rapids if you want to keep afloat until you're past them — you must paddle faster than the current.

I set to grooming myself for the part on these lines. I imagined that I was an international cad about whom there must be no mistake. In brushing up, I practiced on my wife, with some old capers of mine that were familiar to both of us. I often pretended that we weren't married but were only living together, or had just met, or some such. I often tried to look not married when we checked in together at hotels, signing the register furtively and what not, to see if I could arouse suspicion. Well, driving her to town to shop for an aunt's birthday present, that Thursday evening when the stores were open, I imagined that the family station wagon we were in was a low-slung open Jaguar in which I had just picked her up. I was wearing a tweed cap anyhow, and now slouching raffishly behind the wheel I said, "Let's go up to my place and do a little hard breathing."

"Take this road here, it's shorter," she said. "Then cut over to Main Street."

I began to jab with my thumb at a jammed press latch on the glove compartment, to make my wife ask me when I was going to fix it. I jabbed at it several times, reaching across her to do it, and at last she said, "When in God's name are you ever going to fix that thing — or take it down and get it fixed?"

"Women nag their husbands about what they don't do. Men nag their wives about what they do," I said, settling back. " 'When are you going to fix this or mow that?' women say. And men, 'Why must you put chives in everything, what are you forever rearranging the furniture for?' None of that for me."

I prowled down Main Street, steering with my hands on the bottom of the wheel. My wife was poking around in crannies looking for the mate of a glove she had in one hand. "Why can't women lose gloves by the pair?" I debonairly chaffed.

I was feeling my way around in the part, circling for the right vein, and now I felt I pretty much had it: that of a light and informed rascality, a profligate charm that was irresistible even to its victims.

"We ought to pick up a little something for the children, if Maude says they've behaved," my wife said.

"Children! How can you conceive of such a thing? No children for me, you may as well know. The human species is the only one that is devoured by its young." For all this she would soon be at Moot Point, protesting weakly that my kisses drew the marrow from her bones. I dug up a paper-back novel that had got wedged under me. "What the hell is this?" I asked irritably. "Good God, you're not reading that woman?"

"Dip into it waiting for your train. I thought it was up your alley, that sophisticated sort of idiom."

"Every idiom has its idiot." I drew to a stop before the gift shop and reached over to open her door and let her out. "Don't take too long in there. And then let's go up to my place and do a little hard breathing."

Augie arranged for me to see Cornelia the following Wednesday evening. The encounter was to be lubricated by the assumption that I wanted to look at her paintings; having seen which I would proceed to the main purpose of my call. At half past seven on Tuesday evening Augie phoned and asked me to come right over to his studio.

When I climbed through the hatch leading to it, I found him in shirt sleeves, sorting through piles of drawings and sketches which lay everywhere on tables and on the floor. Two new electric heaters had the place hot as a kiln.

"What are you doing?" I asked.

He pointed down at a stack larger than the rest. "Can you let me have a thousand bucks advance on these? There's at least thirty more that you've expressed interest in over the years. I mean the ideas of course."

"What's up?"

He drew a long, harried sigh and hitched up his trousers with his wrists, his hands being black with dust.

"Mean there'll be expenses in any case. Whatever's done in the end, there's things I ought to foot. And if I give her the money — all in a lump sum, and *enough* — there's less chance of anybody coming around here and *asking* me for it. You know — some relative or friend, maybe stirring up trouble or suspicion. I've got to keep out of this."

Now Augie had remained an artist, not by selling his pictures, but by refusing to sell his jokes. Once he took a nickel for them his status would be confused and polluted, not to mention the unlikelihood of a gagman's ever eluding those bourgeois moral laws from which the artist enjoyed exemption. But he was in a spot, and there was no alternative. Was a mistress to force him to take that first long step toward the estate of wage earner? . . .

I stared at the stack. From my point of view, this was the bonanza for which I had been waiting — ours just when the magazine needed ideas, a good new jokesmith. How Blair would rejoice! I didn't feel much like rejoicing now. "I hardly know what to — " I began.

"Oh, the hell with that. You once made me an offer. The letter must be around here somewhere. Fifty dollars apiece for ideas if I went into production, with a quantity bonus if I sold over fifty a year. This is the same as production," he said, waving at the masses of work. "Twenty usable ideas would cover the thousand and I'm sure there's more than twenty there. Go on, take a look."

I could read the caption on the top one from where I stood. One missionary to another in a cook pot as they are about to be eaten by cannibals: "Our work hasn't been entirely in vain. They're going to say grace."

"Look here, I don't see that it's this much your responsibility," I said. "If she wants to be a miss mother, let her be one."

"Don't," he warned me nervously. "I want to do this. The thousand should see her through — well, the first stage. Beyond that let's not look. I owe her this much. So don't go making any bones about this part of it." I realized that he was scared of C.B. — scared, at least, of what she might do — and was determined to put himself in a position of owing nothing, and clear of provoking an erratic action. As he argued about it, he kept glancing instinctively toward the house, and it was vouchsafed me that the philanderer was scared of his wife too! Like any good American husband. "Cornelia can have hostilities. Masculine protest and one thing and another. Showing the world she could get along without a husband was undoubtedly part of that whole plan of hers, at bottom. I understand she's overshadowed by her brothers," he chattered, pacing the sweltering loft.

"Will they be around too?" I asked him.

"Well, they're O.K., from everything I hear. A very cultured sort of family. One's a musician, the other's a literary scholar."

"What's the other one? You said there were three."

"He's a minister," Augie said, looking for his cigarettes. "But they tell me he's not orthodox."

So I had my work cut out for me. I knew what I was to be pitted against. But Augie gave me no time to think about my own problems. "So the poor kid's probably been reacting to her environment. So handle her with kid gloves. Mean butter her up about her paintings," he said. He was pale. Don Wan. The tilted blue eyes had a fugitive look, and the normally neat reddish-blond waves had been thoroughly plowed. Augie was really a very good-looking egg despite a somewhat spoonbill nose, and no doubt there were women who thought that gave him the look of an intellectual Bob Hope. He drew a deep breath and turned again to the drawings. "Now do you want to take these with you and go over them on the train in the morning? Because time is of the essence."

"I don't have to look at anything first. I'll have the agreement drawn up and the check for the advance ready by noon tomorrow. Then you can cash it and — do you want me to take the money along tomorrow night?" I asked.

"I'd appreciate it. She's got a cold and can't meet me outside the house, and I don't want to be seen there. I have other people to think of in this."

"Certainly. Bring the drawings with you when you come to the office tomorrow," I said. I had started to say good night when I thought of something. "By the way, what are you going to tell Isolde is happening to all the money you'll be getting? Because you'll have to tell her you're selling your jokes. It'll be no time before she sees them coming out in the magazine, because I'll be turning them over to the artists right away."

"God, I never thought of that. Yes, she knows all my stuff. What'll we do?" he asked hollowly.

I thought a moment.

"Well, suppose I do this," I said. "Suppose I make the advance a little more than a thousand — the best Blair'll do, say — and you'll have something to show Isolde. Or put in the bank. Keep dividing what you make between the two women, for as long as you have to." I backed gingerly through the hatch and started down the precipitous stair. I paused with my head at floor level. "You'll have to work like a son of a bitch now," I said, and disappeared from view.

The Blys lived in a large white rambling house on the outskirts of Norwalk, the address of which I found in the phone book, and to which I was directed by three cops. Norwalk is built on more hills than Rome, and nothing in it, uncannily, is descended to but only attained by climbing. I had the thousand dollars on me, but to keep in the mood I pretended I had cadged it from a rich uncle who had written me off as a rotter and was only doing it for my family. "This is the last wench I'll buy off for you — from now on you can tidy up your own messes," he'd said, and stridden from the drawing room. I parked the car a block from the house and walked up to the door, unregenerate still.

Cornelia was, of course, expecting me, and it was she who answered the door. "Come in," she said. She was wearing a loose-fitting artist's smock like the one she'd had on at the P.T.A. business — maybe the same one. She led me into a living room lined with books from floor to ceiling, in which two men in their middle thirties were sitting, one sideways in a deep chair, with his legs slung over the arm, reading a book, of which he turned a page as I entered; the other on a sofa before a fire, reading a musical score. "This is my brother Carveth," Cornelia said of him. "Are we interrupting a concert?" she asked, for it turned out that Carveth derived the same pleasure from reading a score as other people do from hearing the composition played — more. "And he'd rather read a recipe than eat the dish," said a voice behind me. "This is my brother Hubert," Cornelia said, indicating the reader who had risen with the book in his hand.

Carveth had studied at Juilliard and Rochester, and abroad at the Paris Conservatory and in Germany and Italy. He was now at home working on a history of music which he said Knopf was going to publish in twelve volumes. He was married, but his wife, an anthropologist, was at present on the Zambesi on a Guggenheim, studying Rhodesian taboos. Hubert was another in a family who had jet-propelled themselves from one scholarship to another. "The best things in life are free," he said, having, at thirty-six, never paid for his tuition. Carveth frequently taught between courses, but Hubert had never sat anywhere but on the student's side of a lectern. No one in the family could enumerate his degrees on the spur of the moment, nor extemporaneously recall the colleges and universities he had attended, which included Oxford, the Sorbonne and the Free University of Amsterdam. He had grazed wide among the humanities, but would seem to have settled on literature, in which he would continue to conduct research until a suitable teaching post turned up. Faculties in the main tended to be chary of him because he appeared to have no specialty. The other two brothers gave him what aid was not supplied by scholarships and grants. He was currently in the East to catch some lectures at Yale, which was his alma mater and to which he had offered to bequeath his brain. He had made this offer several years before, but had not received formal acceptance, only a series of interim replies advising him of the status the matter had reached in the departments among which it was being bandied for consideration.

"Won't you sit down," Cornelia said to me.

We were given brandies in large inhalers, and cigars were passed round. Cornelia declined those Hubert proffered in a humidor, and lit a Between the Acts of her own. I took a cigar, but did not immediately light it. Setting aside his score, Carveth remarked that he'd have been farther along in his work if his old room hadn't been stolen from him by his brother. "You know — the one overlooking Norwalk Bay," he said with a meaning glance at Hubert. "I had thought there was no advantage in the view," replied the other, "since the Bay is something to be overlooked in any case." The fire was prodded and Carveth was coaxed to the piano. He composed impressionistic pieces in the tradition of that pleasant homogenized dissonance come down from Debussy through Delius. He played a suite of three numbers called "Night," being a series of sweet qualms on that subject, then struck out into a group of take-offs. Using the air of "Three Blind Mice," he parodied first a Bach fugue. Then he did the tune as Berlioz would have done it, and lastly, Hindemith. We set down our brandies and applauded when he'd finished.

"The Hindemith needs work," he said, reaching for his own drink which he had set on the piano.

"No, I like it best," Cornelia said, taking another cigarello from its flat tin.

"Oh, really?" Carveth said, rising from the bench. "I thought it needed touching up."

"Oh, come now, that's pure affectation. You know it's perfect," Hubert said from the armchair, over one side of which he again had a leg slung. I saw that there was a tradition of family persiflage here, at which Hubert was most active. He had a way of bringing his head down when he laughed that resembled Cornelia's, except that in his case it often took the form of appearing to dodge an expected blow for his jokes.

"Hubert thinks everything is affectation," Carveth said. "He takes nothing at face value."

"But nothing can be taken at face value. Least of all pure naturalness. That's the ultimate affectation. It's the attempt to cover our masks with a bare face."

"Nonsense. I appeal to the rest. What do you say?"

Cornelia chose to follow the dispute with her musing slice-of-watermelon smile; so they all looked at me. I swirled the brandy around in my glass a moment. "There's a lot in what he says," I said.

I set my glass down and suggested to Cornelia that I ought perhaps to see her paintings, for which I had prefabricated some remarks. She rose from her window seat and, letting Carveth give me another spot of brandy, I took my glass and followed her through a door to the rear of the house.

Her studio was a large, high-ceilinged, sky-lighted room, the walls of which were as covered with paintings, etchings and drawings as the rest of the house was with books (there were bookcases along both walls of the corridor down which we had come).

"Just go right ahead and look around," Cornelia said.

The canvases, which everywhere met my eye, gave me the sensation I often get from extreme modernity in painting — that of smothering under a crazy quilt. The succession of bisected squares and triangles and other mathematical forms were utilized in rendering man, machinery and nature alike. There was a Cubist study of three dancers; a mélange of gears and pistons suggesting visually the roar of many means of transportation; and everywhere color represented as refracted light. Having completed the tour, I took a drink of brandy and turned around.

"These are excellent, but don't you painters ever feel you'd like to break out of your prism?" I said, to find that there was nobody in the room but myself.

I took a stiff slug of what remained in my snifter and returned to the living room, where I found Cornelia curled up on the window seat, listening interestedly to a discussion about poetry between Carveth and Hubert. Sitting down beside her, I leaned toward her and whispered, "They're excellent but don't you think —"

"Oh, thank you," she said. "Did you really like them?"

"But they're not for us. We can't use that type of thing for a cover."

"No, I supposed not." Our attention was drawn to the discussion. At the moment, Hubert was analyzing the transition from Victorian to modern poetry.

"Poets used to be obvious with obscure words," he said. "Now they are obscure with plain ones."

There was a silence in which he acknowledged my return by looking in my direction; it had the effect of an inquiry as to what I might think of this. I set my brandy to rocking in the snifter again, and said, "They go too far."

Carveth saw that there was precious little to rock, and came over with the bottle and gave me another splash. So the civilized evening wore on. Hubert walked the room, drawing on his cigar.

"Of course the whole discussion, our whole view of poetry, is so restricted to what we know of the English that we don't understand there are other traditions. The French, what an entirely new vista they open!" he said. "How much more pure poetry there is there. And how didactic and moralistic so much British poetry seems by comparison."

"The French for the simile of beauty, the English for the simile of health, as it were," Carveth said, carrying the bottle back to the table.

There was a sound of feet coming down a stairway.

"Here comes Emory," Cornelia said.

I stiffened. This was it — the minister. These two chaps I could handle — broad-minded, educated, reasonable liberals both. But Emory was a horse of another color. I gulped down my brandy and steeled myself as he entered.

The cleric was a roan. He had a billow of chestnut hair flecked with gray, and bright blue eyes like glazed berries. He wore a black velvet smoking jacket and carried a pipe in his hand. He was at forty a crystallized bachelor (unlike Hubert who was "interested" in a woman in nearby Stamford). He rapped out the pipe on the underside of the mantel, after we had been introduced, and said yes to Carveth's offer of a brandy.

"I've been on the phone the whole evening with the trustees about that new steeple. Ours blew off, you know," he told me, "in that hurricane last fall. Act of God," he added dryly, and there was a gust of laughter that could not have been less hearty than the gale which had toppled the spire. "I suppose," he continued, spreading his hands to the fire, "I suppose the termites in the beams come under the same category, as well as that plaster that fell out of the ceiling in the committee room."

Hubert winked at us and said, "Maybe each is a punishment for not taking the last more seriously."

"Now, now, let's not have any more of your stuffy theology, Hubert," Emory said, taking the drink from Carveth. "I get enough of that from my parishioners."

So now I saw that the whole family represented the sophisticated progressive tradition, Emory as much as the rest, if not more so. I learned later how advanced he was; how he had no creed, refrained from public prayer, and was known to heckle street-corner evangelists for giving the church a black eye. "Don't you know the Gospels don't harmonize? Don't you see you're stressing nonessentials?" he would fling at them on Saturday nights.

Hubert drew him into an argument about the existence of a personal Deity, which Hubert said there might be more evidence of than Emory admitted. "Tommyrot," Emory said. "In any case, I have never thought of Him especially as a saint. He is a symbol of the whole world's upward struggle — the hard knowledge, not the easy salvation." He went on to say that his quarrel was more with the churchmen he was left of than the scientists he was to the right of. All science had given us is the the specter of a meaningless universe, but its very meaninglessness ennobles our own values, which are the bootstraps we raise ourselves with, and which must be love, not fear. Sacred must not be an anagram for scared, etc.

He sat down and crossed his legs. "Well, getting back to our church problems, let us hope," he said somewhat sardonically, "that a kind Providence will put a speedy end to the Acts of God under which we have been laboring. But enough of my botherations." He looked over at me. "So this is the chap who has our wench in an interesting condition?"

Cornelia opened her mouth to set him right, but an impulse took hold of me. Squeezing my cigar from its cellophane sheath, I said: "Suppose I have."

"Why nothing at all, dear fellow," he said. The others assured me they were not medieval about these matters either; that they did not regard the idea of seduction as psychologically valid. They vied with one another in not regarding the idea of seduction as psychologically valid. Hubert rose and went over to a shelf of books, at a row of which he peered. "Is it Faulkner who has one of his characters point out that women are not seduced, men are elected?" he said, running his finger along a number of titles. "Confound it, where is all my Faulkner?"

"That's beautifully put," Emory said, producing pencil and paper. "I must use it for a text some day."

I sat up in my seat. "It's not a view I share," I said, reaching for my inhaler, which was empty. Carveth replenished it for me, observing that I was a brandy partisan. "I drink to make other people interesting," I said, showing them at a stroke what their aphorisms were beside those of a man like George Jean Nathan.

"Can't find it. Oh, well," Hubert said, coming away from the shelves. "That's what comes of loaning books."

I bit off the end of my cigar and checked the draft. I was aware of Cornelia watching me with an anxious frown as I paused to take another drink from my glass. "You boys haven't seen my latest picture. I've finished it. Why don't you go have a look at it?" she said. "It's still on the easel."

"I prefer the double standard," I said, striking a match. "It enables one to retain the luxury of guilt."

A couple of the men rose. "I'd like to see the new picture," Carveth said.

Having lighted the cigar, I rocked my brandy, cradling my inhaler in one palm. "Affairs are like watermelons. They leave more mess than they're worth."

"Yes, perhaps you two have things to talk about," Carveth said. "Please remember we'll do what we can, which of course isn't a great deal. It's a pity Cornelia lost the suit. She was banking on that rather, and now things have been knocked galley west. I guess she feels now she can't keep the child. We realize you're married — bit of a poser that. Agree with Shaw that mating shouldn't have anything to do with marriage, necessarily. However, if she decides it's best to relinquish the child, that's probably the most intelligent and enlightened thing to do, from the child's point of view as well as everyone else's."

"Just as it's been proved that two dissimilar stocks produce the best offspring, so being reared by a third is very likely an added advantage," Hubert put in. Cornelia sat smoothing out a pleat in her skirt with her palm. "Well, let's go see the picture then. You'll excuse us."

When they were gone, Cornelia said:

"What did you do that for?"

"Augie's name must under no circumstances come into this," I emphasized, pointing the coal of my cigar at her. "As you know, he's trying to negotiate an adoption."

She gave a nervous laugh, ducking her head.

"They mistook me for him. That's all right. That's fine. I have nothing to lose, and I'm glad to do this for Augie. Just as Augie's glad to do this for you." I drew the money out of my pocket and went over and set it on the table beside her. She looked at it without taking it.

"But I don't want anything from him. I'll take care of this myself," she said.

"It's a thousand dollars. It should see you through. If it doesn't, get in touch with me — not him. He must be given a wide berth, now and forever. Is that clear?" I said in firm tones.

"You're very sweet."

I smoked the cigar till I was nauseated, which point was reached when the band which I had left on it caught fire, then I dropped it into an ashtray.

"It's your money. I'll bet it is — isn't it?" she said. "Augie hasn't got it to spare."

"It's his — every mortal penny, and I won't go into what it's cost him here, in terms of his career."

I watched her a moment as she sat with her head bent, smoothing out her skirt, which was flat as a table-top. Overshadowed by her brothers indeed. Was she one of those who must always distinguish themselves heretically — sue clients for defacing her work with the normal number of eyes, get pregnant as a spinster, smoke cigars?

I rose and stood over her again. I spoke quietly and deliberately.

"Some day, mark my word, you're going to meet a nice fellow and fall in love. You'll want to marry and settle down. Have a home life and children," I went steadily on. "But that'll be out forever if you already have one. Don't be a miss mother." I let this sink in. "So do the right thing, by this one as well as by yourself. I mean make it possible for it to have two parents instead of one. Well, now, if you want this — I mean if you want this child to have two parents instead of just one, and yourself to be a wife as well as a mother — now get this because it's important — there's a wonderful place in New Haven called Rock-a-Bye. That's where you should go. I recommend it highly. It's a first-rate place, which you can rest assured is very particular about who they give babies to. They turned Augie down, and so that's why it's absolutely essential that *this is the one place you go and nowhere else* so that — are you listening?" The head bobbed. "So that Augie won't end up adopting his own child."

I followed her responses sharply, ready in case she said anything unreasonable or was in any way emotional or illogical, in which event I would say, "Women! How much easier it is to chase them than to follow them." But I was given no grievance on that head, which irked me to some extent, as I had gone to a great deal of trouble preparing for this interview. Cornelia was the soul of compliance, repeating "Rock-a-Bye" after me as I asked, to make sure it was firmly printed on her mind. And when the brothers came clomping back it was with the same enlightened bonhommie and badinage and broad-minded tolerance as when they had left. I stood ready and waiting for them with my back to the fireplace, now gone cold, holding the snifter in one hand and the retrieved and rekindled cigar in the other, with a forbidding expression. It was the look of a man accustomed to buying his way out of every scrape. Instead of bristling, they "quite saw my situation," that it was "just one of those things," and regarded the thousand dollars, left visible on the table and explained by Cornelia, as damned handsome of me — better than lots of chaps would have done considering the trouble was mostly Cornelia's carelessness and unfortunately ill-timed impulse.

As I went out the door, taking my leave about eleven o'clock, gluttonous for the night air after all those brandies, the cleric called, "Come drop in at my church sometime." The invitation did not pass off without a rejoinder.

"Oh, don't let him do that," Carveth chaffered as I picked my way down the stairs to the sidewalk. "The poor chap might lose his faith."

Eleven

"WHAT happened? How did you make out? What did she say?"

Augie's questions tumbled out.

"Women are like lobsters," I said. "The tenderest meat is in the claws."

"What's the matter, are you stewed?" he asked, raising his voice into the transmitter, for I was reporting to him by phone from a tavern booth later that night. "How was she?"

"Having a mind of one's own doesn't necessarily imply having any mind as such," I felt constrained delicately to lay before him. What a hoodwinker Sex was! C.B. indeed!

"But what *happened?* The coast is clear for a minute so I can talk — but hurry."

I told him. I explained that it had gone quite well on the whole and that everything looked to be under control. There was nothing to worry about that I could see, barring the unexpected. Accounting from a phone booth wasn't very satisfactory, but I had wanted to reassure him. I told him I'd give him a full report the next day.

The excitement of the evening in general conspired to murder sleep, or at least inflict serious injuries on it, in my case, and hours later I was still wide awake. I thought of the days when I had nothing to worry about but a rat in the wall. Would that time come again? Don't lie here revolving on a spit, I told my-self — sleep.

I remembered something I've heard from time to time all my life, namely that the last thought we think before we go to sleep is important because it is amalgamated into the subconscious. I'd read it recently in a magazine and a short time later heard an inspirational counselor on television, expounding it, say, "Dwell on some worth-while or uplifting thought as you drop off. Maybe just a line of poetry. I once lulled myself to sleep with the phrase, 'the darling buds of May.' The sheer beauty of a line like that, taken over the brink with us, can't help permeating us with its moral or aesthetic merit."

While lying in bed, waiting to fall into the arms of Morpheus (or into his hands, rather, as I prefer to think of it, and as you would, too, if you had some of my dreams) I remembered the counselor's suggestion and acted on it. Composing myself between the sheets, I set my mind to the task of selecting something to dwell on. I fetched up with several possibilities, famous sayings and fragments of poetry and one thing and another, but discarded them all for various reasons — not suited to meditation, too flippant, etc. Among them was "Say not the struggle nought availeth," which I felt to be rousing rather than mesmeric in its effect. A capital thought to get up with, say, and face the new day. For some reason, I recalled Samuel Johnson's "Patriotism is the last refuge of a scoundrel," and also that it was he who first said Hell was paved with good intentions. Neither of these seemed quite right for the purpose at hand; one did not want anything "trenchant." I could see that this method was not as easy as it sounded. Then suddenly there swam into my mind a line of poetry that I found as felicitous as the TV counselor apparently had the fragment from Shakespeare. It was from a poem by Dylan Thomas that I'd heard someone read aloud at a party the week before: "Altarwise by owl-light in the halfway house."

I dwelt on that awhile. The cadence of the words and the gentle profundity of the mood they evoked utterly charmed and, gradually, soothed me. An excellent idea, this. I would make a regular practice of it, taking a thought or a line a night and immersing myself in it, giving myself over to its overtones. How much better than indulging in some flabby reverie full of wool-gathering and wish-fulfillment. I reiterated the line hypnotically to myself: "Altarwise by owl-light in the halfway house . . ." Just as I was getting pleasantly drowsy, I sensed something nagging the back of my mind; something about the line. I didn't know what it meant.

I lay with my hands laced under my head, looking up at the ceiling. Did the poet mean to convey the idea of religious experience in middle age under nocturnal conditions? Or was the owl designed to suggest a pagan element (as the bird traditionally linked with Minerva) rather than mere physical nightfall? Or was a note more funereal than either of these intended to be struck? Was the symbolism all private and obscure? After maybe half an hour of this, I glanced at the dresser clock, which was not obscure, being phosphorescent. It said a quarter after two. (I hadn't gone to bed till one-thirty.) This was a hell of an hour to get into textual criticism.

I lit a cigarette from a pack on my nightstand and, propped on one elbow, lay on my side smoking. Was the trouble that the line was torn from its context? Maybe if I had the entire poem, or a stanza from it, it would help, provided it did not open exegetical vistas that would keep me till dawn. I mentally ran over the poetry collections in my library, without being able to think of one that was likely to contain any Thomas. Nor could I remember a word more of the poem as the man had read it at the party, or even what it was about.

My arm felt strained and I straightened to a sitting position. Perched tailorwise on the bed, I myself stared like an owl into the gloom. I was stark awake now. Tailorwise by owl-light in the half-awake house. "The hideous clarity of insomnia." Who said that? Wasn't it Chesterton? Know any more Chesterton? No. How about Chesterfield? "The pleasure is momentary, the position ridiculous, and the expense damnable." Not a very edifying thought, nor one the TV counselor would have been likely to sanction. Turning my back on the deep waters into which I had permitted myself to be lured, and fixing my mind firmly on the names of Longfellow, Whittier and Holmes, as on the lights along the shore, I made for the havens of corn. "Build thee more stately mansions, O my soul." I should have picked that. Or better yet, "Tell me not in mournful numbers life is but an empty dream." Yes, that was the ticket. I would switch to that.

As I mentally intoned my substitute selection, however, curious and persistent alterations kept creeping into it — "Tell me not in mournful owl-light life is but a half-baked dream," and so on. There was no getting ashore; like a firm undertow my original selection drew me back. A question of sportsmanship, the pluck to see a thing through, came into it too. "Altarwise by owl-light in the halfway house." How could a line so analgesic to the ear be so exacerbating to the intellect? "Not by eastern windows only, when daylight enters, comes the light," would soon cover the situation.

I threw back the quilts and groped my way into the hall. Snapping on a light, I squatted before a bookcase there and ran my eye along the volumes on a lower shelf. Through the open bedroom doorway I could hear my wife stir.

"Whah you doing?" she mumbled.

"Looking for a book."

"Can't sleep?"

"No. Do you know where that anthology of criticism is I bought last week? You know, the one with the section on modern poetry."

"Oh, I dah noh. . . . " Her words trailed indistinguishably off.

"Look, are you awake? You heard Fred Hume read that poem of Dylan Thomas's. What does this line mean to you? 'Altarwise by owl-light in the halfway house.' "

"O my God you raven bow this sour a night?" she said, and turned over with a violent groan of the bedspring. "Stew o'clock."

I found the book and took it to bed with me. Tilting the shade of the lamp on my nightstand so the light wouldn't bother my wife, I burrowed down in the chapter I wanted. It had, as I'd recalled from having flipped through the volume when I bought it, several pages on Dylan Thomas.

"The Welsh bard's rich kaleidoscope of images projects a highly personalized, memory-charged idiom," I read, "through which is restored the virginity of the lyric impulse. . . . " There were a number of passages quoted from his poetry — none, however, containing the line in question.

But the reference work turned out to serve its purpose nevertheless. A page or two of "the cistern of Self" and "perpendicularity as distinguished from horizontality of feeling fund," and I felt my eyes grow heavy. I laid the volume aside and put out the light, the raveled sleeve of sleep already half knit up. Drowsily wadding my pillow under my head, I remembered something

Disraeli had once said, to the effect that he didn't know to which he was the more grateful — the books that kept him awake or those that put him to sleep.

And with that thought I drifted off into the Land of Nod.

I awoke from a dream in which I was to get a medal provided I could endure having it pinned on my skin. Didn't make it. Looked over to my wife's bed. Sprawled out on her side with one leg arched up, her thigh exposed under a rumpled blue silk nightgown. A beautiful sleeper, quiet as a Cadillac. I reached a leg across the aisle between us and prodded her with a toe. She twitched awake and smiled.

"I suppose you expect me to marry you now," I said. She yawned and stretched voluptuously, curling her fists over her shoulders. "Well, don't get any ideas, Liebchen. I prefer things strictly à la carte."

"So do I. I don't plan to spend my life washing a man's shirts and bearing his children," said my wife, who occasionally fell in with my rigmaroles when she had the time.

"Can you bear children?" I said, sizing her up.

"I can bear children all right. It's men I can't bear."

I went into the bathroom to wash. She meant well, but she didn't know how to hold her end up in a rigmarole — always said things that were out of character.

I made breakfast, as I frequently do. I brewed coffee and squeezed oranges. As Audrey and I were sitting at the breakfast table, each sipping his coffee and with his separate ruminations, the children began to troop in. First little Phoebe, naked except for a tweed vest; an old salt-and-pepper affair of mine. The implication that she had slept in it was one that I did not care to explore.

Maude said when she came in: "Tell us that joke about Mrs. Obenhaus."

"We mustn't make fun of people's names," I said. "After all, we know the Obenhauses."

The thing was that last night's mood curiously persisted, and I found it difficult to throw myself into the family japes. I could not shake myself free of the role. These poor children, did they dream their father was a viper? How would they take it when one of his numerous scandals broke at last, making his double life front-page knowledge? Would they forgive him in later years?

"Go on," Maude persisted. "We never tell any of these jokes outside the house."

"Oh, all right. Why, we're going to visit the Obenhauses tonight. They've been married ten years and are having Obenhaus," I said, unwillingly. "Is that what you mean?"

Ralph said: "What's a father vexation?"

I looked accusingly at my wife. "I thought we were going to restrict them to kids' programs — no television after dinner. It's bad enough having to explain what a jeopardy sheriff is, but at least Westerns are boys' speed."

"We heard this on a Western," Ralph said. "The bad guy in it had a father vexation."

"Somebody on a dude ranch? For heaven's sake?"

"No, regular out West. He kept holding up the Wells Fargo over and over because he had a father vexation. What is that? There's father vexations and mother vexations I know."

"Just what it sounds like," I explained. "His father vexed him when he was a child, that means got under his skin. Can you understand that?"

"I think I can," Ralph said, giving me a thoughtful look, and returned to his cereal.

I felt more and more isolated from all this; not part of a family picture at all, but separate from it, a stranger to it even, whose sins might be visited upon his children unto the third and fourth generation. I saw it all: the lawyers filing at last into the house, the youngsters being spirited from the vicinity of disgrace, my wife exclaiming, "How could you?" as she paced behind drawn blinds. The scene was so vivid to me that I shuddered and shook my head, as if to shed it from my mind's eye.

"What's the matter with you?" my wife asked, watching me across the breakfast table.

"Nothing. I'll be all right."

The illusion was not lifted — nor the sense of apprehension dispelled — by a couple of the children coming over, as they presently did, and tousling their Pa. That these scenarios were premonitory was revealed in the course of the next week, several days which preceded the descent of Mrs. Mash, but followed certain events out of which was being brewed, unsuspected, a little hellbroth of my own.

Twelve

AMONG the Saturday and Sunday spring and summer suburban nights, germinal to these follies, in which I have tried to show Augie as going from strength to strength, was an occurrence more directly relating to myself, whose role was not always a spectatorial one. It arose out of that old pain in the ischial protuberance that the self-designated peers of the Age of Foible gave me, in particular with that fancy categorical singular, "the artist," which they were forever using on themselves. I decided not to let that one pass the next time it came round.

It came round next in the course of a barbecue, on the beach at Avalon, on a night now so lost among the moral dog days of that summer that I would be put to it to fix it chronologically amid the lawn parties and fist fights that also helped form its social tapestry, except that my wife was at her mother's in Pennsylvania at the time, with the children, on what was supposed to be a last holiday before school started. So it was probably the end of August. I was giving a light to a matchless blonde, not to put too fine a point on it, when someone remarked, "Of course the artist is at odds with the culture of his time."

"So is the editor," I piped up.

Everybody turned and looked at me as if they thought I was nuts.

"So is the what?" someone asked.

"The editor," I repeated, snapping the match away into the sand. "You know. He's at odds with the culture of his time too, very often. So are the auditor and the architect, for all I know, but I can speak for the editor. I can name you several, all top men in their field, who wouldn't take a plugged nickel for ours."

I pestered them systematically with this heresy for the good part of ten minutes, a long lecture for me. I went on to say that I didn't know of an editor worth his salt who was really integrated with the prevailing mores, that at least two editors of my acquaintance had imperfect domestic backgrounds and even histories of sexual digression, as well as other of the stigmata of creativity — not too extreme a word, I submitted, for a profession that often as not involved whipping somebody else's work into shape. Being compelled by modesty to leave out of the discussion what I might have in my private craw, I spoke of the compensatory part the work of editing might play, for the individual. I submitted that the drive to get out a magazine every week could be basically sexual in nature, a kind of sublimation for the person in question. I said I liked to think of the editor as a kind of pimp who brought the artist and his public together.

They nibbled on this with long teeth at first, but gradually came to take a less dim view of it, and to treat me with more respect. I detected thoughtful glances from several, thoughtful pauses in the chewing of chicken meat, that seemed to foretell one's being able to hold one's head up a little higher in one's community.

There was an immediate tangible upshot of the disquisition.

A girl on the edge of the group whom I'd noticed, in the light of the fire round which we were ringed, to have been listening with particular attention, crept across the intervening sand and wedged her way in beside me. The majority (not including me) were dressed for swimming, and she had on a dark blue suit which was still wet from a recent dip.

"I was interested in what you said about editing," she said. "I've written some articles that need cutting and maybe a little other working over — whipping into shape, as you say. A fresh eye is important, don't you think?"

"No doubt about it," I said, running one over her hair, which was like corn silk; her long, luxuriant and, I was sure, native, lashes; her full if somewhat pulpy mouth. She had one of those faces that remind us that prettiness is not a degree of beauty but something else again. While far from pretty she just missed beauty, with the kind of plainness in which you feel that a stroke or two more of the chisel would have meant divinity. I swirled a can of beer I had in my hand — one whose half-dozen predecessors had lubricated my tongue for the harangue, as a matter of fact — and looking into it asked, "What kind of articles are they?"

"Sort of memoirs. About my family?" She had that habit of ending declarative sentences with an interrogatory inflection, as if to add "You know?" "Mainly my father, who was a sort of character? In the town where I grew up in Massachusetts. The sort of thing you use a lot of in *The Townsman.*" She cleared a strand of hair out of her eye, and settling down beside me on the sand said, "I need someone who can sort of look at them objectively. Someone who's not too close to the subject?"

I drank the lees of my beer and pitched the can on a nearby pile of empties. "I'd be glad to look at them," I said.

"Would you?" She clasped her hands, on her knees again. "God, if I dreamt there was a chance of getting in *The Townsman.* Sort of all jelly at the thought?"

A beer later I heard her remark that she loved the country so much every time she got out to it that she didn't see how she lived all alone in the city in a stuffy apartment. Two beers later, and in the dying firelight, I heard myself say, "Perhaps we can discuss them over lunch one day."

She sort of mislaid a hand on my arm and said with a laugh, "There's a whole book of them."

"I eat every day," I assured her with an arch smile. I threw another can on the pile. "This is what is known as a publisher's advance."

"Ish kabibble about that if I can just get some good sound professional advice." She looked into a beer of her own, holding the can in both hands in a way that gave it the quality of a temple vessel, and asked, "Are you here alone?"

"Yes. You alone too?"

"Yes. That is, I came with the McBains. Week-end guest. They're cousins. Do you know them?"

I didn't, except by sight; I hadn't met them till tonight.

The chiaroscuro broke up, with some of the Nereids and old youths charging in for a last dip. The water was so shallow here and the beach sloped so gradually you had to run a quarter of a mile to get your feet covered let alone attain a depth sufficient to fling yourself into with any éclat, so that these dramatic dashes petered out into bathos. A man had tried to commit suicide here once — a local artist who'd had a painting rejected by the Avalon Hardware Company, which hung canvases as a way of displaying wares in its picture-frame section — and had gotten so tired and discouraged walking out in search of deep enough water that he'd turned around and gone back. Gotten a little self-conscious too, as there'd been parties on the beach watching. A few hundred more feet and he'd have been under Long Island jurisdiction.

The girl and I hesitantly rose. "Look, are your people — ?" I began.

"I'll tell the McBains to go on, if you can drop me."

She went to the McBains' station wagon where she also changed back into her street clothes. Carrying a last beer apiece, we went for a walk down the beach.

Strolling along, I recalled my last summer holiday from domestic life, two years before; how I'd begun it in a ferment vaguely related to the hearsay about the "trouble" husbands "got into" when their wives were away. My debaucheries had ultimately consisted of an hour spent in the shooting galleries along Sixth Avenue with a friend named Al Standard; the consumption at Lindy's of great bleeding wedges of strawberry cheese pie and a party at the home of a neighbor, to celebrate his revision of a hymnal for a denomination whose name escapes me. The interlude of lotus eating had been interspersed with plays and movies frenetically gobbled in the drive to "get as much in" as I could, and had ended, one final evening, in the company of an air pilot acquaintance, who confessed a secret desire to write obscenities on the sky.

It was my memory of the general tepidity of that fortnight (and of the sheepish kind of shame that constituted its aftermath) that added, I suppose, a slight undercurrent of resolve to my mood of tingling expectation as we scuffed along through the sand. We fetched up near a breakwater a half mile from where we'd started. We sat down on the sand, turning our faces to the water and hearing nearby the tidal river pouring itself forever into the gluttonous sea; the same sea that wallowed softly or flung its pitiless spume against the rocks at Moot Point.

"A nickel for your thoughts," she said. "Inflation."

"I was just thinking how in all this Everything, there's Nothing," I said. "The more Everything, the more Nothing." It was the old *Weltschmerz* act, which no longer worked with my wife. One arm flung out above my head, I lay back on the sand and went on, "Never to pluck the fruit of meaning or longer be permitted to eat the lotus of illusion — that is the curse of modern man. Never, never and again never to decipher what is written in the stars, or whispered in the ever-murmuring sea shells."

She pushed back the lock of hair the better to scrutinize me worriedly. I dropped my arm down over my eyes, gorging myself on her concern.

"To think that death comes to species as well as to individuals; to worlds as well as species," I continued. "That as we lie here the earth under us is cooling toward the clinker it's bound to become — like the moon."

"Are there then no what-do-you-ma-call-its — values?"

"None whatever," I replied inclemently. I gave a small, bitter laugh. "Except those we scratch out our farcical little day with. Philosophy is the attempt to pick at a wet knot with boxing gloves."

"Are you sure?"

"Positive. Think of the dreams and fancies set humming in this walnut hull." I tapped my skull. It was considerably south of that point that my own fermentations were going on, but anyhow. I stretched a hand upward. "There's nothing or nobody to whom all those boiling stars mean so much as a four-minute egg."

"My father is an atheist too." She rolled away and smiled reminiscently. "You and he are a lot alike."

I was wearing denim slacks, a soiled T-shirt, and a switchman's cap, clothes not exactly suited to the elucidation of *Weltschmerz*, but I did my best to recover the offensive.

"Life is a jigsaw puzzle with half the pieces missing. Millikan tried to add up the number of molecules there are in the Universe, and ended up with a cigarboxful of zeros. There it is — take it or leave it — the Universe."

"The Universe isn't everything," she consoled me.

"What are your articles like?" I sat up.

"Never mind them now."

"Tell me about your family."

I had drawn the bung from a rather capacious subject. She went into detail about her ancestors, who had been fishing people on both sides. An uncle was now curator of a marine museum of natural history in Massachusetts — he had reconstructed an entire whale skeleton from two corset stays, or something; a grandfather on her mother's side was a captain who had gone down with his ship (rocked in the Credo of the deep?). I heard this while Arcturus slipped an inch toward the abyss, and the moon rose like a bloody cliché. She brought it up to date, the story, with an eccentric and wonderfully picturesque father, in the tradition of salty characters, who was the main subject of the memoirs she was working on. "He sues everybody," she told me hilariously. "And always grumbling about the way things are. A lot like you."

Our hands met up like crabs cruising in the sand between us. I lay over toward her as, now, she settled back.

"Are the eyelashes home-grown?" I asked, propped on one elbow.

"Mm," she said, nodding.

I studied her with a morose intoxication. I tried to put a

check on myself by flunking her out of Moot Point, that touch-stone. I had been supposing to myself that Le Corbusier had designed the house, and now I imagined asking her whether she liked Le Corbusier, and her replying, "Love some — with a little Benedictine if you've got it." Thus my imp and guardian floated above me, to sabotage and save. But it was no good. In her eyes was the splintered light of stars, and her voice seemed to echo the murmur of delinquent waters. Her eyes were blue, her skin fair, her lips strategically placed. After I had kissed her, she sat up and fanned her face in tribute to myself. "Whew," she said. "Sort of absolutely flabbergasted."

I could have kicked myself as I drove her out to where she was staying, clear in Southport fifteen miles away, and I knew that I was going to feel more like kicking myself when I got home to my place. So, figuring I might as well be hanged for a sheep as a lamb, I kissed her again and again, when I dropped her.

She sat musing on me from her corner of the front seat. "I had a feeling right from the start that you were going to play on my black keys." She got out a comb and tidied up the mess of pottage for which I had sold my birthright. "Such a Schopen-hauer." She smiled, raking the long soft fleece. "The last boy I went with was a sort of moral fatso?"

I came round and opened her door. "It's been very nice — what is your name?" I said. "I didn't quite catch it at the beach."

"Terry McBain," she said. We walked up to the house. "About the articles. Supposing I phone you at your office. Sort of next week?"

Thirteen

I SPENT the days till then with a nagging conscience. My pricks of remorse were especially keen in the empty house, where my wife's blank pillow and empty bed, the framed photographs on the mantel, the clock ticking into the silence drenched with absence filled me with a sentimental regret. Oh, if I had only kept my rovings to Moot Point! How many pleasant hours, ruminantly alone in my fortnight's bachelorhood, might I not be spending there even now. In the coral gardens of my thought life the figure of Terry McBain did supplant that of Isolde Poole — just as Isolde Poole's had that of her predecessor — like those hermit crabs which inhabit vacated univalves, but only brokenly and unsuccessfully: reality always routed me to account. More than that, my conscience dunned me with claims even for peccancies committed at Moot Point, now, a thing previously unheard of, for Moot Point had always been a sanctuary where I could tell the illusory hours unvexed. "There is nothing wrong," I evoked myself as chatting on the terrace there with Terry McBain, "there is nothing wrong with the birds and bees as a metaphor for sex. For what man has not felt himself pecked and stung to death?" Oh, how I wished I could recall those words now; even that phantom wrong to my wife was gathered into the general circuit of guilt.

This state of mind continued until I found myself in an endless round of wishing I had the truant evening to live over again.

So obsessed did I become with this idea of having another chance that I finally began to ask myself, Why not? Why couldn't I relive that evening? It should be perfectly simple. I would reproduce as closely as possible the circumstances under which I had erred, lead up to the point where I had succumbed, and then not succumb. This, I felt, would not be a mere ritualistic repair of my spirit but an actual moral victory, since the same physical indulgence would be open to me.

The urge to make this token demonstration of fidelity put me in a fume of impatience when half a week passed without Terry McBain calling me at the office, as she had promised. The need to get this whole thing over with before my wife and family got back made me decide that, if Terry McBain didn't phone by the following Friday, I would call her. By Friday noon she hadn't phoned, and, having found her in the book, I rang her up. She was home.

"Oh, hello, hello," she greeted me, instantly recognizing my voice. "I was going to call you. How's tricks?"

"Fine? How are the articles coming?"

"Why, I was polishing and cutting three of them — I wanted to get them in shape before I showed them to you. Sort of trimming away the fat?"

"Well, swell. How do you feel about dinner tonight? Are you free?" Naturally my plan wouldn't work if she just brought the stuff into the office. I had to have an actual temptation.

"I'm free, yes, and I'd love to. I don't know that I'll have the articles done by that time, if that makes any never mind."

"That doesn't matter. How's seven o'clock?"

"Okie doke."

We ate at a place of her choosing called Mrs. Ainslee's, this being a bower of chintz garnished with potted palms and cooled by mechanical zephyrs, where the liquor had to be fetched from a bar next door. Terry was dressed in a navy blue faille suit of provocative sibilance and a blue and yellow ascot that, under the eaves of a floppy yellow hat, set off her amber skin and blue eyes. I watched her mood closely for any signs that her country relatives had supplied a dossier of me at variance with the idea of an unattached man I had permitted myself to be mistaken for, but there were none. Maybe the cousin McBains didn't know me any better than I knew them, if indeed Terry had reported on the sequel to the barbecue at all. She chattered sociably over a dinner of roast beef and Yorkshire pudding, largely about her father, who sued everybody. I asked the waiter whether his neighbors could scare up a bottle of red wine, and one was obtained. We had a dessert whose identity was never clearly established, but it was a kind of cobbler in which apples figured principally. Picking at mine, I said, "Let's go up to your place."

Terry sipped hot coffee through pursed lips.

"I've been thinking, after the other night," she answered gravely, lowering her cup to its saucer.

So she had a moral reclamation of her own to make. Good God, I'd never thought of that! But, of course. In addition to the normal female wish not to seem to be too easily had was the hazard of her appearing to be offering amorous favors in return for editorial ones. Casting couches. On top of all this loomed my owing it to her to tell her that I worked in the art department and had nothing to do with text, hence could be of no use to her. But I couldn't do that quite yet. What a muddle this was getting to be — and with only tonight to play it out. Resistance was the last thing I'd bargained for. If she was going to play hard to get, I reflected as I set fire to a cigarette, we were faced with a hopeless stalemate: she withholding what I would wait forever for the opportunity to decline. Yet without my reclamation the evening would be a total waste.

I began to get nervous and fidgety. When the waiter hove into view again I signaled him over and said, "Have they got any Corbusier? I mean Courvoisier?" He trotted out the front door, and presently trotted back with two glasses of cognac. Dreamily breathing in the fumes of hers, Terry closed her eyes. "Trying to ply me with liquor?"

There was something to that: I would have to seduce her into a state of compliance advanced enough for me to extract some moral credit from it. I turned over the check which the waiter had left. Seventeen dollars and twenty-eight cents.

"Come on, let's go up to your place."

She closed her eyes again and shook her head with a playful smile.

"What if I said it meant a lot to me?" I asked.

She set her glass down. "What if I said it meant a lot to me not to miss a picture that's running uptown? A revival of *Mutiny on the Bounty*."

"I've seen that."

"Well, so have I. Wouldn't you like to see it again?"

"Of course."

The film absorbed us both. Halfway through it, Terry peeled off a glove and slipped her arm through mine. She scratched my wrist lightly with her red talons. We held hands till the end of the picture. Then we walked to her place, which was only a few blocks away.

"Father's a dear underneath. He's paying my rent for a year

while I try my hand at these crazy articles, as he calls them," she said. "Of course Mother's a scream in her own right. I think you'll love her. Mother always says Father's the most even-tempered man she ever met — always surly."

I was unco-operative. "Is he discombobulated? Does his epizootic sagatiate?"

"What's the matter?" She appraised me. "Such a gloomy. Living out there in the country all alone probably. . . . My place is right in this next block."

Slowing my pace, I cast an eye up at the stars.

"Nickel."

"Oh, I was just thinking of the Fourth Law of Thermodynamics, or whichever one it is that says matter is running down. Matter is running down and the universe itself will one day become extinct. An everlasting and immitigable nothingness, in the void of black and absolute — "

"Don't." She gave my arm a maternal squeeze. "You're better off not thinking about those things. We can go so far and no further. Don't torture yourself by delving too deep."

"I can't help it."

I was feeling lousier every minute, because this was among the old routines with which I had wooed my wife, on whose black keys I had also played. It was a vicious circle, this having to use sentimental coin to square myself. Like hocking your wedding silver. But what was I to do?

"This is my door," she said as I sailed on by, upward gazing. "Well, it's been a wonderful evening."

I had once seen a play by J. B. Priestley in which the audience is given alternative endings. One is an unhappy one, the fruit of a chain of revelations about the characters brought on by a trivial question about a cigarette box, early in the first act. The other is a happy, "what if," ending, such as might result had the question not been asked, but some other, equally trivial, deflection intervened, and set the course otherwise. I had to get that optional ending, and get it tonight.

"Just wonderful. Thanks so much."

"Some people wonder how people can do themselves in," I said, looking down at the ground. "I don't wonder about it. That's the only thing I do understand."

"Come on up," Terry said.

I mounted the dark stairs behind her, swinging my hat in my hand.

Terry's quarters consisted of a small living room, a Pullman kitchen, a bedroom and a bath. There was a tiny entrance hall with a chair in it on which I put my hat. She switched on a table lamp in the living room and disappeared into the bedroom, taking off her hat. "Fix us a drink," she said. "You'll find everything in that chest next to the typewriter. And ice in the refrigerator. Make yourself at home. I'll have a bourbon and water."

I mixed two, and carried them to a coffee table in front of a sofa. I sat down on the sofa. I could hear Terry stirring about in the bedroom — a drawer, the jingle of wire hangers, something zipped. Somewhere in the building there was the muffled sound of a door shutting. I glanced nervously at my wrist watch. It was five minutes to eleven. Too late to catch the eleven-twenty home. There remained only the twelve-thirty — the last train to Avalon till the milk runs.

There was a rustle of, I think, Swiss batiste, and Terry appeared in a blue and white dotted dressing gown. She joined me on the sofa. "Sort of making you the host." She picked up her drink and sipped from it. "Strong." She lounged, partly away from me, with one shoulder against the back of the sofa. I was aware of the whisper of negligee and of my senses drowning in perfume.

"Too much nose candy?" she said and laughed. "It's a little stronger than I usually use. Somebody gave it to me."

I wondered had it been the "moral fatso" of whom she had spoken. Something puzzled me.

"You said your last boy friend was a moral fatso," I said. "Just what does that mean?"

"Oh, he thinks, like, Mother's Day has become too commercialized, and the government is getting into things that are none of its beeswax?" She sat closer and slipped an arm through mine again. "I can imagine what marriage to *him* would have been like. The type who'd be out every other night because he'd be sort of secretary-treasurer of everything? And the rest of the time he'd be downstairs with his woodwork hobby, making the sort of trays you'd have to have standing around on end."

"And when you went on vacation with him, he'd mail everybody live turtles," I said, feeling I was getting the hang of this thing. "Kind of a Mortimer."

"His name *is* Gerard."

We laughed together, having Gerard's number so.

I stole another look at my watch. Still too early to go, without appearing abrupt. I said, "What was the one before that like?"

"Him. He was a genius, but he had two pages missing."

"He had two pages missing?" I said softly.

"He invented things. He'd invent something you'd attach to an open window so that if you weren't home it would close automatically when it rained, by the wet shorting out the electrical circuit. Only it turned out that the dew shorted the circuit the same way, so the bedroom windows would keep sliding shut all night?" She smiled up at me. "Jealous?"

"Tell me, Terry, did your father ever see either of these guys?"

"Father!" She sat up, sloshing her drink in the hilarity of remembering something. "I'll never forget what he said about Albert — that's the inventor. Well, Albert worked his way through college selling magazine subscriptions, you see, and when I told Father that, to build him up, Father said, 'And after he graduates from college he'll *still* be selling them.'"

I laughed, a soft laugh of private security. The whole thing had resolved itself into a kind of double or nothing, so to speak, and Terry's apparent willingness to have me stay the night would leave me with the debt paid off and a substantial moral balance in my favor. Cautiously I tested my position. Running the ball of a forefinger along the rim of my glass, I asked, with a tongue grown surprisingly dry, "What time is breakfast around here?"

"Breakfast is any time anybody wants to get up, but it won't be around here quoth she. Not with a Schrafft's nice and handy in the next block." She watched me, sipping. "Have you ever eaten their grilled Johnnycake?"

"Very often indeed," I said. "I love it."

I finished my drink and then waited a few minutes more. Then I stood up.

"Look, I think I'd better be getting along."

But the retrieval of my self-respect was not to be effected without a grave hitch: the loss to Terry McBain of her own.

"Well, will you make up your *mind*?" she said, her eyes brighter than I had yet seen them. She set her drink down on the table. "Is this a habit of yours — flipping through samples to find something that strikes your —"

"No, it's not that at all."

She rose. "I'd like to know exactly who it is you're trying to make a fool of," quoth she, tucking together the lapels of her dressing gown in a gesture not without truculence. I seemed to see ranging, generation on generation behind her, the granite New England spirits out of which she had professedly been hewn.

"Myself, I guess. I'll probably hate myself for this in the morning," I went on, attempting a humorous subtlety that I was far from feeling, and, to tell the truth, far from comprehending myself.

"Just what the devil does *that* mean?"

I smiled and looked at the rug, pinching my nose. "It's just that I think you were right earlier in the evening, back at Mrs. Ainslee's — where, by the way, I was amused at their having to run out for liquor all the time. Incidentally, I wonder what the legal arrangement is in a case like that — who pays the tax, or what."

"Where were we?"

"But the thing is, people shouldn't lose their heads."

"They shouldn't blow hot and cold either," she tersely answered.

"You're right there. You've a perfect right to call it that," I said fairly. I shook my head. "Sex," I said, as though the grievance and the weariness were equally mine.

It was, I sensed, my apologetic air rather than my philosophical one that somewhat mollified the girl. Undone of my aplomb, even of my *Weltschmerz*, of which nothing remained but a hangdog look, she felt a little sorry for me. At least she relented. But the revival of our footing was only temporary. "Well, let's forget it this time," she said. "Run along if you want. What I was going to ask was if you're interested in going to a cocktail party at some friends' of mine in town here. It's a week from Sunday."

Panic clawed me, in the need now to get everything cleared up.

"Look, I don't know whether you know I'm married or not — "

"Married."

"Yes, I thought the McBains told you."

"The McBains don't know you from Adam — but they may," she said flintily.

"Oh, Terry."

"They couldn't place you when I asked them about you — "

"But I took for granted — I mean all of us at the same party. Of course it was a large party, one of those enormous affairs, sponsored by local groups, that are so typical of Avalon community life, especially, I might add, in the summer, with our miles of beaches. But what I meant to say is, I sort of took it for granted you knew the dope about me. That I only meant I'd come to the barbecue alone — not that I was single. Had I only dreamt — I mean if that angle was important to you." I gave this up and now did hang my head. "I suppose I'm a rotter."

"Oh, don't go giving yourself airs!" Terry turned smartly to the window. "Well — married." She turned back again, and, her arms folded, regarded me with displeasure, "Can you give me a little better idea what this is all about, including the double talk?"

"Why, yes, I'll do my best." I drew a long breath and looked up, like a public speaker preparing an answer to something put to him in the question period. "I've seen you twice," I began.

"The first time was accidental, as you know, a case of where one thing led to another, as they often do. I was sorry for it."

"I'll bet you were, the time it took you to call me back."

"I'm coming to that. So we have a sheep-through-the-gap, a husband momentarily fallen from grace. Oh, a thing common enough in itself, but still, leaving an aftermath of regret, for basically we are moral creatures, however emancipated we pride ourselves on being intellectually." She breathed sharply and rolled her eyes up at the ceiling. "Now we come to why I called you back. You see, I wanted to prove to myself that I wasn't a cad. That I was made of better stuff. And besides, I owed it to my wife."

"What about what you owed me?" she said, tucking shut the negligee with the same bellicose gesture. "When are we coming to that?"

I was like a man who, thinking to pluck up a negligible strand of briar, finds he has hold of a mile of twisting root. I pursued the subject with a kind of tense interest, wondering how I would handle it. Moving a step, I caught sight of myself in a wall mirror. My complexion blended harmoniously with the color scheme of the interior, which was an off-white, very attractive against drapes of oyster and a bottle-green rug.

As I was collecting my thoughts, Terry started toward me with deliberate steps. "Do you know what *I* think I owe you?"

I shot a glance at a vase on a nearby table. Among my Moot Point *délicatesses* was a scene in which a spitfire I have up for the week end aims a piece of earthenware at me and I duck. "Darling!" I nimbly return. "I didn't know you were domestic." It wouldn't have worked in here, that much was clear.

"Did you ever see a play by J. B. Priestley with two endings?"

I jabbered in a dry voice, backing into the vestibule and toward the door.

"I can think of a lot of things to do to you — " Terry said, still advancing.

"A grim ending and a happy one. I just wanted to run through this incident again up to a certain point, and then sort of switch to the happy ending, like in the play. A very skillfully woven thing it was, the sort of thing the British do so much better than we. Think of my intentions!" I protested. "Get this thing in its proper perspective. I might as well have come up here to put you on a pedestal."

" — but they're all too good for you. Like hanging!" she continued, ignoring my rebuttal as she had my parallel.

"*Dangerous Corner*," I said, feeling for the doorknob behind my back. "That was the name of the play. It ran for quite a while," I added, feeling as if I had done so myself — or as if I might.

"I could call a cop to say you're annoying me. Or the janitor to throw you out." Terry was talking like that.

I opened the door, snatched my hat off the chair, and scurried for the hallway stairs. I picked my way down them gingerly but rapidly, in a tailwind of invective for "my sort" that grew in volume and intensity as I negotiated the two twisting flights to the street, and drew tenants to their doors as well as sped my departure. A rather muscular and formidable-looking woman in a dark bathrobe glared at me as I shot on down. The words abated as their author apparently sensed spectators to be accumulating on the lower landings, but they echoed in my ears as I scuttled through the one remaining door into the safety of the street, and continued to echo long afterward: the sound, justly respected, of an injured woman.

Fourteen

SO now I felt rotten about Terry McBain. Now it was she I had on my conscience. I felt I owed her something. I could still see the hurt in the fronded eyes, in the anger of that skirmish I couldn't shed the recollection of. It was with a view to now paying *that* account, and if possible closing the books on this entire matter before my wife got back (in five days), that I phoned her to offer my good offices with the articles.

It took no thinking out to decide that that was the one clear kindness I could do her. No strings attached, no ulterior motives, nothing in it for me. Just a favor.

I went out to phone her, not wanting to put a call through the office switchboard girl, who had a sharp ear for the rhythms of folk speech. I slipped out for a late lunch, winding up in a Howard Johnson's that had just been opened in the neighborhood. I wasn't terribly hungry and my stomach was upset, but I'd have liked something like a broiled chop of some sort. "Could I have a lamb chop?" I asked the waitress, waving off the menu she extended. "I don't want much to eat and so as little vegetables and so on as I can get."

"I can give you the children's portions if you'd like," she suggested. "In fact, the lamb chop happens to be our Simple Simon Special."

"I'll have that and a bottle of ale. Bring me the ale first, please."

"Well, now, I couldn't give you the ale on the Simple Simon — I mean if you're thinking of a substitution for the milk. You have to take the milk, and a little ice cream for dessert, if you want it on the lunch."

"That's all right. Just bring me the Simple Simon Special and a bottle of ale," I said, feeling we had reached the nadir of human relations. I was mistaken. She was back in a trice with no ale and to announce, "We're all out of lamb chops. Would you like to see the children's menu?" She held out a small bill of fare which I declined. I leaned back against the wall of the booth I was in and viewed her.

"I understand there are twenty-eight of these places," I said.

"That is the number of flavors. There are over four hundred restaurants."

"All as good as this, I trust?"

"I was only trying to help. You don't have to bite my head off."

"How else would you suggest getting anything to eat around here?" I took the menu wearily and donned my spectacles to consult it. I was persecuted by a flow of designations such as the Peter Piper Plate, Little Boy Blue and the Humpty Dumpty Lunch. My stomach gave a low growl, like a displeased dog. However the Humpty Dumpty looked O.K., the entree being described as "small chicken salad," which seemed to be on the snacklike scale I was in the market for.

"I'll have the Humpty Dumpty," I said, handing the card back to her, "and a bottle of ale. Black Horse if you've got it."

"We have," she said, making off.

I spied a trio of hens watching me from the next table with

that "the types you meet in public" expression. As I pocketed my glasses I cowed them with a slow burn, which scattered their regard. The ale came, and then swiftly the Humpty Dumpty, with roll and butter.

Having restored myself on these viands, I went to the telephone booth and called Terry McBain.

"This is me," I plunged in the instant I heard her voice. "Look, I'm sorry about last night and the whole thing and all, but let's forget it. Now what about the articles? I'd still like to see them."

There was a long pause. Then, "You would?"

"Very much. Of course it isn't my department, I'm in the art end — " I rattled off at high speed, to get *that* debt of clarification out of the way — "but I can see that they get into the right hands, and maybe give you a little steer on them myself."

"Of course last night was one of those ridiculous businesses — better forgotten."

"When can you drop the pieces at my office?"

"Sort of after while? I've been touching up the first few chapters, enough to give you an idea what the series will be like. Fifteen in all. I could be there at fivish, if that's O.K."

She spent the first five minutes in my office browsing among the mulch piles of sketches and drawings on every desk and table and on some of the chairs.

"Sort of a pool of blood last night."

"Well . . ." I shrugged.

"So this is the funny-pitcher factory. Fascinating, to see all this stuff in embryo stage."

I could see she was interested, so I said, "Would you

mind if I took one second to get this memo off? Then I'll be free."

"Go right ahead. Love to rubber."

I drew the mouthpiece of a dictaphone toward me and said into it: "Memo to Mr. Blair. On the attached idea-to-be-worked-on, suggest the bus conductor be changed to two barefoot street fanatics in sackcloth and carrying the usual 'Repent' placards, watching a colleague down the street whose sign reads, oh, something like, *Patronize the Gotham Ecclesiastical Supply House — Hymnals, Collection Plates, Other Religious Accessories*. One of the two fanatics saying to the other, 'I never thought I'd live to see Ebenezer go commercial.'"

I paused and saw that her back was listening. I released the catch on the dictaphone and showed off some more:

"Memo to Mr. Blair. Catch no fetal heartbeat in attached fencing-school idea, however offer this notion which I'm afraid is a rather complete switch. Two fencers in dueling school having a fist fight. Their rapiers lying on the floor. One observer to another: 'It all started when one of them made a crack about the other's form.'"

I rose, handed the dictaphone record through the doorway to my secretary and came back in, closing the door behind me.

"Well, then."

We walked on a light crust of formality and tact, like a snow crust you try not to step through. She wore a brown suit and had a silk ribbon in her yellow fleece; she struck at my vanished youth and my disreputable sorrows. She was holding a brown Manila envelope, disquietingly fat. Seeing me appraise it she suddenly took a tighter grip on it and moved to the door. "This is ridiculous."

I reached over to prise the envelope from her grasp. She

jerked it behind her back, and in my struggle to snatch it she banged against the closed door with a thud that rattled the latch. We scuffled against the door. I heard my secretary's typewriter stop in the outer office, and the sound of a chair scraped back as by someone rising in alarm.

"No," Terry said. "Don't."

I pinned her against the door. Holding one of her arms, I reached behind her with my free hand for the envelope. My embrace crushed a cloud of scent from her clothes. At last I wrested the envelope out of her clutch and dropped it on my desk.

"I'll look forward to reading it," I panted, smoothing back my hair.

She tugged her coat and skirt to rights. "Well . . . You'll call me?"

"Yes."

"Well, good-by then. And thanks a lot. You're very sweet."

She had not reached the elevators when I had the envelope open and the manuscript in my lap. It began:

"Father was always suing everybody. At the drop of a . . . " I shuffled through the pages reading sentences at random. "Father would say, 'The mean temperature for July has been ninety-one point five, and that's pretty mean. . . .' For years Father put no stock in 'this allergy business,' but later came to believe in it to the extent of being convinced that he was allergic to his own hair. . . . Dressed in his fur coat and coonskin cap, Father was a sight to behold. . . . "

I put the manuscript down and walked to the window. I looked down into the gulch of Forty-seventh Street, twiddling the Venetian-blind cord. Father was that star codger and ubiquitous nuisance who had still not been written out of the national system. Father McBain was a trifle overpicturesque for *The Townsman*, that much was sure — and his daughter not yet out of the building.

I phoned Father's daughter shortly after noon three days later, by which time I'd read the manuscript through and so had the fiction editor Hackett, who'd sent it back to me with the note "Too reminiscent."

"Look, this is good stuff, but not just up our alley. And they're stocked up on reminiscence at the moment." I made a slip of the tongue and said "reminuisance" first, or almost did.

Long silence. "I see."

"I enjoyed reading it myself. A lot."

"I'll bet."

"Come, come now. There are lots of places you can sell this."

"I know. I've tried them all."

"Well . . . " I hesitated. It wouldn't do to just mail the stuff back to her, or leave it at the receptionist's for her to pick up. I couldn't seem to get my foot out of this thing. "Can you have a drink?"

"Can I *have* one! I need one."

We met in the Biltmore lounge, and this time she had on a salt-and-pepper tweed suit and a "courageous" little hat of butterscotch color with a pompon on it.

"It's junk," she said instead of hello, as I set the envelope on the table where she'd been awaiting me. "Junk, junk, *junk!*" she repeated accusingly, with such ferocity I thought she was going to reach across the table and scratch me.

"Stop this nonsense," I said. I signaled a waiter and ordered a Manhattan. She was already drinking a Martini. "You act as if your whole life was at stake."

"Well, it is. I'm twenty-five, time to find out if you've got anything or should go back to Squeedunk. What's the matter, don't you like my hat?"

"Yes. I was just admiring the way you wear it — so nice and casually." I made another *lapsus linguae* and said "casualty." She called me on it and also brought up the one I'd made on the phone, which had not escaped her.

"What have you been doing, chewing slippery elm?" she said. "Well anyhow, if the stuff was only good for *some* magazine. I was always afraid to try *The Townsman* because that was where I wanted to be. Now I know." She sighed and broke her hands apart. "I suppose I might as well quit."

I wished she would quit — quit talking like this. And I wished that damned woman at the next table would stop too — she was delivering one of those "ices" monologues to a female friend. "So ices if you think you deserve a better job, go in and tell him ices. Ices you've been in the bathroom-fixture game long enough to have that right, and if you don't blow your own horn nobody will. Right ices? Ices nobody ever got anywhere hemming and hawing — take the bull by the horns ices to him."

"Let's get out of here," Ices to my own companion, after ten solid minutes of this. "What — what are you doing for dinner tonight?"

She gathered up her bag and gloves and the Manila envelope. "I'll fix dinner for us. We'll stop by and get some veal for scallopine. Don't try to talk me out of it. I have to do something with my hands when I'm in a stew."

Outside in the street, she threw the manuscript into a city trash basket, taking for granted of course that I would fish it out, which I did; but I felt very put-upon having to dive in head first, as I did, because the basket had been recently emptied and the manuscript lay at the bottom. I almost fell in. I carried the manuscript the rest of the way to her apartment, where I gave it to her. She threw it into a wastebasket. I ignored these proceedings.

She clattered to work in the tiny kitchen, conjuring utensils out of an area no larger than a phone booth. I tied an apron on myself, but then sat reading a newspaper because every time I offered to help I was jostled out of the way. At last, after much beating of flour into the veal with the rim of a saucer, she had it simmering in sherry in the skillet.

She turned and took me in. "Nickel," she said.

"I'm reading the newspaper."

"Nickel," she demanded.

"I was thinking that we all learn by experience, but some of us have to go to summer school," I said, with an air of aphorism that was undone by a wet paper napkin sticking to the bottom of my cocktail glass as I raised it to my lips.

"What would you tell your wife if she came in here now?"

"That we were cutting capers in the kitchen," I said with a rather engaging smile, and slipped another inch behind my newspaper.

"We ought to have some wine with this. Besides this sherry." She turned and stooped, and from a lower drawer dug a bottle of claret which she said someone had given her the previous Christmas. (I wondered was it the moral fatso, or the chap with two pages missing.)

"Have you ever had mulled claret?"

"Well, hell." I crossed my legs under my apron.

"I'd like some now. That's just what I feel like." She got out spices and began to mix them briskly into the claret. "You know what mulled claret is, don't you?"

"I know what mulled claret is. It's a cure for alcoholism." I wanted to read my paper. "You need a poker to heat it with anyway. We don't have one."

"The janitor has. Downstairs in the basement, a poker left over from the coal furnace."

"But that's ten feet long!" I protested.

"What of it? If you want mulled claret, do it right. Go on down and get it. If the janitor isn't there it won't make any difference. He won't mind. Just go through that door you've seen in the front hall and down the stairs. Go on."

"Oh, all right," I said, with that reluctance familiar to husbands when they are routed out of their easy chairs on some domestic chore. "I'll get it."

The janitor wasn't around, but I found the poker. Carrying it up, I met a woman on her way down. I stood back in a corner of the landing to let her by, holding the poker up like a spear. "Mull some claret," I explained with a giggle, so she wouldn't think I was up to some kind of violence.

The poker wasn't ten feet long, exactly. But I stood clear in the living room in order to heat the tip over a kitchen burner; and to plunge the hot end into the claret, which was on a table in the living room, I stood in the bedroom doorway. But it made a fine hiss, and I suppose the cups of claret tasted better for the observed ritual.

"There's an autumn tang in the air," Terry said, in defense of our doing this.

There was no autumn tang in that apartment. I went around in shirt-sleeves opening windows. Superimposed on the spirits in the scallopine, the mulled claret made me begin to feel a little mulled myself. Bustling about setting the table, we'd accidentally touched hands and felt a spark fly between us from the electricity scuffed up by our feet in the carpet. Terry found this amusing and wanted to do it with our lips. I did not feel these kisses "counted"; indeed, since they represented bodily contacts which I made no effort to develop, I saw them as actually piling up additional credit in the moral balance I had on deposit.

Suddenly she said, "All junk," and sat down and dropped her head on the table, after clearing a space in which to do so.

"Now, now," I said. "It isn't that bad."

"Isn't it? I told you my father agreed to pay my rent for one year. The year's up, without me coming through. And now I've got to 'give up that nonsense.' But I don't want to do anything else. You're right — we're better off dead."

"Don't talk that way," I said, putting my hand on her shoulder.

She rose and was around, and I felt the clutch of a hand that advertised her warmth and demon. "Put me to bed."

This affair, then, had no status and cohesion of its own but was purely a framework for its emotional concomitants, in which alone it had any shape and perseverance, like those old barns which, themselves in a state of collapse, are supported by the vines to which they have given rise.

I staggered into the bedroom with her and laid her on the bed. "Thanks for the dinner," I said. "It was swell." Starting for the door, I was arrested by the thud of a thrown shoe, which clattered to the floor after making a lesion in the wallpaper.

She removed and threw the mate, with a vigor which gave new force to the professed need to be doing something with her hands when upset. I hesitated in the doorway. "Close it," she said.

I stood there as she peeled off her stockings and then the

rest of her clothes. I still hesitated — I couldn't offend the girl. She stood on a rug in the middle of the room, and through no fault of my own I saw the teacup-sized breasts and the lyre-shaped loins, the whole symmetrical edifice of youth in the light which dimmed when she came over and swung the door closed almost.

"Why are you an atheist?" she said.

Her hair hung down like the velvet in old collection bags.

"God only knows."

I couldn't get the knot out of my tie — my hands were shaking so. I slipped the noose over my head. My teeth chattered like castanets. Somehow I got my clothing off. I felt a cold breath from Betelgeuse, and somewhere a chunk crumbled from the Polar Cap whose thawing would one day flood the continents and blot us all from view.

"Hurry," she said from the bed.

My knees knocking together, I picked my way across the cold floor, stepping carefully over Myerstown, Pennsylvania, where my mother-in-law lived, to the bed. I lay in it shivering from head to foot.

"Sorry," I said later. I wished to Christ I was at Moot Point, where all this was so much easier.

"It happens to everybody." She lay back smoking a cigarette, the sheet drawn to her chin. I watched the coal of her cigarette, like a pulsing jewel when she drew on it. She put it out and said, "Guilty wilty?"

She threw back the covers and went into the living room from which she returned with a bottle of whisky and a couple of glasses. She poured and handed me a drink. I took it like a man receiving medicine, and drank it off. A spark shot between our hands again, reviving her interest in that lark.

"You're a regular dynamo on this rug," she said. "Come on, get up and try it. Relax, for God's sake."

I climbed out of bed and stood on a shag rug with her, compliantly wiping my feet on its nap, to work up electricity.

"Say, I've got an idea," I said, as I did. Some association, some accidental connection in my mind, had given it to me.

"What?"

"About where to send your articles," I said, steadily generating current. "Or the first one anyway. *The Reader's Digest.* Your Most Unforgettable Character. Lots of people have done their fathers or some other relative."

She stood openmouthed with pleasure. "I never thought of that. But, of course — it's a natural. Why, what a wonderful idea. Why didn't I think of that myself?"

"Because you kept thinking of him as a book. Forget that. He's a one-shot."

As she digested the proposal, I slipped over to where my clothes were and started to pick my way into a cold shirt.

"No, no," she said, seeing me. "Let's drink to the idea."

Three or four drinks in rapid succession produced a bonfire in the pit of my stomach; which warmth soon spread up my limbs and into my head, suffusing me with a delicious drowsiness; on the crest of which I floated off with the last reflection that, when I awoke in the morning, it would be to the assurance of having slept with another woman only in the literal sense of the word.

I awoke to find myself on the living-room sofa. How had I gotten there? No matter. Some filament of conscience, some tropism in the dark, had led me to it — to finish the night in a tableau of rectitude. Twisting about under a slipping quilt, I felt a crick in my neck, cramps in my legs, all morally usable miseries. Was that a dream of having been at Moot Point that I vaguely remembered? A clock on a desk said two-thirty. How could it be this light so early? And with all the shades drawn. I got to my feet and stole a look into the bedroom. It was empty; so was the apartment except for myself. My head ached and my tongue was parched.

I went into the bathroom and there met a poltergeist in the mirror. I took a closer look at him. My hair was mashed every which way, like grass after a storm. My eyes looked like swatted moths. I drank cold water and doused my face with it. I felt a relief that was a kind of crystal exhilaration: I had come off all right. In fact I was glad it had all happened — it put me in the light of having better instincts than I'd supposed. I was like the doors on that Italian church which had all along been assumed to have been bronze, but were discovered on cleaning to be gold.

When I went back into the living room, I took a look into the wastebasket in which Terry had thrown the manuscript. It was empty.

Fifteen

I HAD just been to the latest 3-D movie and was resting my eyes on some bas-relief at my favorite museum, and chatting with its curator, a man in a white coat who was polishing the establishment's collection of crystal. His name was Frank.

"Experience is the shortest distance between anticipation and regret," I said.

He nodded noncommittally, and looked out at the moist, suddenly autumn-like street. "It's been an all-day drivel," he said. He set a furbished glass on the back bar. I dug a handful of change out of my pocket and set it on the bar.

"The coins of desire are counterfeit; those of love have numismatic value. Neither can be spent." I shoved a fraction of my wealth across the wood and said, "Give me another Rhine wine and spritzer."

"I like these all-day drivels," he said, contentedly scratching his briskets. "Pleasant." He came over for my glass and refilled it. "I'm glad to see you switching to white wine and soda. I don't make as much out of it, but it's a damn sight better for you." Pouring in the soda, he asked: "What made you so philosophical? What started it?"

"Oh, many things, Frank," I answered, "but mainly, I think, flunking philosophy. It was my first intellectual disappointment, and gave me that sense of proportion about myself that one so sorely needs. Had I lightly mastered those great German noodle floggers, I might have gone on indefinitely without acquiring that philosophical viewpoint that is so indispensable.'"

"It comes in handy around here all right." He set the drink in front of me. "You sure get all kinds in this place." He rang up the money, glancing at me in the mirror. I was wearing a reversible raglan which was new but showing the strains of repeated adaptations to the fickle weather prevailing previous to today's (which had been largely as Frank had said). For the better part of a week, we had been through such abruptly alternating fits of sun and shower that, weary of reversing the raglan, I had put it on tweed-side-out and left it that way. "How come you got a topcoat that's part raincoat and then when it rains you wear the topcoat part on top?"

"How much wood would a woodchuck chuck if a woodchuck would chuck wood?"

"And then no hat to boot."

"I like the gentle rains myself." I drank. "They speak to me of peace. Of the peace at last when these upholstered bones — " I broke off and said, "All right. I know. Let there be no moaning at the bar."

But my heart was not in this. Because now I found that I had my wife back on my conscience again — to some extent. And now that she was home I wanted to make some final, resolving gesture of affection, something in the way of a coming-home present.

The present idea, I thought, turning it all over in my mind, would blend very nicely with the anniversary of our first date, which, searching for some occasion that she probably wouldn't remember and that would hence put me ahead of her, I recalled was to be Saturday, tomorrow. The day would most likely go unnoticed by her, as she did increasingly forget the incidental occasions she had once set such store by. But this was the eleventh hour, and I was still racking my brains in vain for something to give her.

I had left the bar and was hurrying through Frank's drivel to catch the five-thirty home when my eye was caught by something in the window of a liquor store. It was some bottles of a variety of Moselle known as Piesporter, which were on sale as a closeout for three dollars and eighty cents a bottle. The year was '37, a great one, which meant that at this price, and thirty-five dollars a case, the stuff was a steal. I went in and snapped up a case.

"Can you get it out to Avalon, Connecticut, tomorrow?" I asked the salesman, an oppressively natty man in blue pin stripe, and with a blond mustache waxed and twisted into two tines. "I need it tomorrow and I'm not driving."

"I'm sorry, we can't deliver across the state line," he said. "Regulations."

"I see." I pondered my problem. There was only one solution, short of making a special trip by car for the goods, if I wanted it for the week end. "I'll take it with me," I said.

"The whole case?" the salesman said, boggling at the thought. "Can't you take a few bottles home at a time — I mean if you come into the city regularly?"

I explained that the purchase was for a present, and that I did not want to dissipate the gesture by executing it piecemeal. I had made more forbidding portages on Christmas Eve, I had him know, and wasn't going to be daunted by twelve bottles of Piesporter. Besides, I had a plan all doped out in my mind. "Make two parcels of five bottles each," I instructed him. "I'll carry one of those in each hand, and a bottle in each of my raincoat pockets. Make the parcels good and strong with lots of stout twine to hold them by. And I'll phone my wife while you're doing that, if I may, and tell her I'll be on the next train."

It was a figure laden on the above lines that the rush-hour throngs saw toiling down the ramp at Grand Central Terminal, bent over double and plashing audibly, his eyes popping and the veins in his neck standing out like whipcord, his hair pelted into absurdity by the sudden downpour into which the all-day drivel had changed. Moselle is a reasonably light wine, but not by avoirdupois, and I was now proceeding on the remnants of strength left by sprints for cabs which had punctuated the quarter-mile walk in the rain (fruitless sprints, with all that ballast), dashes across traffic intersections, and that broken-field running that makes up so much of a commuter's life. My pace, as a consequence, had slowed to the next thing to a dead stop. My arms felt as if they were coming out of their sockets, and the parcels grazed the floor as I moved. The effect was a little like that prowling gait that is the trade-mark of Groucho Marx, except that it didn't go very well with a wet sheep dog look. Bangs to my chin, I continued down the incline. I paused and set the packages down to brush my hair back, and also to button my raincoat; the two bottles in it made that feel like a millstone around my neck, and I thought that by fastening my coat they might be less of a "dead" weight. But fastening the coat only made it bind unendurably, and I stopped to loosen it again.

I had exactly two minutes to catch my train. What remains in my memory is a small nightmare of exertion. Somehow I got through the main waiting room and, strolling exhaustedly through the gate, heard the conductors yelling "All aboard!" A train let out of its air brakes a series of snorts not unakin to my own stertorous pants. How we pay for sex! I thought. Still I experienced a certain pleasure in my pains, feeling them to be giving me "what I had coming" and thus to that extent closing the score against me. Yet had I dreamt that this was not the end of what I was to pay but only the beginning I believe I would have sunk to the floor and died. In a final spasm of effort I swung aboard the forward platform of the last coach of my train, which was the first platform open to me. I dropped my cargo in a corner of it and stood with my back to the door.

Breathing heavily, I thought of the affectionate dedication behind the production of such wine as this, how the workmen in the German valleys climb the steep terraces on which the vineyards grow, nursing the fruit into maturity by constantly rearranging individual pieces of slate in the soil so that each grape will get the benefit of reflected sunlight, effort more painstaking and back-breaking than what I was going through on this end to acquire the product, but not much. But now I had the bottles, to take home and lay at my wife's feet, which, God knew, would be about as high as I could lift them.

Lurching through the tunnel, I felt a hand on my shoulder. "Are you all right?" a man asked. I saw out of the tail of my eye, as I turned my head a little, that it was a conductor.

"I'm O.K.," I said. When he hovered, solicitous, I repeated testily, "I'm O.K."

"All right. I was only trying to be helpful. It's my duty when somebody looks — " He hesitated, then went on, "Last week we had a case of acute indigestion."

"This is a case of Piesporter," I said, without turning around.

My arms still hung in a simian fashion for I hadn't yet straightened my back — I couldn't. Add to this the fact that he was seeing me from behind, and I suppose there was sufficient ground for his anxiety.

"A case of what?"

"Piesporter."

"That's a new one on me," the conductor said, removing his cap and rummaging in his hair. "Piesporter. What's it like, if I may ask?"

"It's a growth in the Middle Moselle."

So apart from the stiff back I was quite myself again, such as that may be, and by the time we rumbled out of the tunnel and up the grade toward the 125th Street stop I was seated in the car, near the front door where I could keep an eye on the vestibule, for I had left the packages out there. My coat with the two bottles in it was folded carefully on the luggage rack overhead.

The walk from the Avalon platform to the station wagon in which my wife was waiting for me was no problem, being only ten feet. Though I could feel the parcel cord biting into the crop of water blisters I had sprouted in the course of my New York heats. The rain had stopped.

"What are those?" my wife asked me as I stowed the packages in the back of the car.

"Don't you know what for?" I asked mysteriously. I set my raincoat out of sight on the back seat. "Don't tell me you've forgotten what day it is tomorrow," I said, springing into the front seat beside her.

"Tomorrow?" she puzzled, starting up. "What day is it?"

"Why, the anniversary of our first date." I looked wounded. "You've forgotten."

She looked at me suspiciously. "It is at that, isn't it?"

"Yes. Oh, don't feel too bad about it," I said, reaching to take her hand. "Anybody could forget." Everything was going well; going according to plan.

"What did you get me?" she said, withdrawing her hand.

"Now, now, just be patient. Tomorrow's the day, not today."

However, that evening as we sat in the living room reading, I began to wonder what the Piesporter was like, and a marked thirst came about. I put my book down and rose.

"Look, I know you're dying with curiosity," I said. "It's only an hour and forty-five minutes till midnight and, well, I wouldn't mind. It's also a kind of coming-home present for you. So want to open it?"

"Could I?"

Well, nothing would do but that I get the packages out of the closet where I had them hidden and bring them into the living room. I kept the two separate bottles out of sight as they would have tipped the present off. "I can't wait to see the expression on your face," I said as, with an eager smile, she knelt on the floor to open the first of the parcels. She drew out one of the bottles.

"Well, wine," she said. She read the label. "Piesporter?"

"It's that Moselle you're so crazy about."

"I am?"

"Yes. We had it at Hans Hoffman's that night — remember?"

"I see. Well, gee, thanks." She looked over at the other package. "Now I'll open this one."

"That's Piesporter too," I said. "I got you a whole case.

You'll notice it's a '37. A great year for German wines, and for a lady too," I added prettily. She got to her feet and dusted off her skirt. "Also, it's a *Spätlese*," I pointed out, tapping the label of a bottle which I had picked up. "That means it's from selected grapes which have been allowed to become dead ripe, which is another — where are you going?"

"Just back here and sit down."

"Which is when those grapes are at their best," I continued. "It's a condition the Germans call *edelfaul*, when the grapes are *edelreif*."

"Yes. Well, thanks a lot. That's wonderful."

She picked up the magazine she'd been reading, from the floor where she'd dropped it; but it lay unread in her lap. At last she said:

"Did you mean that women are at their best too, when they're — what did you call that when the grapes are dead ripe? *Gestalt?*"

"No, no — *edelfaul*. I believe that's the way Hans pronounced it. Hans went into the whole thing with me after dinner while you and Elsa were playing duets. It's a fascinating subject. I'd like to know more about it. Why, certainly women are at their most attractive when they're mature. That goes without saying."

"Then why say it?"

"I didn't say it."

"No, but you implied it. With that remark about the vintage year and age and all." She dropped the magazine on the floor again; I put the bottle back and sat down. "This is the fifteenth anniversary of that first date already. Do I look thirty-seven?"

"You do not," I answered with sincerity and alacrity.

"When are you supposed to be middle-aged? Thirty-five?"

"Oh, I don't think till forty. And even then . . ."

"Even then what?"

"Even then a woman is only just beginning to get into her, to get into this — " I wriggled restively up in my chair. "Well, into this *Gestalt* — I mean *gefülte* — Oh, damn it, you've got me doing it now. The French have a term for it too. What do they call it again? Oh, yes — *pourriture noble*, I believe. It means a noble ripeness. When the grapes get so they're ready to fall off the vine."

There was a silence.

I said: "Age is a guarantee of body and perfume."

The silence deepened. She looked over at the cellaret on top of which stood a bottle of Canadian Club. "I think I'd like a drink," she said. She rose and started for it.

"Why not open one of these?" I said, indicating the Piesporter. "Come on, let's start celebrating! I'll have one chilled in a jiffy," I added, picking a bottle up and bustling into the kitchen with it. "I can't wait to see the expression on your face when you taste it."

We sat regarding one another moodily across an ice-filled saucepan from which the neck of a bottle of Piesporter protruded like the muzzle of a gun. However, I had a fresh white napkin if not a wine cooler, and I poured and served the Moselle with style. I toasted the occasion, and we drank.

"God," I said, working my lips. "Beautiful?"

"Mm," she agreed, nodding. "Quite nice."

"Get that delightful fruitiness characteristic of all your fine Moselles." I was relieved to find the wine good, because I'd suddenly remembered something about Moselles having to be drunk young, which meant that mine was pushing senility, and also shed a little light on it as a shopping coup.

"What did you do while I was gone?" my wife asked, looking at the largess strewn about the floor.

"Oh, nothing much. Like I told you — movie or two, dinner here and there, and once I ran into Al Standard and had drinks with him. Like I said. Why do you ask?"

"Oh, nothing," she said, stroking the stem of her glass between her fingers.

Holding my wine aloft and appraising its hue, I said, "A very funny thing happened at one of the restaurants I tried, down in the Village — a misprint on the menu. It was one of those hectograph menus? It said, 'Dreaded veal cutlet.' "

She shook a cigarette out of a package and took another tack. "You're really getting to like wine, aren't you? Especially white wines."

"What do you mean by that?"

"I mean you like white wine," she answered, a flintiness in her voice which recalled the great Chablis. "You'd love to lay in cases of it, have a cellar, but it's too expensive. Unless you're buying a present for somebody that you'd be expected to spend that much money on anyhow — "

"I think that was uncalled for," I said, going over and giving her a light. But it was what I wanted. I moved cautiously in quest of a grievance, luring her inch by inch toward saying something she would be sorry for. "I remember distinctly you were crazy about the wine we drank at Hans's. You exclaimed about the Piesporter we had first, and you exclaimed about the bottle he opened later. It was a 1937 Rüdesheimer Hinterhaus Riesling Auslese — "

"You *have* to exclaim at Hans's. Or he sulks."

"I'm not through yet. I remember that bottle because I memorized the label, as a sort of a gag." I started over from the beginning. "It was a 1937 Rüdesheimer Hinterhaus Riesling Auslese Wachstum und Original Abfüllung Grafen von Francken-Sierstorpff."

"Don't make so much noise," she shushed with a warning jerk of her head toward the sleeping children. "Why, do you bone up on the subject during those tough three-hour lunches you have to go through in New York every day?"

Now she was close. In a moment she would wound me, if I worked it right. Then I'd be in the catbird seat. Carefully, I cued her; carefully because this called for egging, and a hair's-breadth too much could in a twinkling reverse the advantage by making the other one the injured party.

"You mean while you're curled up here reading a book? Like that one there?" I said, pointing to a volume spread-eagled on the ottoman.

"Not curled up with it, exactly, but trying my best to wade through it — it and the rest of that set of Trollope you bought me on my last birthday because you were dying to reread him."

That did it. That was the shaft that went home.

I turned a hurt face to the window and said, "I don't think that was a very nice thing to say. What puts you in such a defensive mood? I don't understand it, darling." I faced about with a hand spread. "Is it because you thought I'd mind your forgetting our little anniversary? How could you know me so little as to think I would?"

"And speaking of anniversaries, there hangs my last wedding-anniversary present." She nodded to a Reginald Marsh over the mantel. "That painting you just had to have. I can't wait to see what I get on the next one. A nice silver ice bucket probably."

That stung me to the quick; so much so that I could not be content with wounds but must take up spears.

"This is the thanks I get for carting this whole damn case home," I said. My arms still ached for me to wave them to any great extent. "Are we going to start appreciating some of the finer things of life, or are we going along on the level of taste here in Subourbon Heights?" Since the gag was a visual one it made no sense to her whatever, and I was too proud to spell it out. I expanded on the subject of the portage. "All the way across town during the rush hour and in a downpour, and then halfway across two states. At least the conductor on the train showed some concern — he was really worried. Why, the distance I lugged this stuff to get it home on time is big enough to put in all the vineyards between Braunsberg and Schweinfurt!"

She may have thought I was swearing at her, because she ground out her cigarette, rose and started to leave the room. I stepped athwart her path.

"Take a look at these," I said, spreading both hands to display the rows of blisters I had acquired. "Talk about edelfaul!"

My wife passed around me, after an accommodating glance at the lesions, and marched on into the bedroom with great dignity.

"Good night," she called back satirically. "Sleep tight."

"Don't worry, I will," I said, drawing the Piesporter from its ice even as I reached with my other hand for my glass.

Well, I patched it up though. I smoothed it over. I smoothed it over with another present. It was a series of recordings, by Casadesus, of all, but *all* of Ravel's piano music. Three records — six sides, that is, and long-playing — which I was lucky enough to pick up in Avalon the next morning. It made a nice remembrance, I think, because it's the sort of thing I can't abide.

And a couple of weeks later Terry McBain phoned me in an absolute tizzy to say that the *Digest* had bought her Most Unforgettable Character.

"Episode," I said to myself, "closed."

Sixteen

SO things were back to normal again. And back to normal up at Moot Point too.

With what nostalgia had I not in the interval hankered for its enveloping graces, and how tonic now the resumed hours there among my growing ranks of guests! It was on one of the evenings soon after my return that we invented, a group of us, in a spate of extemporaneous mirth, something we called Loony Latin, the idea of which was, of course, later pirated and transposed into Gallic as Fractured French. It was basically the same thing. For example, a *hic jacet* was, we said, a sport coat worn by a person of provincial, or corny, taste; *ad nauseam* meant a sickening industrial advertisement, and the like. We didn't mind the theft; indeed, we followed with amusement the solemn commercialization of what had sufficed us purely as an evening's toy. "Limitation is the sincerest form of flattery," I laughingly observed to my circle as we passed the plagiarism around one night. But we never publicly belittled the volume, or the foolish napkins and highball glasses that succeeded it either, as that would have been rather a breach of suavity in the brightest constellation, as our set had by now come to be called, in the Eastern social skies.

How did things stand in Avalon, and what of Augie Poole? He was far from being without interior resources of his own, as

I very soon came to see. One evening I went over to his house to borrow an ice crusher and found Isolde in tears. Now what? Everything had seemed under control. Augie had kicked in with another five hundred dollars, which I'd taken to Cornelia the day before. Augie was laying low, as was proper since he was under very strict surveillance now in the Crib's final checkup before approval. Cornelia had told me she'd gone to the Rock-a-Bye people, as I'd urged, and they were fine; all confidences were honored and nothing demanded, but anything putative fathers felt they could give was appreciated. Hence the extra five hundred, the original thousand being regarded as covering medical expenses as such. Augie walked the chalkline, holding hands with his wife in public and being knightly in many other ways and at all times. Then, happening to glance in the window after ringing the bell to get the ice crusher, I saw Isolde drying her eyes as she rose from the couch and came to the door. My heart sank: all the beans had been spilled.

"Oh. The ice crusher. Audrey did call about it, I forgot. Come in."

"I hate to . . . " I stepped inside, closing the door.

"No trouble. I'll get it."

She went into the kitchen. No Augie in sight. I thought I heard a creak in another room. Was the ex-satyr in hiding?

Isolde was in the kitchen long enough to touch up her face as well as get the grinder, without very good results.

"What's the matter, Isolde?" I said, taking the ice crusher.

"You know." She dove into the couch and buried her face in the cushions.

"Augie?"

The head bobbed. "I suppose you've known about it all along."

I set the ice crusher on a table. I reached down and touched her hair awkwardly. "Augie's basically a good egg. . . ."

"Good!" She tossed around into a sitting position, her hair flung up at me as if in reproach. "Is that all you can say? Is that all you can say for the most wonderful guy a woman ever had? To do a thing like that."

"To do a thing like what, Isolde?" I said, confused.

"Sell his ideas of course. What are we talking about? Give up his career and settle down to being a hack idea man. A gagman! So he'll have the kind of family-man, steady-income quality the agency wants in a husband. He's doing it all for me." She broke into fresh wails, giving me time in which to collect my thoughts.

It didn't take me long to get the pitch. The old bastard, I thought, angrily navigating the room. Making moral capital out of what his sins had made inevitable. Getting on deposit a lump sum so big he could draw on it indefinitely — pretty sly. Why, it would keep him liquid till the day he died! For when would the time come when his wife must now not be grateful to him?

"Where is he now?" I asked, wondering if he was around here but too ashamed to come out.

"He's in his studio." Isolde gave her nose a tweak with a handkerchief. "He's pretending he doesn't care, the lamb. Did he seem to you to be cut to pieces?"

"Not exactly. Well, in a way." I veered bewilderedly in my loyalties. I had a sudden flash. Was he even more saintly-like-a-fox than seemed? There was the likelihood, my intuition told me, that Augie had come to realize at last that he didn't have what it takes, and would have sold his ideas anyway. So it was next to nothing that he had managed to parlay into martyrdom. Maybe this was speculation, but it was valid speculation, and

I felt Isolde had a right to any consolation it might afford. Therefore I said:

"Baby doll, don't cut yourself to pieces. Because there's this about it. Eventually — well, let me put it this way. There comes a time in every man's life when he realizes he isn't wielding a rapier, but only laying about with the kitchen poker — "

"Oh!" she brought out in a reproving gasp, and turned away. Then she said: "But of course that's the way you've felt about him all along. This is what you've always wanted."

"I was only — "

"I know. Trying to make it easier for me. I'm sorry." She stood at the window and worried a handkerchief through her hands. "I wish I didn't nave to take this from him. I told him I wouldn't have it, but he insisted. He almost got angry about it. But I sure wish I didn't have to take it from him."

"You may have chance enough to pay him back," I said and, picking up the ice grinder, beat a hasty retreat.

I couldn't get home fast enough.

"Well, Audrey," I said, carrying the crusher into the kitchen where she was preparing for a couple of after-dinner callers we expected — people who liked stingers and frappé drinks, which is what the ice crusher was for, "Guess what your wicked Augie has done now."

"Been arrested with a chorus girl?"

"He's given up his career for his family," I said, a trifle smugly. I hadn't mentioned any of this yet, having hesitated to break the news before Augie did. "It seems the agency would feel better if he had a steady income, soo he's selling his ideas and becoming a gagman. A gagman! You know what that means. Burying his dreams of becoming an artist. Forever," I added when there was no response.

"Well, that's fine," my wife said, reaching into the refrigerator for something.

"Is that all you can say? It's fine? Why don't you admit 'my boy,' as you've ironically been calling him, has come through with flying colors? I hate to say I told you so, but I think you ought to give credit where credit is due."

"I do." She closed the refrigerator door and turned. "I give him plenty of credit, if this is what he's really doing. But is he giving up for Isolde any more than Isolde has given up for him?"

"What do you mean?"

"Her acting. Or have you forgotten? That was a career too. I won't say she has a terrific amount of talent, but it's as much as Augie's any day. Maybe more — because Isolde at least has had a few bit parts."

"Augie's sold things."

"What?"

"To us. That cornucopia full of frozen foods — probably other things in the future."

"That cornucopia." She smiled. "Really now. That dinky little Thanksgiving spot. You called it a one-shot yourself. No faces to draw, which is the real test of a cartoonist — you keep saying that yourself. Don't go away yet. Oh, you've started the oil furnace again. One second, I want to make this point. It makes me so furious I can hardly talk. When a woman gives up something to be a housewife and mother, it's taken for granted — that's just Nature. But let a man make the least concession and there's all this hoopla. It's always the man marriage is a trap for."

"I'll keep my own shut and save ours," I said, and walked with a broad smile to answer the door, for our guests had arrived.

On returning to the office from lunch the next day, I found a telephone message on my desk:

Miss McBain called at 12:35. Would like you to call her back. Urgent.

What could be urgent? Probably some revisions on Father that she wanted help with. Well, that was hardly urgent from my point of view; I had a few pressing matters of my own to attend to. I was deep in a raft of correspondence I'd let pile up when the phone rang and it was Terry again. Her voice said "trouble."

"I hate to bother you," she said, "but something's happened and I just had to tell you. Something terrible."

"What?"

"Can't you guess? Think hard."

There was a pregnant silence.

"Does it concern me?" I asked.

"Indirectly. Have you guessed?"

"Terry?"

"What?"

"Have you been drinking?"

"No. I'm so embarrassed and — ashamed. Such a fool. I might have known."

"Known, Terry?"

"That I was asking for it."

"Yes."

"You've guessed — the inevitable. . . . Hello, are you there?"

"Yes. You mean that when I was drunk and didn't know what I was . . ."

"What do you mean when you were drunk? The thing is, I've told Father — "

"What?"

" — and he's already talking about lawyers."

"Bu-but." I rose on rubber legs, gored on a vision of armed nuptials; except that no blunderbuss in Father's hands could bring about our union. Blunderbuss: a mistaken kiss. "I'm already ma-ma — " My voice bleated away into a thin squeal, like Laurel's of Laurel and Hardy when he is about to cry. I picked weakly at a kink in the phone cord. "Your father won't shuh-shuh-shoo — "

"What on earth is the matter with you?"

"Will he shoot me?" I laughed feebly.

"Don't worry," she said, laughing herself. "I won't even mention your name." I felt a partial relief — but only partial; like a genuflecting pack beast relieved by ten pounds of a load a hundred in excess of his capacity. "You're a brick, Terry. Look, can I call you back? Are you home?" I wanted to get off the office line.

"Yes, but I won't be here long. I'm waiting for a plane reservation to come through, and if I can't get that I'm going to catch a late afternoon train home. That's why I wanted to get in touch with you right away. I wondered if you had any ideas."

"It's too late for what would have been my main thought — not to tell your father."

"I know." She sighed. "But he would have found out anyway."

"Not necessarily. Those things can be . . . "

"He'd have found out. Somebody would have told him and then it would have been twice as bad. Of course it isn't a sort of desperate rush. It'll be months before — "

"I'll call you back, Terry. You know how terrible I feel about it, of course — "

"Don't. It's not your fault." She heaved another long sigh. "But it is the ruination of everything. It's just the end."

"Courage," I babbled. "I'll call you back."

My legs growing steadily number as under a prodigious dose of Novocain that was freezing me from the feet up, I sat staring at the blotter-pad on my desk. Papers materialized upon it and were removed by my secretary's hand. It had a lace cuff at the wrist. My secretary found me, sometime later, affixing my signature to letters of which I was the recipient, and reading without comprehension correspondence I had just dictated.

"What's the matter?" she asked at last. "You look pale."

"I'm all right. I don't feel so hot. Open a window, I'm roasting in here." I lay down on a couch I had in my office and said, "I won't take any calls for a bit."

I heard the phone ring in the outer office and my secretary's crisp voice, "He's out just now. Is there any message?"

After a while I went downstairs and into a drugstore, where I hauled myself into a phone booth and dialed Terry's number. There was no answer. I let the phone ring several times and then hung up. Back in my office, a telegram awaited me:

COULDN'T GET YOU AGAIN TO SAY GOING HOME TRAIN THIS AFTERNOON SORRY NOW BOTHERED YOU BECAUSE YOU SO UTTERLY DUMPS BUT FELT HAD TO TELL YOU AND PROMISE NOT BOTHER YOU AGAIN SOMETHING MUST SEE THROUGH MYSELF.

So she was leaving the burden of gallantry up to me. She was giving me an out, but only after I had learned the facts. I couldn't honorably take it. I would call her back, of course, next week, and the week after that if she hadn't returned. Meanwhile what? Meanwhile how much money could I dig up and where? I couldn't pay out anything like this called for without it showing on my bank balance. Too much to smuggle under Miscellaneous in a family budget. I'd have to touch the office for it. Pay it back a few dollars a week; go without lunch maybe; or such fancy ones; or pick up a little fruit at a Sixth Avenue delicatessen. We all overeat. *There are lots of good reasons for being good.* Get hold of yourself is the main thing at the moment. There mustn't be any sign of this *Angst* to anybody. *Angst,* there's a word for you. Say it over and over to yourself till everything becomes a joke. *Angst, Angst, Angst. Weltschmerz.*

At home, we got the notification from the agency that Mrs. Mash was coming to interview us about the Pooles. Now the whole picture was changed. Now it wasn't the danger of Augie adopting his own child, but of his adopting mine. Mathematical "odds" are no comfort to a man in *Angst.* Not this type of *Angst* anyway. A possibility is a possibility, and the submicroscopic mote of this one bloomed into monstrous likelihood: Terry, sent into the snow by a Biblical Father (like the girls in the cartoons we were always running), coming out to stay with the only people she knew who could take her in, the McBains, friends near Avalon who would see her through, help her get in touch with some nice local agency — *Angst.* Did I have the whole thing to do over again? Why didn't I die in Grand Central, lugging the Piesporter? Why didn't I die on the walk home in the heat, back in that other time?

No wonder I lost my voice (in more or less the same fading squeal as on the telephone) when the Mrs. Mash woman marched into the bedroom.

I got it back the next day. But I didn't let on to anybody. I didn't want to be quizzed on why it had conked out. Not till

I had the answers all worked out. I wanted time to think. I continued, on the whole, in bed, jotting bulletins and words of encouragement to my wife and such of my children as could read — Maude and Marco — and the story was given out that their father had been stricken with quinsy and might be laid up indeterminately, this being also the explanation phoned in to the office when Monday came and my absence from it had to be accounted for. Of my Moot Point considerations nothing remained; "escapes" never avail us when they are really sorely needed — they appease only the gray hours, not the black. I sat in a cockpit of the bedclothes and drank highballs. Tuesday afternoon I heard my wife on the phone when Blair called. "Why, he's under the weather, Mr. Blair. Quinsy . . . How's that, Mr. Blair? . . . Because he's allergic to it." (To penicillin, which he'd asked why I hadn't taken.) When my wife suggested she call Dr. Vancouver for another look at me, I rolled my eyes as if to say, "That hypochondriac." However, she called him.

He peered gingerly down my throat again, asking me not to breathe on him as the epidemic was still going strong and many there were who depended on his good health. I held my breath, but gagged on the stick he put down my throat, causing him to avert abruptly. He sat facing away from me till my gasping had subsided. His examination over, he rose and said, "Again I can't find a thing. A thing, that is, but a little tightness of the anterior muscles that you might get with *globus hystericus*. But *globus hystericus* couldn't possibly last this long, so maybe you've got an aphasia. I've never seen a true aphasia." I glanced at my wife and then modestly at the counterpane — for a true aphasia would give us great status in the psychosomatic belt. Vancouver stowed his flashlight in his bag and snapped the tongue depressor in two and gave it to my wife to dispose of. Then he went into the bathroom to gargle.

"If there's anything troubling you, tell me," he called later above the sound of washing his hands. "Or if you don't feel it's any of my business I'll have Dr. Printemps look at you."

"Who is Dr. Printemps?" my wife asked.

"He's a psychiatrist."

The very word was like magic. I cleared my throat. They turned and looked at me speculatively. I put a hand to my throat and smiled: not able to talk yet, but it seemed to be loosening up in there. Before Vancouver left, I was able to whisper a word or two. Well, good, but it still might be wise for him to give Printemps a ring and — I shook my head and waved him off. I would be all right.

The ringing phone was a further tonic: every time it did I jumped, wondering whether Terry, if she'd returned, would be indiscreet enough to call me here; I must be getting back to New York, and calling her to forestall any such thing. The possibility of Mrs. Mash's reappearing gave further spur to my recovery, though I devoutly hoped I had been washed out as a witness.

That evening, my wife and I sat in our wonted living-room chairs. I drew on a cigar of the size, smaller than a panatela, known as a doll. I had a flannel rag around my throat which gave me a vaguely tragic air. She occasionally paused in her knitting to watch me.

"Now that you can talk," she said at last, "what's it all about?"

"I was hoping you wouldn't ask me that. I'd really rather not go into it," I whispered, my voice threatening to depart again.

"You've got to."

"No."

"Yes."

"Our union has been blest with issues," I said with great good humor, fingering the rag around my throat. "No, I feel it's fairer to all concerned to drop it." I drew on the doll and, frowning at the coal, let a trickle of smoke out of the side of my mouth.

"I'm your wife," my wife said, hooking up a strand of yarn with her little finger. "It would never get any farther as far as I'm concerned."

It was of course no use resisting; her curiosity would never let me rest. I twisted the cigar out morosely in an ashtray; then suddenly buried my face in my hands and said, "Oh, my God." I peered at her through a latticework of fingers, and saw that she was knitting steadily, her face overcomposed; a little pale.

"How do you feel about — well, extramarital affairs, as they're called?" I said. My plan was to pay out as little rope at a time as I could, till she was satisfied. "Kinsey has shown us that the majority — "

"You mean Augie's been sleeping with another woman?"

I nodded. "Yes."

"That's all?" Her manner was suspicious. "That sent you into such a tailspin?" I would have to pay out more rope.

I rose and, flapping my hands at my sides, said: "I suppose it's no use trying to hide anything. The woman is with child. That was it."

Standing at the window made no sense: the draperies were drawn. But I couldn't bring myself to turn around. My shoulders may have hunched a little as I steeled myself. I heard the click of the needles stop, and a rustle as she put her knitting in a basket on the floor beside her chair. Then I turned around.

We can seldom adequately foretell how people will react in an emergency or to extraordinary tidings, even people whom we know intimately; I had supposed my wife's disapproval of Augie's deeds would ring out proportionately to this their fruits. Nothing could have been more mistaken. She sat quietly a moment, after my announcement, greeting it with only a stare into her lap. "I'm sorry to hear that," she said.

She reached over for a package of cigarettes and dug one out. "Yes," I said, "so am I."

She sighed with her whole body.

"Well," she observed philosophically, yet at the same time a shade more censoriously, "people sleep together with their eyes open."

Seventeen

BACK in town once more, the next day, I drank three whiskies in rapid succession and dialed Terry's number. I shut my eyes and gritted my teeth as the ringing phone drilled into my brain: once, twice, six times, eight. No answer. This failure was blessedly repeated the next day, and three days later — five times in two weeks. And then the operator said, "That number has been disconnected."

It would be idle to disguise my relief. It was as though a stone had been lifted from my chest. She had been as good as her word then, "seeing it through" herself; and I as good as my vow to meet the demands of honor. Terry had undoubtedly gone back to her family, and I had not the remotest idea where in Massachusetts that was. There was nothing more for me to do — but try to forget.

My agony sloped off to a vicarious concern, once again, with Augie's. My wife did not press me for details; in fact, she wanted to know as little of them as possible now that she knew the gist, out of a feeling of loyalty to Isolde. I gave her to know that the situation was "contained," and proceeding toward a satisfactory resolution. Of the good this ill wind blew she needed no reminder: that was obvious in Augie's conduct. The account he gave of his reconstruction, on standard breadwinner lines, was enough also for Mrs. Mash, who troubled me no more. I suppose the woman had concluded that the opinions of a zany such as I were worthless in any case. The Crib O.K.'d the Pooles. It was now simply a question of settling down and waiting till the agency had "something that seemed right for them." For such an institution goes to as many pains to choose the child for the parents as it does to choose the parents for the role.

Typical of the new Augie were certain burning moral wants, a tendency to take inventory of himself in preparation for the role; in particular, to contemplate the awful symmetry of the circumstances under which he was about to assume it. We had long ethical discussions, of which the fruit was the conclusion that this was all a moral charade which had elicited his best and must now be forgotten, in favor of preparing himself for his new duties, the faithful discharge of which would give him quittance in full. This was a premise to which he clung, but one he insisted tirelessly on rehashing, like a man punching out a pillow on which he is trying to rest his head. We recapitulated it on long hikes we took with the aim, also, of fatiguing him so he could sleep, and on which he insisted on dragging me along (the word is an apt one for I am no lover of walks) both to keep him company and help hammer out a coherent position. So while we chose varying terrains to traverse on foot, we covered the same philosophical ground so often we were letter-perfect.

"You see, it's a sort of moral charade, no more," I puffed as we mounted a stile and struck out across an open field, one Saturday afternoon. "Your right hand will cancel out the debt contracted by your left."

"How can I be sure?"

"Because every man fathers a child and then rears one. You will do no less."

"But the two are not the same. Someone else will rear mine."

"And you will rear another's. All life is random. We conceive in blind happenstance even what is our fleshly own," I replied in a fairly turgid passage we had worked out in numerous marches across the stony meadows of Connecticut. I built dutifully to my climax, though breathing hard from exertion. "What are we but ciphers in the manswarm, grains in the anonymous dust. Nameless we come out of darkness, nameless return to it." Some of this was Augie's, some of it was mine, and some of it was Thomas Wolfe's. "But there is no point in flailing ourselves with fruitless reproach."

"You certainly seem to have done a lot of thinking about this," Augie said.

"Yes."

"Tell me the fable of the Roman mother and her child."

"Oh, not that again," I groaned, making for a stone wall. "Let's sit down here and take a breather."

We did. I took off my hat, a gray homburg. I have a great difficulty with hats which stems from the shape of my head, which is long and narrow like that of a football, so that a hat which fits from front to back will be too wide. I had recently gotten a haircut and so this homburg kept slipping down with each impact of my heels on the hard ground — the way you bring an ax down on its helve by pounding the other end on something. There were times on these marches when it dropped down over my eyes. This naturally obscured my visibility and once nearly cost me my life when I stepped out on the road in the dusk and into the path of a car whose driver had not yet turned on his lights.

I squeezed off a shoe and nursed a foot which had a large blister (edelreif) on it. "Life is a fortuitous conglomeration of Adams," I said. I looked up at the sky. Augie followed my glance. Appraising the dark wooliness of the clouds he said, "I wouldn't be surprised if we got one hell of a snowstorm. There's one due, you know."

"Yes," I said. "Does look like it. Let's go home."

Hobbling along down a road along which cars whizzed steadily, I said at last, "I don't know about you, but I'm going to flag a ride." So we hitchhiked, and at last a man we knew named Hal Mansfield came by and, recognizing us in the dusk, stopped. He took us both home. I remarked that it looked like snow, and Hal said heartily, "Yes. That reminds me of that sleigh ride party we've always talked about getting up. This time let's do it."

"I'm game," I said, glad for the lift in the warm car.

I had once defined Reality as "a shuffled deck of cards." That sleigh ride party turned out to be the Joker in the pack.

There were close to twenty of us half-yokels in it. Sleigh rides were constantly being gotten up or talked about, there in Avalon; the impulse at work was, I suppose, that nostalgia for simplicity that motivated a population a third of whom lived by taking in one another's antiques. Forgetting that true simplicity that lies in the flip of a thermostat switch on a cold winter's night — and reminded by Hal Mansfield of my promise — I agreed to turn up at his house the following Saturday night, "if there is still snow." There was, a frozen coat of it, in a temperature plunging toward zero and below.

A few feelers were put out about postponing the lark, but bravado carried the day, and half past seven found me upstairs sheathing myself in successive layers of cotton shorts and shirts. At this point my wife, whom I had thought busy scratching together a getup of her own, came into the bedroom where I was dressing and lay down, with the statement that she believed she had a cold coming on. Murmuring persiflage about the Spartan spirit, I drew on vest after vest. I donned a coat and then wormed into a mackinaw I remembered I had in the closet. When I crowned this improvisation with the homburg — the only "old" hat I had — my wife turned her face to the wall and pleaded a sick headache. "You're the doctor," I said humorously, and feeling more upholstered than clothed, descended the stairs, pocketed a pint of brandy, climbed into the station wagon and drove off. The Pooles were visiting Isolde's grandmother in another part of the state.

I found a sleigh in the Mansfields' yard, and standing beside it a man in a decayed blazer, flapping his arms. A cap that he wore with the earlaps down, a muffler one end of which was flung over his shoulder, his guarantee that he had newspapers under the blazer, and a mustache on which icicles had begun to form indicated that no detail would be lacking in our search for an Arcadian pattern.

"Where's everybody?" I asked.

"Inside," he said, pausing to adjust the harness on a steaming roan. I turned to the house with visions of warmth, eggnog and cancellation dancing in my head, but at that moment the door opened and people came tumbling and laughing out of it, their arms laden with blankets and heated bricks and stones. Hal Mansfield led the way to the sleigh, on the floor of which muffed and mittened people disposed themselves under quilts. "Hop in," somebody said, and handed me a tepid rock.

The possible alternations of sexes having run out, I scrounged down between a former tax assessor of perhaps forty-eight to fifty and the tail of the sleigh. He and I were supposed to share a warm stone, as well as a blanket, but the stone became speedily indistinguishable from our shoes, with the result that the former tax assessor and I kept feeling for each other's feet under the robe. Tiring of this rigmarole, he finally kicked the rock into the middle of the sleigh with an oath. He talked briefly about how the speedometer of his car had squeaked on the way up, owing to the cold's having rendered the grease in the mechanism ineffectual; then conversation died between us.

There was some friendly ridicule of those who had begged off. To the insinuation that their courage had failed them, someone replied that it had served them — we'd not the guts to back out, nor the sponsors the intelligence to call it off.

"We couldn't," Hal Mansfield said. "We've made arrangements to meet the other bunch, you know."

"What other bunch?"

"There's a party heading this way from Southport. We're to meet up somewhere between the Yacht Club and Grove Corners, on Grackle Hill Road. That gives us about eight miles apiece."

The connection between group misery and mirth is a boon on such occasions, but I never reached the stage evidenced by the hoots and buffoonery of my companions. Mile after mile I lay quivering under the robe, my teeth chattering, the homburg crushed indifferently under my head. I began to feel what is, for me anyhow, the first symptoms of really bitter cold — a pain in the eardrums. High time for a nip, I thought, and bit off a glove. But my fingers were too frozen to fish the bottle out, and after a few moments of fumbling among the stratifications of my clothing, I laughed weakly and said to the former tax assessor, "There's a bottle in my right inside pocket. Maybe you can get it out."

No maybe about it. In three seconds he had rummaged it out

of my ribs and was unscrewing the cap. "Ah, brandy!" he said, taking a pull.

"Brandy!" someone else shouted. Word went round and then the bottle, with many a lusty slug and many a good word for me. More impotent than either hurt or angry, I saw it passed from one mittened hand to another. There was some left when it got back to me, but my hands were so stiff half of it trickled down my chin, where it speedily froze. Then, settling down as far under the blanket as I could, and as nearly in the shape of a hoop as is humanly possible, and in a state of hopeless discouragement, I tried to concentrate on the localized glow in my stomach.

A sister-in-law of Hal Mansfield's, a woman named Mrs. Kipling, revived the spark of life in me with something she said. It was a reference to "the real sou'wester" she had on, which someone was admiring. I remembered her having once related being aboard ship "in a terrific nor'easter."

I hauled myself around and into a sitting position against the side of the sleigh. The woman was opposite me and one to the right. Pushing the homburg out of my eyes I asked, "Are you originally from New England?"

"Yes. Well, that is, Papa and Mama moved up to Vermont when I was eight." She smiled. "Are you?"

"No. I'm from the Mi'est," I said. "I went to Nor'estern."

This wasn't definitive parody being largely due to my jaw's being so stiff I couldn't manipulate it well enough to talk any better than that; but I stood a hundred per cent behind the way it came out.

"Have you lived in New England all your life since then?" I pursued.

"All my life except for three years when I was abroad."

"Oh, you were a broad at one time. How long ago were you a broad?"

"In my twenties."

"That's the best time to be a broad," I said. "What's it like, being a broad?"

"Oh, wonderful."

"I imagine it must be."

I gave this up, being engaged in another foot joust with the former tax assessor who had hijacked a hot jug from his neighbor. We were rewarded with a warm trickle on our trousers cuffs, having kicked the stopper loose. I reorganized my limbs on the floor again. As I did so, I heard someone up front ask Hal Mansfield, "You're sure they're on their way? This is Grackle Hill Road," and Hal Mansfield answer, "Positive. I talked to Ned McBain on the phone just now before we left."

That rang a bell somewhat louder than those tinkling on old Dobbin's harness. Rigid as a figure on a catafalque and steadily more garnished with ice, I lay in a fixed stare, contemplating the brass tacks in Cassiopeia's Chair. A young woman next to Mrs. Kipling, imagining herself to be guessing my thoughts, glanced up at the sky and said softly: "Isn't it majestic? Think of it — in just the Milky Way alone, all those billions and trillions of stars."

"I don't have my glasses with me," I said.

"Each one a world. And all billions and trillions of light years away. All swinging through inconceivable reaches of space."

"It's all right if you like that sort of thing," I said.

"Doesn't it fill you with reverence?"

"No. It just makes me sick to my stomach."

"Then what have we been put here for?"

"To freeze."

"You think everything is futile?"

"Yes."

"Then why not commit suicide?"

"That's futile too."

My jaw having worked itself loose a little in this colloquy, I turned to see what other groups in the party I could throw cold water on; but almost all the rest were clustered now at the front, watching the road ahead for the other sleigh. I turned to Mrs. Kipling.

"Have you ever been to We'inster A'ey?"

"No," she said, giving me an icy stare; and heaving herself to her feet, picked her way to the front.

A cry went up. "Here they come!"

Bells on bobtail rang as we sailed to the summit of Grackle Hill and slid to a stop. A second horse snorted and stamped nearby, and the merrymakers boiled down off the sleighs and mingled on the road, shouting and laughing and thumping one another on the back. Those in our sleigh stumbled out past and over me, till only the former tax assessor and I were left; then he climbed down. "Coming out for a stretch?" he said. I murmured something negative. I had caught the name McBain again.

When our sleigh was empty, I raised myself cautiously on one knee and peered over the side. They jigged and chatted in the snow. Everyone had that tearstained and kind of fiendish look that people have in extreme cold. Which of them were Terry's cousins? Suddenly my eye caught a glimpse of a face above a woolen scarf, which made me duck down out of sight again. A moment later, I heard a voice that went with it.

" — Mother always walked into the house backwards in

winter, because she claimed that kept her glasses from steaming up? Never did though."

I lay in a paralytic trance, hearing the bright cries shuttled in the air around me, like swirling flakes of sound. We were there five minutes, ten, maybe more. I didn't concern myself with time. Because now I began to feel an ominous comfort, and I thought of that slow-creeping, delicious warmth with which doomed travelers are said to lie down in the Alpine snow. Remotely, I heard something about going to Shively's for hot chocolate. Then figures came pouring back into the sleigh, tumbling over me and taking their places again. Then we were off, again in a tinkle of harness bells. We took another hill, and I kept my eyes on the stars, for it was toward these that we seemed to be mounting.

"Excelsior!" the former tax assessor said. "Why couldn't somebody think of putting excelsior in this damned thing? Pad the floor as well as warm it up."

I turned and gave him a dull look, fancying that my neck squeaked as I did so, like his speedometer. I knew what the "Excelsior" meant. I felt a pleasant sleepiness, now. Things receded; all words fused in a general babel, and had that remote and elfin sound of voices that trickle through to you on the telephone from another connection. Indifferently, I remarked the fluency with which two women gossips clacked their tongues; because at this point I felt that my own would retain any position into which it was bent, like lead. I put it out weakly to wet my upper lip; it slid across it, there having occurred under my nose a marked thickening of the filigree that goes with death by freezing. I laughed softly at a rotting star. Already I could feel my spirit, like gas let out of an uncorked bottle, drifting toward the blue pavilions of eternity. I turned my head toward the open tail of the sleigh. A moon was rising, like a bad orange.

Shively's was a large ice-cream place on the Post Road. I heard them piling off the sleigh, and, still more dimly, off the other one, and into the store.

I thought, after a moment, I mustn't lie here. I must get up and take a bus home. Maybe I could even find a cab. But I remembered — I had no money. I laughed helplessly as my hands fumbled at a pocket, then crept to a standstill, like some numb arachnids.

Two figures hove into view at the tailgate. "There he is. What's the matter?"

"I have no money."

"We can let you have money. You can't stay here — you'll freeze to death."

I smiled. It took quite a while, being like something making its way through silly putty. Yet I had at the same time, as they helped me over the tail of the sleigh, the most extraordinary sense of lightness, like a window mannequin any one of whose limbs could be disjointed and laid aside. They helped me across the sidewalk and through Shively's door.

I sidled into the first booth I saw empty, hoping Terry wouldn't recognize me even if she saw me. I couldn't pull the brim of the hat down over one eye as it was a homburg. There was little danger of her spotting me immediately in the confusion; a mauve nose and generally glacéed features kept me incognito for a good ten minutes. But then, as I was raising a cup of hot chocolate to my lips, I happened to glance into a booth in which Terry was looking over, her elbows cocked up on the table and a cup in both her hands, studying me. Her mouth opened in an inaudible cry of recognition. She excused herself

to some companions I couldn't see, rose, and carried her chocolate over. Dressed in a buttoned coonskin coat, she slid in
across from me.

"I didn't know you were here," she said. "How've you been?"

"I tried to get you, I tried every which way," I said, looking
her steadily in the eye. "How are you?"

"I'm fine."

"Let's go over where we can talk," I said, pointing to where a
group of teen-agers were making enough noise around a jukebox
so no one could have overheard us. But just then the jukebox
started up, and it seemed all right to stay where we were. A
loud vocal streamed across the huge premises:

> The way you bugged my heart
> You snowed me from the start,
> I was a cornball and a cow;
> But now I'm in a puff
> Over one who's got the stuff
> And everything is Roger now.
> So don't try to bug me back
> Or wig me when it's slack
> 'Cause everything is Roger now.

"I tried to phone you, oh, many times. Your phone is disconnected. You — came out here?"

"Yes. I have a room at the McBains' now. That's them right
over — there." She pointed at a middle-aged couple gotten up
largely in leather. "I earn my sort of keep around the house a
little, sit for them et cetera — and scribble a few hours each
day."

She bent her head to sip from her chocolate. Raising her
head, she parted the hair away from her right eye and made a
study of me. "You're blue."

"Just what did you expect of me?" I asked.

She watched me, drinking.

I slid down as far as I could in the booth, till my chin was almost on a level with the table-top. "How many months are you gone?" I asked in a hollow voice.

"What are you talking about?"

"The child."

"Child? What child? What in God's name are you talking about?"

I slid up again in the booth. "Isn't there a child?"

"Where did you get such an idea?"

"What was all the — what was it you called me in such a state about?"

She opened her mouth on an unuttered laugh, then put her hand to her forehead. Then she said, "I thought you understood what I was talking about. That was about the article. My Most Unforgettable Character?" I nodded impatiently. "Father threatened to sue."

"Sue you?"

"Well, *The Reader's Digest,* actually. He wasn't going to be anybody's Most Unforgettable Character. Soo, they sent the article back." She spooned up the frothy chocolate. "I was sorry I bothered you about it, but I felt so low I just had to tell you."

My mind flew back over the telephone conversation. "Have you guessed? The inevitable. The thing is, I've told Father. I'm so embarrassed — so ashamed. I might have known. . . ."

I asked her, "What are you writing about now?"

"Mother." Her face lit up and she leaned across the table. "Mother was always trying to outwit pests in the house. Like the other night, when the McBains found one of Ned's suits all chewed up by moths, I remembered how Mother would always throw an old piece of flannel on the floor of the closet, so the moths would eat that instead?"

I laughed heartily. "That's rich," I said.

"Mother won't think being somebody's Most Unforgettable Character is a disgrace to the family. I've already cleared it with her. So when I'm finished, if you could find a minute. . . ."

The jukebox boomed out across the room's expanding hub-bub:

> You played me for a schnook,
> You're blotsky in my book,
> You never built a bonfire in my hall.
> You're soggy and you snowed me
> And he's the one who showed me,
> I know that he will fizz me with his call.
> Now that I really dig you
> Don't wait for me to wig you,
> 'Cause everything is Roger after all.

Members of both sleigh parties rose and began to draw on mittens and mufflers. "Right home for me," somebody said.

"What's the matter?" I called, hysterical. "We soft?"

I got home about a quarter to twelve, to find my wife reading in bed.

"What kind of a time did you have?" she asked, looking up from her book.

"Terrific." I took a hot bath, drew on flannel pajamas I'd set to warm on the bathroom radiator, and returned to the bedroom.

My wife set her book aside. "Did you really?" she asked me,

interested. "Because, you know, I didn't actually have a sick headache or anything. I got cold feet at the last minute."

And none too soon, old girl, I thought as I pulled the covers back and popped blissfully in between the sheets.

Eighteen

THE peak of Augie's conventionalization took, in terms of outward symbols, the form of his joining us all for a church supper one evening. Seated on folding chairs in the church basement, we put our minds to cutting roast beef without dissecting the paper plates on which it was served; and this with meat only moderately amenable to surgery. A jab of particular force not only cut through my plate but made a slight incision in the trousers fabric of the knee I was holding my food on, and I felt a trickling warmth which gave new meaning to the term "lap supper." This was in the early spring. I had on a white linen suit for the first time that season, and lifting my plate I saw a stain the color of hemoglobin spreading on the pants. My companions fared better, having asked for and gotten well-done meat instead of rare. My emotions remained pent up, as we were seated within earshot of the minister, a pale, seraphic man with eyes the color of lentils. Still, what words I would have cared to utter would have been unfit for a brothel, let alone a house of worship. To some profanity that did escape under my breath my wife said under hers, "Please. We're in church." To which I answered, "Only in the basement." I looked around me, and wondered what their religion really meant to the commuters I saw on every hand. I have never heard of anything being converted in Connecticut but old barns.

Looking a little like an intern calling it a day, I rose and, with Augie, took all the empty plates back to the serving counter. There we got four dishes of ice cream and four cups of coffee, and joined our ladies with them. They were deep in a conversation during which Isolde, as we approached, cast an admiring glance at her husband in the course of something she said. Sitting down, we learned what they were talking about: the slowness of the agency in not having, even yet, come through. She was clearly chafing under the delay. Which the Crib explained by saying that at the moment the demand exceeded the supply, and anyhow they hadn't had anything that seemed right for the Pooles — for, as they emphasized more than once, they made a point of matching the parents with the child as closely as possible. This concerned the latter's extraction (what was known of it), color of hair and eyes, and other details of general appearance on which comparison might reasonably be made. Audrey was quick to corroborate this to Isolde, from her own experience with friends who had adopted, and so was Augie, out of what appeared to be widespread private researches of his own.

"Augie's certainly gone out of his way to find all this out," Isolde said. "So interested." She blew him a kiss across me.

A moment later, as we were watching a diversion at the serving tables where somebody had dropped a loaded tray, Isolde suddenly set her dessert spoon down in her dish and said: "I know what we'll do."

"What?"

"Try again with Rock-a-Bye."

Augie's face turned the color of the ice cream he was raising to his own lips, which happened to be pistachio. "Why do that?" he asked.

"Why not? Lots of couples try more than one agency. Or even more than two, before they succeed. That right, Audrey?"

"Well, yes, that's true. The Haleys tried I don't know how many agencies before they got something."

"Well then." Isolde spread a hand as at something elementary. "Why should we stick with the Crib?"

"But would shopping around be fair to them?" Augie protested. He laid his ice cream aside.

"Yes, why hurt their feelings?" I chimed in.

"Feelings!" Isolde laughed. "What's that got to do with it? I've got feelings too. Look how long they're taking. They might keep us on the string indefinitely. What can we lose by getting our name on two lists? If the Crib has something for us first, fine. If Rock-a-Bye, fine too. There's every reason to believe Rock-a-Bye should change its mind now. Augie's changed. And so has his whole financial picture. We never did get a clear answer on why they turned us down the first time, but I think a lot of it was this stable breadwinner idea. Besides, I think we owe it to Augie himself to make them reverse their verdict. I'll call them tomorrow." She emphasized this with a "so there" nod of her head.

I started to protest again, but Augie warned me off with a shake of his head, for fear of arousing suspicion.

Some suspicion had been already aroused several weeks before, when Augie's 1099 form arrived from *The Townsman* office — the statement for Federal income tax return, which specified how much he had earned from the magazine as a free-lance contributor the year before. Isolde had fished it out of the mailbox and opened it, to find that he had earned considerably more than he had declared to her. He explained the discrepancy by saying he had been putting money a little at a time into a separate savings account with which he had wanted to surprise her.

"It's like flaws turning up in a perfect crime," Augie'd said to me. "I sure as hell never thought of that. I wonder what next." To cover his story, I arranged for another advance from the office, and he hurriedly put the money into a new savings account which he did thereupon start.

The next link in what Augie called the infamy of events was revealed at a folk dance in Bridgeport to which we and the Pooles went, separately, early that summer.

For a long time people in our crowd had been trying to get me to folk dances. One of the most persistent was Sid Walters, the clear poet. Sid's obsession with things of that nature formed, as is often the case, part of a generally political concern with society, and, conversely, my indifference to them has been vaguely deplored as somehow indicative of scrawny thinking and bourgeois leanings. Just how my refusal to watch large numbers of strangers exert themselves rhythmically in upstairs rooms is evidence of how I vote has never been clear to me. My blind spot on the colloquial arises in part, I suppose, from folk singers I have heard in New York night clubs, where though the entertainment may be produced on a zither the charges are not necessarily computed on an abacus. But it also dates back to a milking certain Avalonians, myself included, received at the hands of a minstrel with a guitar, who wandered into town off of a freight car and thence into our hearts with the story that he was an ex-convict, a detail which gained for him an extra status among a small but discerning minority. A purse was gotten up for him to which I contributed twenty-five dollars. Intimations that Solitary, as he called himself, was better than any predecessors, including Lead Belly, were liberally nourished by himself and others, and he had acquired a substantial vogue among the intellectuals before he was exposed as an impostor who not only had no criminal record but possessed a background spotted with nothing more than a fear of work and a few jumped hotel bills. I always thought the bastard should have been arrested. However, he disappeared from local view and was never seen again. Uppermost in his repertoire was a number entitled "I was a stranger and you took me in," a ditty that I always think would have a fine relevance if I ever met him long enough to sing it back to him.

Sid Walters and my wife, in the end, whisked me off to a dance by conspiracy. He broke into the house one night flourishing a mimeographed handbill for a Hungarian revel when I was asleep in an armchair. "It's tonight! In Bridgeport! Let's pile into my car and go," he said. Audrey clapped her hands with what I was too dopey to see was a faked extemporaneity, my shoes were fetched, and before I knew what was happening, Mrs. Goodbread materialized and I was being led off between the two plotters to the waiting automobile. It was raining. "Some night to drag a man out to a recital," I grumbled, climbing into the back seat behind my wife.

Studiously buttoning a glove, she said, "It's not a recital, actually, but a real dance."

I reached for the door handle but it was too late.

"This will be the real thing," Sid said, shooting away in second. "Ah, those czardas rhythms. What they do to a man."

"Czardas — didn't Hoagy Carmichael write that?" I said, determined to be as much of a Philistine as possible.

Sid sketched in something of the history and background of Transylvanian forms, and as we headed up the Post Road toward Bridgeport, talked at length about ancient folkways. I have had enough about folkways, especially when dished up with psychiatric-anthropological analysis. I slumped down in the back seat and spent the remainder of the trip trying to think up some new folkways.

One folkway I thought of was an annual so-called Week of Good Report, during which people would go from door to door repeating nice things about their friends, to "atone" for the gossip spread the balance of the year. During this week the populace would eat nothing but tongue in penitential admission of the length of their own; thus they would "take everything back" for the twelvemonth by symbolically eating their words. Then I imagined an annual ceremony involving the hanging of an anthropologist. Another possible folk custom that occurred to me was something that would fall on a day known as Maybe Tuesday, a day nationally observed by building on the already emerging folklore of the quiz show. The quiz show would be reversed. Television crews in every city and town in the country would enter homes and instead of giving away money and gifts for questions answered correctly would take away some article of furniture or other possession for everyone that was not. This would be a long ceremony, lasting all day or till the family were completely stripped of their belongings. Neighbors would gather to watch. This is of course a modernization of the scapegoat ritual, and is called Maybe Tuesday because, as the expression would go, maybe next time it would happen to you.

The dance was held over a restaurant called the Romany Café. I knew from this that it was probably genuine, all right. All authentic folk affairs are held on the second floor. Anybody taking you to one that is on the first floor and representing it as the real thing is either lying or himself the victim of a misunderstanding.

The hall was large, and filling up as we arrived. We met a man in a pea-green jacket who was doing a thesis on some aspect of the dance for his master's, a friend of Sid's who showed my wife how to skip. "That's damn well what I'd like to do," I mumbled in an aside. My wife shot me a glance which enjoined me to either keep my mouth shut or stop acting like a peasant. "Get around and mix," she said, and disappeared on one foot. I did, and presently found myself running into friends from Avalon. We stood out, not favorably, by contrast to the many Old World costumes of the neighborhood folk; in our herringbone and banker's flannel we were dreary to a degree. One by one, or rather two by two, the suburbanites stepped out onto the floor, and were lost in the avenging swirl.

I drifted over to a table where a heady wine punch was being served, and had two or three. There I made the acquaintance of a girl of Slavic extraction named Anna, who spoke a patois derived from coast-to-coast hookups, Broadwayese, and official bebop. "That orchestra is cool," she said, rocking her head. The band was playing a popular favorite at the moment, but she expressed appreciation of a polka that followed in the same terms, and belittled czardas with, "Why don't they get it off the ground?" She taught me a few of the folk steps. The Tokay in the punch reached my head and my feet simultaneously, fostering an illusion of acquired skill; my fourth drink was soon my seventh; single sensations dissolved, over the flying hours, in a general haze of wine and rhythm. About eleven o'clock I happened to glance toward the main doorway and saw the Pooles arrive with another couple. Isolde said something in my wife's ear and they embraced happily. I guessed what the good news was from Augie's long face.

"We've been accepted by Rock-a-Bye," he said, taking me to the sidelines.

"I see."

"We got the report today."

We sank together onto folding chairs which bore the name of a local mortician.

"Let me think," I said.

I was in a mixed frame of mind. Only half of me seemed to sober up while the other half continued to revel, like a street shaded on one side and in sunlight on the other, or possibly moonlight.

"You couldn't steer Isolde away from it?" I said.

"You know I couldn't. It was for me she did it."

"Then we've got to steer Cornelia away from it — if there's still time."

"Would you?"

I got to my feet. "I'll call her right away," I said, oblivious of the hour. I looked around for a phone booth.

"Are you sure you're in shape to?" Augie assessed me worriedly. "You look three sheets to the wind again."

"I'm all right. There's no time to lose."

I found the booth and put in my call. Hubert answered.

"Cornelia's not here, old man," he told me. "I just got back myself from a lecture tour. I can't tell you where she is, but I expect to hear from her. I'm leaving again the first of the week."

"Is Carveth there? Maybe he can tell me."

"He's up at a planning committee meeting for Tanglewood, old man."

"How about Emory?"

"Popped off to Rome on a Fulbright. Got it all of a sudden and arranged for a year there, while his assistant takes over. He's studying Papal history."

"Well, when you say she's not there do you mean she's in New Haven?"

"Oh, yes. She's packed up and gone."

I sat a moment in the booth after hanging up, wondering what to tell Augie. I decided not to tell him anything that night, since he couldn't do anything about it anyway. I would take counsel with myself tomorrow, when I could think more clearly. He was waiting for me near the booth when I came out.

"Everything's O.K. Don't worry about it," I said.

"You talked to her?"

"Yes. There's time to work something else out. Come on, have a drink."

I had three or four myself in an effort to recapture my earlier vinous mood. I danced a couple of polkas with my wife. Everybody was having a good time. I remembered nothing much from midnight until the next morning when eight o'clock struck, like a hammer on my head. I was reassembling the night's impressions in the shower, later on, when I placed what was weighing on my mind — Augie. I spent the next two days mulling over whether to tell him the truth. After all, there was nothing he could do about it. But maybe there was and I couldn't think of it. Or maybe he would want to know, or should. What a responsibility. I stepped over to a mirror to see what an effect this was all having on me. I looked very discouraged, and not a little bitter. No, it was too much to shoulder alone: I would tell him.

"I've been trying to decide whether to break this to you," I said to him, "and I figure you probably should know. I didn't talk to Cornelia. She's already settled in."

"God," he said, clutching his head, as though he were a newel post about to come apart.

"Not necessarily," I said. "Now let's take a good, hard and calm look at this thing. What are the chances of — well, the Sophoclean windup to it? I take it you understand what I mean — you've read Sophocles?"

"Easy does it."

"To begin with, there's only a fifty-fifty chance that Rock-a-Bye will be the one to call you first. Right?"

"They said something about thinking they'll have something for us soon," he said in a dry falsetto.

"Secondly, even if you do draw Rock-a-Bye, the chances of Fate doing what we're afraid of are mathematically so — "

"And the time'd be just about now . . ." he went on to himself. "And the way they make a special point of doing everything in their power to match . . . Christola."

Here I began to rummage for the moral in Augie's life. Did it lie in this burgeoning irony, that the very virtue he had come to present might at the last make him vulnerable to calamity? Was the point that he had not been a complete rogue, only half a one? That if he had really told everybody to go to hell he wouldn't be behind the eight ball now? I had hoped it was the reverse: that it was in the fires of illicit fatherhood that he was to be shriven for the respectable. I had to believe that.

"Well, anyway, there's nothing you can do about it," I said. "There's a kind of relief in that — in pure helplessness. Nothing to do now but wait and see."

"Yes," he sighed. "I guess you're right. It's in the lap of the gods."

Nineteen

IT was a viewpoint from which I would have distilled more comfort had I not the sense of its being partially in my own lap. From being merely privy to Augie's affairs I had progressed to a condition of intimate involvement in them, so intimate that the same quivers of apprehension charged us both. We were emotional Siamese twins, to the extent, at least, of being in a three-legged race for whose duration we were fraternally lashed. And one of the length of whose course we had no foreknowledge. It was, therefore, with a simultaneous plummet of fear and wave of relief that I heard Augie say, having called me at my office from the suburbs, "I've got news for you."

"Make it brief and end on a note of hope."

"One of the agencies just called. They've got something for us. It's a boy."

Tracing with my eye the spirals of the phone cord, I asked: "Which one?"

"Rock-a-Bye."

And so out of whatever reserve of fortitude, caution, poise, or maybe just capacity for outrage, with whatever we had between us to give that this might yet take, we prepared to face the final step. The agency expected Mr. and Mrs. Poole the next afternoon at one o'clock sharp. By noon both of them were in such a swivet that they asked us to drive over with them.

It was Saturday and I was home, so we all piled into our station wagon, which would better accommodate the five we expected for the return journey, or even the four of us going out, than the Pooles' coupé. I drove, and sitting beside me Augie chain-smoked. "The nervous father," Isolde laughed from the back, where she and Audrey sat with bunting and other gear. Augie essayed some sign of amusement too. "Probably have to carry me in," he said.

It was not true — we had to carry him out.

Rock-a-Bye headquarters was a long, narrow, one-story building of white clapboard, set in a square of clipped privet. We were greeted in the reception room by a smiling gray-haired woman named Mrs. Larch. Audrey and I stayed behind in the reception room while the Pooles went back together, ushered by Mrs. Larch.

I lit a cigarette and walked the floor. Audrey smiled at me from a chair. Both were pleased by the stew their husbands were in.

"You look funny," she said.

"I feel funny."

"This happens every day."

I let it pass. I was twisting out the butt of my cigarette in an ashtray when Mrs. Larch thrust her head in and cried, "Come quick!"

I shot through the door ahead of Audrey and pursued the trotting Mrs. Larch up a broad corridor and through another door beyond which a nurse in white was throwing water on Augie from a paper cup. Augie was spread out in an overstuffed chair with his head back. The nurse was dipping her fingers into the paper cup and baptizing him as a housewife does her ironing. Mrs. Larch took the cup from her and dashed the contents into Augie's face. His eyelids began to flutter, and I looked elsewhere.

Disposed nearby above a silk coverlet reposed a blue and gold parody of the features being sprinkled and slapped, unless strain had laid both Augie and me open to hallucination. Yes, that must be it, I told myself sternly, taking in the tilted blue eyes and the blond hair with reddish glints. I blinked, as though to clear my head of a mirage. With a sudden cavernous yawn on the infant's part, the mirage did vanish. Or had *that* been an illusion?

Behind me they were feeding Augie brandy from a regular glass.

"Are you O.K., sweets?" Isolde said, chafing his wrists as Mrs. Larch tipped his head toward the brandy.

He nodded and tried to get up. Mrs. Larch persuaded him back with a firm push of her hand on his chest and said, "Let's move him to the front, there's a sofa there he can lie on." Augie made a gesture of protest, but she signed for me with a shake of her head to ignore him, and I took him by the ankles while Mrs. Larch grasped him under the arms, and we bore him to the front.

"These make the best kind of father," Mrs. Larch stated. "You can keep your casual husbands."

"*In other words there's nothing unusual about this*," I said, walking with my back to my burden. "You keep brandy on hand."

"You'd be surprised what we use brandy for," the nurse said.

"What are some of its other uses?" I chatted.

"Are you all right, lamb?" Isolde asked. She walked flanking Augie, like a handler talking to his prize fighter in cartoons you have seen of boxers being borne from the ring.

"Certainly I'm all right. Let me down."

"All the strain, and now the excitement."

The collapse of an iconoclast is not among the more impressive sights in the world. Pain has been called a natural anaesthetic, once it gets unbearable, and I suppose some such process made me begin to giggle now that this thing was getting really awful. Presently I shook with laughter. I laughed so hard I damn near dropped my end of Augie. I had to pause to secure my grip on his ankles. He kicked and squirmed. "Let me down," he ordered.

We let him down only on the sofa, where he promptly sat up. The nurse gave him the rest of the brandy. We watched him as he finished it. I felt I could have done with a spot myself but didn't dare ask for it.

"What are some of its other uses?" I persisted, when I'd got my voice under control.

"We rub it on the gums during teething," Mrs. Larch told us. "Matter of fact, we sometimes put a drop in baby's formula when it won't sleep at night." She laughed. "You might remember that when you're walking the floor some night, because I can see this is one daddy who's going to take his job seriously."

"I think I'll report you to the state authorities, serving liquor to minors," Augie said. We were all glad to see him kidding again.

The nurse brought in the baby.

"What, what a dumpling," Isolde said.

"He's asleep," Audrey said, over the nurse's other shoulder. "Sweetest thing I ever saw. So aloof and kind of amused."

The nurse beamed at it. "I don't suppose you want him."

"Why, have you others?" Augie said.

"Oh, sure, take your pick," the nurse said, really going along with this joke. "Who'd want him? Angel."

"Yes. I think we've done you proud," Mrs. Larch said. "He even looks a little like you."

"Water." Augie held out the empty glass which I took and filled from a cooler that was pointed out to me in a small adjacent office. "Little chaser," Augie said, taking it. I walked over to the group of women clustered round the child. I thrust a hand in and chucked it under the chin. "Kitchy kitchy coo," I said, a delicate chill going up my spine.

We had to wait while Mrs. Larch took the parents into the small office for a few final formalities. She closed the door, but I couldn't help overhearing snatches of conversation that were none of my business.

"As I've said to your wife, Mr. Poole," Mrs. Larch said, "we can tell you that the mother is a fine intelligent woman with artistic background, like yourself. We try to match all those things, you know — intelligence and all, as well as physical similarity. But of course any woman can make a slip. The wrong company — you know."

When we got away at last, I drove home as though I was trying to claw my way out of an opera. "When the duke discovers that the child he has adopted is none other than . . ."

"Not so fast," my wife called from the back seat where she and Isolde sat with the new addition. "Do you want to kill us?"

I had work to do and lost no time.

"I see what they mean about a vague resemblance," I said. "He does have Isolde's coloring, sort of; her complexion. And of course those blue eyes."

"Augie's too," Isolde said.

"Mm, yes. Yes, I see what you mean."

"I thought that was what Mrs. Larch meant — that it was Augie he looked like."

"Oh, really? Perhaps so."

"Those slant eyes and that hair that isn't quite blond or quite red," Isolde said.

"Don't be deceived by reddish hair in a baby," I said. "Remember, dear, how we thought every one of our kids was going to be redheaded, till we realized it's because it's so thin and the scalp shines through it?"

Augie snapped a cigarette nervously out of the window. "I never saw a baby they couldn't see resembled everybody on both sides of the family. Babies look like everybody because they look like nobody. You can't tell anything about a baby that age. Let me hold the nipper awhile."

I thought we were handling it rather nicely. Now if the women could continue in their sentimental and rather touching belief that Augie had gone to pieces out of excitement, and meanwhile just go on dithering so over the infant they couldn't see what they were looking at, why, everything might yet be all right.

But Augie himself was far from confident. He started to take me out on those long hikes again, to hash things over. I did my best to reassure him. "Stop and consider the odds against such a thing," I said, and when I said stop I meant just that. I led the way to a large rock, where I sat down to nurse another boiled foot. The sun was sweltering, and I had spots in front of my eyes as thick as shad roe.

"You know damn well the odds are just the other way — we've been through that," he said.

"Shall I try to call Cornelia again? She may be back now."

"No. I'd rather be in doubt."

"Well then be in doubt. Don't be so stubbornly sure."

"It struck you that way, the first look. You admitted it."

"Why didn't it strike the women that way?"

"Because they weren't looking for it."

"And we were. So we ended up seeing things. You always end up seeing what you're afraid you will."

But Augie was not convinced. "So now I set out across the high wire," he said presently as we rose to resume the walk. "Because if there's any resemblance, time will bring it out. Not blur it."

"Don't even think of it," I said, grasping his arm — more in the need of something to hold on to than to steady my friend.

Because now we needed everything we had. This would take all our nerve and caution, all the faith and courage we had between us and that high reasoning we had pledged in our earlier walks and talks, everything we had thought and said and stolen from Thomas Wolfe. For while our position had been cooked to a cinder by the turn of events and we had suddenly to reverse the direction from which we drew our strength — having to exchange the philosophical peace implicit in the idea of a patternless anonymity for the solace of apparent Design — a great deal of what we'd settled on was still true. The lines fit anyway, and that was a God's mercy, because if we'd had to work out an entire new routine I don't think I'd have been able to face it.

"Think that you turn out in the end to get what was always yours," I said, galloping along a step behind him. "That out of all the manswarm — "

"Cut it out about the manswarm," Augie said. "The important thing is to watch the women. Watch them like hawks, to see if they suspect."

"Well let's start back," I said. "It'll be getting dark soon."

Dark brought the added risk of his being moved by the stars to some cliché about Infinity, whose infested reaches and galactic turmoils I so deeply deplored. Even allowing for the likelihood of "pattern," and subtracting such histrionics as there were in my *Weltschmerz*, there remained a legitimate irritation with the Cosmos which, if I had to put it in a word, I would describe as the basic indignity of being constantly required to look up into bottomlessness. It's not the kind of thing to which I am by temperament suited, though everyone, of course, to his own taste.

We got home before dark, all right, and when I did I found a letter from the new president of the P.T.A., outlining some projects she had been turning over in her mind for the coming season, soliciting my earnest and active co-operation, and expressing the hope that we would all put our shoulder to the wheel to make this a banner year.

Twenty

AUGIE seemed now, rather than the contrary, to have acquired a certain dignity. An added stature, if you will. We might once, for his truancies, have called him "small." There was nothing small about the scale on which he was now cast. The thing is, he had become invested with a sort of classic Greek irony. He had adopted his own son, and if this does not cloak a man in the Grecian absolutes then nothing in this world will.

Watching Augie go down the street in his too-short top-coat (and the soft hat, pulled down over one eye, to which he was partial that season) you would not have suspected that here was a man who walked in the cool Sophoclean symmetries. Pushing the pram in which reclined the cargo that made it so, he would have struck you that much less as a character headed for rhetorical doom. But he knew he was and I knew it. The child grew daily more the spit of his trundler, with the jolliest impersonation of his father's grin. Strangers pausing by his pram, and neighbors also ignorant of the adoption, invariably remarked on the resemblance. "Chip off the old block," they would say, slapping Augie on the back. Now there was no need for us to watch our wives like hawks — that was how they watched us. Audrey was the first to suspect, or the first to come out with her suspicion. One evening I was aware of her looking at me over the rim of a magazine. I picked one up and got behind it myself.

"It's Augie's, isn't it?" she said.

"Augie's?" A thin smile clung to my lips, like a postage stamp insecurely pasted to a letter.

"I didn't see that was why he behaved the way he did at the agency because I didn't want to see it, I guess — one of those things your mind shuts off. But it's getting clearer every day. It's true, isn't it?"

I refilled my highball glass and then went into the kitchen for some ice. "I won't say it is or isn't," I said, returning. "I'll say, suppose it is? Result: the Pooles have now got what they've tried — how long is it now? — to get. Leave Augie out of it for a minute. Just think of Isolde. What used to stand in the way of their getting their heart's desire was the fact that he was irresponsible. Now it's because he was that they have."

"How do you figure that out?"

"It's the fruit of his lechery — "

"If we can't discuss this without using words like the fruit of his lechery then let's drop the whole subject. How do you reason all this out — that they're getting their heart's desire thanks to his wrongdoing?"

"Because if it hadn't been for his having a child out of wedlock they wouldn't have any in it," I said.

"They'd have gotten another."

"Not necessarily. In fact very likely not. If you'll recall, what finally cleared them with the agencies was his reform, fiscal and otherwise. But he reformed and settled down and became a breadwinning husband, because he was scared into it. And he's becoming more of one every day, as I can tell from the books. Well, if he hadn't sinned on the scale he did the chances are he

wouldn't have reformed on the scale he did. Think of Augie —
this will help — as a kind of Everyman, combining the good
and bad in us. Remember that if it weren't for babies born
illegitimately there wouldn't be any for the salt of the earth to
adopt. Augie was just his own source of supply."

We talked like this long past midnight, and when we gave
off were a long time getting to sleep. I was feeling ragged the
next day when Augie phoned and asked me to go for a
walk with him. It was a Sunday afternoon, and he was going
to take the little mimic out for a turn. That meant an easy stroll,
rather than one of our grueling marches, and I agreed. I was
waiting for him at the road in front of our house when he
appeared, pushing the buggy at a brisk clip at that.

"Isolde suspects," he said as I fell in beside him. "What does
Audrey make of this? She looks at me oddly. You've told her,
haven't you?"

"I couldn't get out of it," I said.

A man carrying a fat Sunday paper was walking toward us up
the road, smiling broadly. It was Mr. Goodbread, husband of
our sitter (now also the Pooles'). Goodbread had been a
gardener for an estate on the Sound which had been recently
closed and put up for sale, and he was now working a day apiece
for several of us more modest home owners. He stopped to
say good afternoon and to dote into the pram. He had on his
working dungarees. A brown cardigan full of blowouts and a
knit cap bound at the tip like a wurst expressed his indifference
to nonessentials.

"Is nize boy," he said, with an accent that was the product of
his having lived in both Germany and Russia. He grinned and
bent to pinch a cheek. "Look just like Daddy. Everybody say."

"Oh, God," Augie said when Goodbread was gone. He

clenched his fists and looked where God lived. "I can't stand any more of this. I can't stand Isolde's not coming out with it. I'm sitting on a powder keg, waiting every day, every minute, for it to blow up. There's only one way to end the suspense."

"How?"

"Set it off."

I clutched his arm. "Now cut it out," I said, "and get hold of yourself. You'll set no powder kegs off and maybe have something get back to the agency."

"Why?"

"Because if they find out it's your child they'll take it away from you. What ails you? Have you forgotten this is a probation period? It's a year before you sign the final papers. You can do what you want then; until then, *shut up*."

But Augie knew what there was for Isolde to put two and two together with: the discrepancy about the income declaration; a mysterious and hastily terminated telephone call or two to think back on; nights spent in town. Singly they meant little; together and in the light of the growing resemblance, they formed a basis on which to reassess the fainting fit. And Augie didn't have enough of a moral balance in the bank of domestic relations to cover what they added up to. He felt it to be only a matter of days before Isolde blurted out a query of some sort; and he sensed, too, the at least slight advantage to be gained by confession, as against being called to account; and so he warned me not to be surprised if I heard him blurt something out first. "Yes, I might very well do it when somebody's around — cushion the shock. I don't think I could stand it just the two of us together. But I want to get the explosion over and done with, and let the dust settle and see what we'll see. Get the damned thing on the agenda."

Isolde accosted me in the hardware store and told me that Augie had been acting "queer." He went about with an abstracted, at times distracted, look. "He tells me things he's said before," she related. "He'll get at things around the house he's already fixed. He talks about moving back to New York." She paused, frowning at the floor. "And now he has this idea he should be playing the piano all hours."

I gave her what reassurance I could: that suburbanites thought continually about moving back to the city, that it was no rarity for people to become suddenly obsessed with hobbies (which were in any case a preservative rather than a threat to stability) and that as for repeating things, everyone did that — I did it myself, now and again, when tired.

"Have you ever taken the car down to have it greased twice in the same day?" she asked. "Or been so tired you got up to play the piano in the middle of the night?"

No, I admitted, I hadn't. Nor had I seen Augie for some weeks. "Has this come on all of a sudden?" I asked.

"Yes, more or less. Drop over tonight if you're free, and see for yourself," she suggested. "Isn't tonight when Audrey's having the Brownie mothers?"

It was, and so I promised Isolde I'd look in.

I arrived about eight o'clock. Augie was sitting at the piano, playing Christmas carols.

"Rushing the season, Augie?" I said, shaking off my topcoat.

"I guess I am," he said. "The middle of October."

Isolde and I exchanged glances. It was the last of November.

"But I like the old carols," I said, rubbing my knuckles on my palm as I entered the living room. "I don't see why we shouldn't play them oftener."

Augie swung round on the stool. "It's funny nobody writes

any new Christmas carols — except old Mrs. Likely. Remember her, Isolde? I ran into her the other day. That's a handsome jacket you've got on," he complimented me.

"Thanks," I said.

We sat down with brandies; Isolde and I did, that is — Augie walked about the room.

"How's little Augie?" I asked.

Augie turned vague eyes to me. "Who?"

"The little nipper."

"Oh, he's fine."

We talked about him some, and I learned his latest achievements. Which reminded Isolde to slip in and see that he was covered. When she returned, Augie said:

"Did I tell you that I ran into old Mrs. Likely on the street?"

"Yes, you did."

There was something wrong here. And it wasn't long before I thought I had my finger on it.

Augie had recently phoned the magazine office about a cost-of-living adjustment check he had coming, and I remembered the punctuality of his inquiry as well as the notable accuracy of his estimate of the figure due him. No want of mental clarity there. Nor in other details relative to business matters, other dates and sums pertaining thereto. So it was borne in on me that I was witnessing a performance, like that conducted at Elsinore. His object was, of course, to portray himself as not responsible for his actions. He was using a broad brush because there was no time: events were closing in on him.

Presently I perceived something else.

"Augie hasn't been sleeping well lately," Isolde said.

"Not just lately," Augie put in. "It's been over a year, actually, though I've tried to keep from worrying you with it. It goes back to when — " He hesitated, then went on: "Maybe you remember the fantods I had once last July? I never told you about it, but at that time I sank a thousand dollars into some stock that turned out to be worthless. It was the first of July. I don't know what could have come over me. I suppose even then I wasn't myself. . . ."

So that was part of the plan. He was trying to establish his incompetence as pre-existing far enough back to cover the time of the act responsible for the pickle he was in; was trying, in other words, to make it retroactive. But good God, I thought to myself, don't lay it on so thick. For now he bent down to peer at and finger the goods in my coat. "That's a mighty handsome jacket you've got on," he said. "Did you have it tailored?"

"No," I said miserably and a little resentfully, looking into my brandy glass and crossing my legs. "I bought it at Rogers Peet. They had a sale."

Isolde set her glass down. "Who'd like a game of Scrabble?"

"I would!" I said, glad for any escape from the form of scrabble we were in as it was. Augie excused himself, pleading fatigue. "I'll kibitz," he said.

He sat down and rambled at the piano, however, soon after Isolde and I had started a game. Giving that up, he went over and turned the radio on. He got some recorded classical music and, shading the volume to our joint liking, went over and stretched out on the sofa, which he affected not being able immediately to locate. From there he kept up a sporadic chatting.

"Guess who I ran into in town the other day, looking exactly the same as ten years ago. Old Mrs. Likely. I asked her if she was writing Christmas carols and she said yes — the church choir was going to sing one this season."

This attempt to offer a disintegrating façade was one I was

able to be tolerant of as well as see through, because of my own Weltschmerz act which was a degree of the same bid for consideration. But it was a difficult transaction at best, and I was dying to tell him that better men than he had failed to bring it off, and for God's sake in any case to put on the soft pedal. At this rate it wouldn't be long before Isolde saw through it herself. Even already, I felt some response on her part to my own ill-concealed skepticism. Finishing a turn at the Scrabble board, she leaned back and said: "Augie, what was the stock you bought?"

"I don't want to bother you about it, baby," he said. "It's water over the dam. I don't even remember the name of it."

"But you remember the date you bought it."

"It was around the Fourth of July." He laughed through his nose. "I guess some connection about burning money up, like fireworks. Oh, well." He went to the radio, on which a recording of a quartet by Bartók had begun. "Do you mind if I get something else?" he asked. "Bartók always makes me want to walk sideways."

I felt Isolde looking at me.

"That's exactly the effect he has on me, Augie," I said and, laying out my letters, sat back. "Your turn, Isolde."

She pushed back her chair and rose.

"I'll be right back," she said. "I want to take another look at that baby."

So Augie saw that Isolde saw that he could tell a hawk from a handsaw, all right, and that he wasn't bringing this thing off. Yet he abandoned the act with the keenest reluctance. Isolde's refusal to credit his lunacy was a bitter blow to him — in fact it almost drove him out of his mind. I suppose his pride was involved. The two lived under a steadily mounting voltage of constraint, exposed to one another's nerves as to live wires. Somebody had to give, and soon. That was why I avoided going to the Pooles' as often as I could, remembering Augie's stated hope for a buffer when the situation broke. But I couldn't decline invitations indefinitely, and so at last I let my wife accept one for dinner on an evening in the middle of the week.

There was a *Turf Guide* in evidence when we got there, suggesting that Augie had lapsed into an interest, long suspended, in the horses. That was when I made the famous crack about posting with such dexterity to racing sheets, putting us all in stitches at the table. Augie, however, resumed a look at once remote and edgy, and when, as we settled down to coffee in the living room, he cleared his throat to say something, I threw in hastily: "Have you ever noticed what a ringer Mr. Goodbread is for Tito? One of those amazing resemblances."

"Oh, you must hear Augie's imitation of Mr. Goodbread," Isolde said. "Do it, Augie."

"Oh, no."

"Please do," we all said.

"Oh, all right. De sep feeds de gress like de blod de vessels. Dis wary good ting, big horse lawn mower ronning over de gress make de blade lay down flat if no sep — but if sep, springs ride beg op again."

"Priceless?"

"Wonderful."

Augie drew a deep breath and continued nervously:

"So de otter day I was over to see Hinkle de dog catcher aboud how much topsoil he'll need in his beg yard, wants to seed it, and I was explaining how de gress needs deep ort what can nourish de sep, when who should ring but de phone. Hinkle rons in de house a while, and pretty soon comes beg out mad. 'Woman calling me op because dead dog in de road in front of her house,' he says. She says, 'Can you come right over and pick it op?' I says, 'No.' She says, 'Why not?' Says 'Big horse.' She says, 'Big horse why?' Says, 'Big horse I only dill wit live dogs. Dad's my jurisdiction — I'm de dog catcher.' She says, 'Who shall I call?' Says, 'I don't care, lady. Call de ondertaker. I only pick up what I have to catch.' She gets med flies off de handle. Dad's the poblic for you every time. Dey're worse dan anybody' — Look, I'm the father of that child."

I don't know why Augie chose that particular moment. His take-off had gone well, we were having a good time. Maybe that was why — an impulse to spring it in a state of grace. Or maybe the very unreality of the moment was useful to him. Maybe it was for both of these reasons, or neither, or one altogether different. But he sprang it and there we sat. The damn thing was on the agenda. Not only on the agenda, but before the house.

Augie went over and raised a window. He wiped his brow with a handkerchief and came back to his seat. Isolde was running her forefinger round the rim of her cup. My wife and I were looking into our laps.

"There was a child, you know. This is it. There's no doubt about it. Why try to hide it, why pretend? I suggest we hang me from a sour apple tree. I suggest we cut me up into little pieces for fish bait. I hate to do this to Dick and Audrey, but they wouldn't be spared it anyway — I'd have to face them finally, so why not now? I figured we might as well get it all over with in one crack." He rose and walked toward a crib in a far corner of the room where Junior was parked tonight. "I'll do anything you think fair. This little cherub — "

Isolde came over and thrust herself between them, her back to the crib. "Don't you dare touch that child!" she said.

"Now, Isolde," I said rising, not knowing quite what line I was taking.

"Get out," Isolde said to Augie.

"Forgive me."

"I'll forgive you if you get out. Get out and don't ever let me see you again."

Augie stood looking at her with his mouth open. I stood with my hands spread. Audrey got up. "I think we'd better go."

"No, stay. I'm glad myself about that part of it — now I won't have to tell you myself. And I'd rather not be alone tonight," Isolde said.

"Well, then I'll leave with Augie," I said. "Audrey and you can stay together."

"You want to do that then?" Audrey said. It was all getting idiotic — as though we were discussing who would ride with whom to a party or something.

Augie turned to us. "I have a few more things to say." I supposed he meant in castigation of himself, but couldn't be sure; because Isolde strode to the door, flung it open, pointed through it, and said: "Get out! You — coyote!"

There was once a movie — perhaps it was *All About Eve* — in which some actress had done that to George Sanders and he'd said, "You're too short for that gesture. Besides it went out with Mrs. Fiske." Isolde was short, but she wasn't too short for the gesture. And Augie got out. But he hesitated first and said, "I ought to pack a few things."

"I'll send your things. Just get out now."

"Forgive me."

"Later."

"Then we'll let it that way. I'll let you know through Dick where to send my things. I'll probably stop at the Algonquin."

"You wouldn't stop at anything," was another rejoinder I recalled, this one from a musical comedy, in a brisk exchange also involving hotels. The mind has its own shock absorbers when emotions are under stress.

When Augie started for the closet to get his coat and hat (having shut the door a moment because of the draft) I went for mine too.

"Wait," Audrey called to me. "I'd like you to stay a minute and tell Isolde all the things you told me the other night. You know — how if it hadn't been for Augie's bad side there wouldn't be this good, and so on. How it's thanks to that and all."

"Well, all right," I agreed, though I'd have liked an hour or two alone to prepare a few notes. I was certainly more than happy to do all I could to help my two friends get this straightened around. I stood with my overcoat in my hands. "But shouldn't I at least drive Augie to the station, if he's going to New York?"

"I'd rather walk," Augie said. "It's only two and a half miles."

So we watched as he got into his coat and put on his hat. He opened the door and then paused, as if waiting for something. I felt we were waiting too — for what? For something more substantial than a mere exit, perhaps, something more clarion and conclusive, as befits a man who through Spanish living had come to a Greek end. But there was nothing, and the moment passed as a hesitating doubt whether he should wave or not. And at last he didn't wave, but gave us a rather charming smile and then, glancing into the corner where the crib was, went out, closing the door quietly behind him. We heard his footsteps a moment on the gravel outside and then no more, a faint sharp dwindling sound which seemed to give us something of the recessional touch we missed, like the last color fading from a sunset clothing some particular doom, leaving to us a silence in which we could only suppose that we had seen the last of Augie Poole, a figure already vanishing up the road, a memory and a means, a phantom digested by the evening shadows.

Twenty-One

CONFESSION is good for the soul only in the sense that a tweed coat is good for dandruff — it is a palliative rather than a remedy. Augie's admission solved nothing and helped nobody. It eased one tension only to create another as bad, or worse. What was to become of the Poole family, now three? Isolde, who must be judge and jury, realized soon that this state of affairs could not continue without reaching the ears of Rock-a-Bye. Agencies by no means relax their vigil of a house after they have given it a child. Rock-a-Bye would still be many months on the watch. A representative dropped in less than two weeks after Augie's expulsion, as a matter of fact, but it was during the day when there was no need to explain his absence from the premises. But Isolde knew agencies have ways of finding things out and was constantly afraid theirs might get wind of the rupture. Still she could not find it in her heart to take Augie back. So she delayed: hesitating, doubting, weighing. And waiting. As though something would turn up to help her make up her mind, or make it up for her.

"But those things don't happen," Audrey and I remonstrated with her, time and time again. "You've got to make your mind up to take him back or that's the end of it."

Augie, meanwhile, lived unhappily at the Algonquin in New York City. His work went poorly. He got no new ideas. We gave him a steady part-time job at *The Townsman*, developing germinal ideas we had in the office, or ideas that were nebulous or imperfect; situations of the kind to which Blair always attached the memo, "Something here. Work on." Augie was very creative on these. His "switches" were often completely new contributions, and he saved many a joke we had been ready to scrap. He worked on the captions of bought cartoons, too. He came in three days a week to the office. He languished. He loved Isolde — that was plain now. And he loved the child. There was no doubt he missed them more acutely every day.

"He's dying to see you both," I reported to Isolde. "Isn't that worth something?"

She smoothed out a pleat in her skirt with a stiff hand and frowned. Pride held out. Augie had now been gone five weeks.

"What'll I tell him?" I said. "I'm going to have dinner with him in town Thursday. Any message?"

No message. She needed time.

Thursday I quit work early and had several drinks at as many bars in restless preparation for meeting Augie at a bar we had designated. The higher I got the lower I got, as it were. When I turned up at the appointed place, which was my personal favorite, the curator looked at me narrowly.

"I see I got competition," he said, wiping a glass. We were again momentarily alone.

"Give me a straight rye," I said.

"I don't know."

"Come on now. I'm a steady customer here."

"You're not very steady tonight."

"Then give me a white wine and seltzer."

Frank complied, but advised I make the drink last as it was all I was likely to get from him in the very immediate future.

He went silently back to his work. I nursed the drink moodily, turning over something extra I had on my mind. Moot Point had fallen off.

All the grace and charm seemed to have vanished from that pleasure dome, now apparently past its modish peak and sloping into its long decline. The sequels to those delicate humoresques, each an étude illustrative of some aspect of the sexual harmonics, with which I had so often detained myself in times past, had become unremittingly banal and gross — mere carnal intervals, encounters with shopgirls whisked up there for the most elementary of purposes. Why? Was my fancy not what it used to be? Or were its latest products secretly willed, out of that hankering for the vulgar, that nostalgia for the loam of things, that haunts overspun man? In any case I was spared nothing. I visualized to the last detail the breakfasts which, once the last fine fillip of communions given and taken there, were now the penalties of its debauches. Indeed their horrors were often the whole of my scenarios. Thus I imagined myself, in trying to render somewhat more literate the conversation going on over bacon and eggs with one of these grisettes, as wondering aloud whether Cummings would live, and her replying, "Is he sick?"

I slumped across the bar with my hands to my face.

"What's the matter?" Frank asked.

"Unholy mess."

He shook his head.

"What defeats me about you educated fellows is you have everything a fellow could ask for, well-spoken, good jobs, fine families, and you sit around here like the last rose of summer. I don't know. It's too many for me. Believe me if I had your job."

"I know," I said. "I've got everything."

"Then get that mailbag off your lower lip."

Frank turned and watched something on the sidewalk outside. I followed his gaze and saw a blonde six feet tall and wearing a mink stole, looking in.

"She meets a guy here once in a while," Frank explained.

"I tell you what you do, Frank, if she comes in here. I'll be sitting here like this, my tie straightened, new homburg on, a drink in front of me, my briefcase on the next stool — a fellow outwardly prosperous, you understand, and yet with a definite touch of something lost and lonely. Then you go over to where she's sitting and say to her, like a bartender in a cartoon, you see — now, get this. You look over at me and say to her: 'It's a sort of Marquand story — a basically independent nature sacrificed to the externals of achievement.' Have you got that?"

"Oh, go to hell," Frank said. "Here she comes now."

The woman went to the farthest stool and set a gold mesh evening bag on the bar and drew off a pair of pink gloves, which she folded and laid as carefully on the evening bag as she had the bag on the bar. She was smooth-featured and clear-skinned, with durable Panelyte laminated plastic top designed to resist stains, scratches, heat and moisture. Finely crafted, meticulously detailed, legs tipped with satin brass ferrules. Complete with synchro-mesh, spatter shield and automatic three-heat timing switch. All this plus the wonderful economy of Frank's budget-pleasing prices. Hurry! Hurry!

"*C'est l'époque*," I said, lightly tapping the ashes from my cigarette.

"What did you say?" asked Frank, who was mixing her a whisky sour she had ordered.

"It's the age we live in. A general, almost stylized, ennui has taken hold of us. Security, intellectual attainments, these mean

nothing; subtlety is a hindrance to peace as often as its source."
I saw from the woman's reflection in the bar mirror that the
ripe mouth had fallen ajar. It closed, however, on a cigarette
presently thrust into it. Every hair was in place. She had obviously never been hissed at by a lamb chop, or by anything else
in a frying pan. I got her in trouble. *O my God!*

"The human mechanism," I continued, "has become too
finely tuned. We are shattered by vibrations from which denser
natures were exempt. The path to death and decay is not an
easy one, and to presume to untangle the skein of things is
worse than in vain. It is vain."

"I thought you di'n't feel good," Frank said, serving the newcomer her libation. Watching him strike a match for her cigarette, I thought to whet her interest with something in a lighter
vein, something from my store of incidental quips and sallies.

"You change that bar rag about once a year, Frank?" I twitted.
"He changes that bar rag once a year — on New Year's Eve.
Every New Year's Eve he wrings out the old, wrings in the new."

The woman took a sip from her sour and scratched an instep.
I tried a fresh tittup.

"Man in a small Southern town killed his mother-in-law, his
sister-in-law, two cousins and an uncle. He took the bodies down
into the basement, boiled them in washtubs, and puréed the
remains through a sieve. What was the upshot?" I twisted my
cigarette out in an ashtray. "Strained relations."

The woman presented a face wreathed in smiles. I was about
to smile back when a pair of masculine shoulders three feet wide
brushed past mine from behind and the woman was joined by
a new arrival. A better example of the "denser natures" to which
I had just alluded could scarcely be imagined. I'm not saying
his eyebrows and hairline merged, but the image will be met-

aphorically helpful. He was dark, and weighed at least two hundred and fifty pounds. He patted the woman's head with a little endearment, from which she drew back. "Can't a fellow touch the girl he's in love with's hair?" he said.

"Get me all mussed up."

"I like those eyes even when you're sore," was his rejoinder. "You hypmatize me."

I beamed benevolently on the scene and winked at Frank. "Let us all be terribly Spanish, for there is not enough time to be Greek," I said.

The primate who had just come in stepped over to me.

"What was that crack, Bud?" he said.

"That was no crack," I said. "I was just — "

"I can hear. I got ears. I don't like remarks passed about nobody's nationality. See?" the primate replied, helping himself to a handful of my lapels. "In this country we don't care where people came from. This is a democracy."

"It was in the spirit of that assumption that I — "

"And talk English."

"Yes, sir. Yes, siree."

"O.K."

He released me and went back to his hypmatist. The bartender scowled at me and I scowled back. I would take my custom elsewhere were it not for the appointment I had in this dump — that was what my glare said. Finally the door opened again and Augie hurried in.

"Sorry I'm late," he said. "But I just had a phone call from Isolde at the hotel."

I was instantly tense. "What about?" I asked.

He gave a nervous shrug. "You got me. She just said for me to come out, she wants to see me. Something's up."

"Wants to see you when? Tonight?" I said apprehensively.

"Tonight. Give me some Bourbon and water, will you?" Augie turned to me. " 'Had to see me' was the way she put it — not wanted to see me. What could that mean?"

"God, I don't know. I hope the agency isn't on the warpath."

"Don't even say it." Augie glanced over his shoulder at a wall clock. "It's seven-thirty now. The next train isn't till eight ten. Time enough for a couple. I sure need 'em."

"I told you not to stir this up."

"Cut it out. Mean only a storm could clear so foul a sky."

Augie had a couple, in the course of which I phoned Audrey and told her I'd be on the eight ten with Augie instead of on a later train for which we had made arrangements that morning. "Isolde wants to see him. Something seems to be up. What's going on?" I asked.

"You'll find out when you get here," she said. "I can't talk about it over the telephone."

"Well, what is it?"

"You hurry home."

Augie and I walked the three blocks to the station. On the train we buried ourselves behind magazines — not that we read them. We were both on tenterhooks. The train was a local and the trip an eternity. But at last we arrived at Avalon, and there were Isolde and Audrey both waiting for us on the platform. Their eyes were red. They had clearly both been crying.

We got into our separate cars and started for home. I could see the Pooles' car tailing us in the rearview mirror. We had gone a short distance from the station when Audrey burst out with:

"You'll never guess what's happened."

"What?" I said. "What the devil's going on out here? Is it something about the agency?"

"No."

"What then?"

"Isolde's going to have a baby."

As everyone knows, childless women often become pregnant after adopting an infant. The experience of maternity itself supposedly thaws out the fears and self-doubts that had previously thwarted its accomplishment. That had happened to Isolde, in only the few months' time in which she had been a practicing mother. She had always wanted a child at the same time that she'd feared it, and naturally the swell of emotion released by the realization of her long-hungered-for condition swept her back into a tide of feeling for her husband. She had suspected her condition for a couple of weeks, but only today had medical reports proved it beyond a doubt.

I don't know what reconciliation scene was enacted in the Poole home that night. I can only imagine it — the tears, laughter, protestations, embraces.

On that night, which now seemed so long ago, when Isolde had called Audrey and told her of their wish to adopt, Audrey and I had been lying in bed unretired, in the way we have — she reading a book, I smoking and musing and listening to sounds in the plaster. Neither of us was reading this night. We nursed a drink apiece and talked long past midnight about the Pooles. I thought I heard a faint rustle in the wall and remembered the rat that had visited me the other time. We had no more rats now — they were gone. No thanks to either Nebuchadnezzar (who had died a few months before) or the cat the Pooles had loaned us; thanks only to a terrier we had acquired. Jake was his name. Perhaps it was only Jake, scooting and scrabbling about in the basement, who had made the noise. Our four children were of course long asleep, dreaming their peculiar dreams. Phoebe (now firmly representing herself as Alice) often dreamed of letters of the alphabet, or so she told us at breakfast.

The phone rang. Audrey bolted out of bed and got it on the third ring — par for that distance. It was Isolde. They talked for half an hour or more, and when Audrey returned she said: "They want to celebrate. All of us together."

Celebrate we did. We made a night of it in New York. Our old foursome. Happy once again, with a difference perhaps — but happy. The Pooles carted Augie, Junior over to our place in a carrying basket and Mrs. Goodbread sat with all the children there. We dressed. The girls were visions in new frocks; the men, in tuxedos now slightly tight for them, looked like exploded baked potatoes. We had dinner and then went to a night club. We drank champagne. We raised our glasses.

"Here's how," Augie said.

The child was born in the early fall and was a girl. Anita is her name.

That was only a few years ago and yet the children seem to be already growing up — the Pooles' and, certainly, ours. Mrs. Goodbread sits regularly with the Pooles' two, but our Maude is now old enough to leave with the rest. Old enough also, though, to be going out on her own now and then. Mr. Goodbread still mows lawns for several of us and detains us widely as a raconteur. Dr. Vancouver has left general medicine and settled in pediatrics; there is still a lack of baby doctors in growing Avalon and he has made a good thing of it. Isolde takes her kids to him and reports he is O.K., but still a good deal of a hypochondriac — though less apprehensive about catching things from babies than he'd been from adults. Terry I never saw again. The McBains moved West, and they and she have dropped from sight. Now and then I pick up a copy of *The Reader's Digest* and look for the article about her mother, but I never see it.

So Augie was gathered into the orbit that claims us all at last. So the damnation is that there is no damnation; the peal of doom is a penny whistle, the Good Humor bell calling the children at evening. So the years glide along. I never go to Moot Point any more. There is nothing doing there. A new six-lane highway goes by the door, and Moot Point is a silent ruin. It would have been much better had the state survey hit it directly — then it would have been condemned by eminent domain and torn down, with reasonable remuneration at market value. But the government does not recognize near misses or what they call consequential damage to property deflated by scenic blights. So my old haunt stands, throttled by the encroaching forests, choked with bushes filled with guzzling bees or tufts of winter snow. Cars and fume-dispensing trailers bowl past the front all day; the Maine waters murmur everlastingly behind. I hardly think about it any more — I can't stand to. But sometimes I'm reminded of it, and then my heart breaks. As a valley dweller drinks from streams which bear rumors of the cold purity of mountaintops, so I can in chance moments of daily life catch echoes and glimpses, intimations of that ideal typified by Moot Point at its best. A woman's wit and animal ease, splinters of hotel gaiety, these quicken memories of that lost Babylonian grace, that quicksilver common to all those who were seen there in the old days.

I've been looking for another site; or I should say we are — because my wife has taken the initiative in our search for a summer cottage. We've had our eye for a long time on a lakeside plot up in New Hampshire, and it looks as though we're going to buy and build on it. Nothing pretentious, you understand, nothing fancy, just a little place we can call our own. It won't be named Moot Point, by a long chalk, but probably something like Pines and Needles, or even Drowsy Dell. Because instead of the suave adulteries and worldly company for which Moot Point was famous in its heyday, this will be strictly a family affair, with youngsters romping on the lawn and splashing in the water. We'll have the Pooles up a good deal, I expect, for long week ends and summer holidays with all the children, of whom ours are approaching the age when they'll have friends and school-mates of their own to ask up. Maude already has a boy with a popping car, which leaves half its organs in my drive. Inciden-tally, I often come upon Maude making entries in a book which she refuses to let me see, and keeps locked in a drawer. She says it's a diary, but I don't know — it looks more like a notebook to me. Could that, then, be the end? "Father always started the oil furnace when he stamped his foot. . . . Father would make Mother presents of his favorite wines and of the books he wanted to read. . . ."

"Everybody has to get away," Mother remarked over her needlepoint one evening, as plans for the summer cottage were being completed. "And don't you think it'll be a real retreat for both of us?"

"I don't know about you," Father said, pouring himself a glass of ale as he settled back with a sigh in his easy chair, "but it's certainly a retreat for me."